"HURRY—"

"Why, darlin'," Bo murmured, bending his head so that his jaw brushed hers. "All you had to do was ask."

Yeah, yeah. She followed him back into the office, watching over her shoulder to see who was looking, shutting the door to give them some privacy. "Now." But one look at Bo had the words falling right out of her head.

He was unbuttoning his shirt.

"What are you doing?" she asked weakly.

"You said hurry." A wedge of sinewy, tanned skin appeared. He shrugged the shirt off his shoulders, exposing his chest, the defined pecs, the correlated ridges of his ribs, his belly—

"No. Bo, I didn't mean—"

His hands went to the buttons on his Levi's.

Pop.

Pop.

"W-wait!" She forced her gaze up, up into his. "Seriously, I didn't mean—" But at the laughter in his eyes she trailed off, her eyes twitching. *He was messing with her.*

She slapped her hands over her eyes. "Get your clothes back on!"

The Novels of Jill Shalvis

Get a Clue

Out of This World

Smart and Sexy

Strong and Sexy

Superb and Sexy

Instant Attraction

Instant Gratification

Instant Temptation

Anthologies Featuring Jill

Bad Boys Southern Style

He's the One

Merry and Bright

Published by Kensington Publishing Corporation

Aussie Rules

JILL SHALVIS

B
BRAVA

KENSINGTON PUBLISHING CORP.

www.kensingtonbooks.com

KENSINGTON BOOKS are published by

Kensington Publishing Corp.
119 West 40th Street
New York, NY 10018

All Kensington titles, imprints, and distributed lines are available at special quantity discounts for bulk purchases for sales promotion, premiums, fund-raising, and educational, or institutional use. Special book excerpts or customized printings can also be created to fit specific needs. For details, write or phone the office of the Kensington Special Sales Manager: Kensington Publishing Corp., 119 West 40th Street, New York, NY 10018. Attn. Special Sales Department. Phone: 1-800-221-2647.

Kensington and the K logo Reg. U.S. Pat. & TM Off.

ISBN-13: 978-1-61773-786-2
ISBN-10: 1-61773-786-0
First Kensington Trade Edition: June 2006
First Kensington Mass Market Edition: January 2009

eISBN-13: 978-1-61773-787-9
eISBN-10: 1-61773-787-9
Kensington Electronic Edition: May 2016

10 9 8 7 6 5 4 3 2

Printed in the United States of America

Chapter 1

If you asked Melanie Anderson, nothing was sexier than flying. Not an eighty-five mile-per-hour ride in a Ferrari, not any chick flick out there, nothing, not even men. Not that she had anything against the penis-carrying gender, but flying was where it was at for Mel, and had been since the tender age of four, when she'd constructed wings out of cardboard and jumped out of a tree on a dare. Unfortunately, that first time the ground got in her way, breaking her fall.

And her ankle.

Her second try had come at age eight, when she'd leapt off her granny's second-story deck into a pile of fallen leaves. No broken ankle this time, but she did receive a nice contusion to the back of the head.

By age twelve, a time when most girls discovered boys and their toys, Mel had discovered airplanes, and had taken a job sweeping for tips at a local airport just to be near them. Maybe because her own home never seemed happy, maybe because she didn't have much else to look forward to, but the magic of flying was all she ever dreamed about.

She wanted to be a pilot. And not just any pilot, but a

kick-ass pilot who could fly anywhere, anytime, and look cool while doing it.

Now she was twenty-six and she'd pulled it all off. She ran her own charter service: Anderson Air. That Anderson Air consisted of a single Cessna 172 and a not-exactly-air-worthy Hawker was another matter altogether. Having fueled her dreams from cardboard wings to titanium steel made her proud as hell of herself. Now, if only she could pay her bills, things would be just about perfect, but money, like man-made orgasms, remained in short supply.

"Mel! Mel, sweetie, the oven is kaput again!"

Mel sighed as she walked through the lobby of North Beach Airport, a small, privately owned, fixed-base operation. The cozy, sparsely decorated place was dotted with worn leather couches and low, beat-up coffee tables and potted palm trees— low maintenance to the extreme. A couple of the walls were glass, looking out onto the tarmac and the two large hangars, one of which housed the maintenance department and the other the overnight tie-down department. Beyond that lay a string of fourteen smaller hangars, all rentals. And beyond that, Santa Barbara and the Pacific Ocean, where Mel could routinely find her line guys and aircraft mechanic riding the waves on their surfboards instead of doing their job.

The far wall held a huge map of the world, dotted with different colored pushpins designating the places where she and everyone else had flown on various chartered flights. Red pins dominated. Mel was red, of course, and just looking at the map made her smile with pride.

Just past the map, the wall jutted out, opening up into the Sunshine Café, an ambitious name for five round tables and a small bar/nook, behind which was a stove, oven, microwave, and refrigerator, all crammed into six hundred square feet and painted a bright sunshine yellow. On the walls hung photos, all of planes, and all gorgeously shot from the ground's viewpoint.

Charlene Stone stood in the middle of the kitchen nook, bottle-dyed maroon hair piled on top of her head, her black lip gloss a perfect match to her black fingernails. She'd turned forty this year and wore a T-shirt that read TWENTY WAS GOOD BUT FORTY IS BETTER, and a pair of short shorts that rivaled Daisy Duke's. As the eighties had been Char's favorite decade to date, she had Poison blaring from a boom box on the counter while staring into the oven. "I can't get my muffins going," she said in her Alabama drawl.

"I thought *I* was your muffin, baby."

This from Charlene's husband, Al, the photographer who'd taken the pictures on the walls, who despite being forty himself had never outgrown his horny twenties. Medium height, built like the boxer he'd once been, he waggled a brow and grinned.

They'd been married forever, had in fact raised two kids while they'd still been kids themselves, but they had empty-nest syndrome now, and were currently revisiting their honeymoon days—meaning they talked about sex often, had sex often, and talked about it some more.

"People come here for my muffins," Charlene said, and smacked Al's chest.

"I love your muffins."

"You're just kissing up now."

This brought out a big, hopeful grin. "No, but I'd like to." He shifted close, put his hands on Char's hips. "Kiss up, and then down . . ."

Char shot Mel a long look. "Men are dogs."

Mel tended to agree with that assessment but she knew enough to keep her tongue. "I'll get the oven fixed."

"Oh, honey, that'd be great. I know you're swamped and this is the last thing you need."

Yep, on the list of things Mel didn't need, the oven going on the blink fell right behind a hole in her head. "We need the oven. I'll get it fixed ASAP."

"Good, because if I keep disappointing the customers, we aren't going to be able to pay our rent this month. Sally will freak."

Ah, yes, the elusive Sally.

Sally was the owner of North Beach Airport, and everyone's boss, from fueling to maintenance to hangaring. Mel herself rented space from Sally for Anderson Air and in return for a lower fee managed the whole airport for Sally. Since Sunshine Café happened to be one of the few profitable segments of North Beach, the broken oven fell into Mel's already-overflowing pot of responsibilities. She pulled the radio off the clip on her belt to call their fix-it guy, who sometimes fixed things, and sometimes didn't. Mostly didn't. "I'll get Ernest."

Charlene sighed.

"Yeah, yeah." Mel brought the radio up to her mouth. "Ernest, come to the café, please."

No answer, which was not a big surprise. No one was sure exactly how old Ernest was but he'd been at North Beach as long as Mel could remember. According to other sources, he'd been around since the dawn of time. Only thing was, he was grumpy as an old goat and was rarely anywhere he should be when Mel needed him.

Like now.

"He's probably rescuing a spider." To Al's credit, he said this with a straight face.

Ernest loved spiders. He actually carried around a special species book in his back pocket so that he could characterize each and every spider he came across, and here just off the Santa Barbara coast, in the shadows of the Santa Ynez Mountains, he came across a lot. The only thing he loved more than spiders was computers. The man, strange as it seemed, was a computer god. He probably could have gotten a job anywhere for more money, but undoubtedly he couldn't nap on the job anywhere else so he stayed at North Beach.

"Ernest," Mel said again into the radio. "Come in, please. Ernest, come in."

"No need to shout, missy."

Mel nearly jumped out of her skin at the low, craggily, grumpy voice behind her. Ernest stood there, all five feet of him packed with attitude, from his steel-toed boots to his greasy trousers and long-sleeved, button-down plaid, to his bad comb-over, which was rumpled now, telling her he'd been sleeping in the storage closet again. The crease on his cheek that resembled the side of a can of oil was a dead give-away. "The oven's down," she told him.

"Eh?" He cupped a hand to his bad ear. "Speak up!"

Mel would have fired his curmudgeonly ass a long time ago except she couldn't afford anyone else. "Oven! Broken!"

"You never talk loud enough," he grumbled. "Sally's the only one who talks loud enough."

Ernest hadn't actually spoken directly to Sally in years, but arguing with the man was like betting against the house.

Never going to win.

"Can you fix the oven?" she yelled in his good ear.

"I'll fix the damn oven soon as I fix the damn fuel pump!"

Mel's stomach dropped. "What's wrong with the gas pump?" Muffins they could live without. Getting fuel into their customers' aircrafts, some of which landed here daily for the fuel alone, they could not.

"Nothing I can't handle." Ernest was already walking away, his pants slipping down because he had no hips to hold them on. He stopped, hitched them up, then kept moving.

The radio squawked with the announcement of an un-scheduled plane arriving in twenty minutes. Mel waited for one of the linemen, Ritchie or Kellan, to respond to the news, but neither did. Once again she lifted the radio to her lips and called for her employees.

No response.

"Gotta love those brain-dead college students," Char said.

Mel resisted the urge to smack her own forehead with the radio. "If those two are in the back hangar getting high again, I'm going to kill them."

"We're falling apart at the seams." Charlene hugged Mel. "Look, honey, you've got your hands full. I'll go see what I can wrangle up without the oven, 'kay?"

"I'll get on it," Mel promised her just as the Poison CD ended.

For one blessed moment silence reigned before a new CD clicked on. Journey. "I just wish we could give this place the makeover it needs," Char yelled over the music.

Mel wished that, too. They were making ends meet, and they all had jobs, two really good things, but no one was getting rich, that was for sure.

Not that she wanted to be rich, but comfortable would be nice . . .

Al followed his wife into the kitchen, his hand sliding down her back to squeeze her ass.

"Albert Edward Stone!" Charlene said in her most Southern-genteel voice. "If you think that instead of cooking muffins, I'm going to 'cook' with you—"

"Come on, just a quickie—"

"That's what you got just last night!"

"Hey, that wasn't a quickie, that was some of my best work!"

Mel covered her ears and walked away. She didn't need the reminder that everyone was getting quickies and she was not. So it'd been a long time for her, so what? People could live without sex.

Or so the rumor went.

"Mel? Mel, are you around here somewhere?"

At Dimi's voice drifting through the lobby from the front receptionist desk, Mel changed direction and headed that way, wondering, what now?

Dimi Wilmington sat perched on the edge of her desk, head tilted as she studied the view out the window of sweeping coastlines bisected by the magnificent Santa Ynez Mountains and a typical low-lying morning fog. Willowy, with legs long past the legal limit, Dimi had a body and face that could launch a thousand ships, make the fat lady sing, and put grown men on their knees to worship at her altar.

She used them to her full advantage, too, rarely coming across a man she didn't like—which probably explained the new whisker burn along her jaw.

Terrific. Everyone was getting lucky except Mel.

It was said she and Dimi were night and day, a modern-day odd couple. Mel being the anal one. The one who gathered worries and stress like moss on a tree. She also tended to gather the heartaches and responsibilities of others much like a fraught mother hen, bitching after all her little chicks, pecking at them until they did as she wanted them to.

Dimi was more a live-and-let-live type of soul. She cared, deeply, she'd just rather light incense and meditate than actually solve a problem. She was both a thorn in Mel's side and her closest confidant.

She wore a multicolored, filmy, gauzy miniskirt and a snug, white cap-sleeved tee with a pink heart in the center that brought the eyes to immediate attention of her brand spanking-new breasts. But the thing that never failed to amaze Mel about Dimi was that she could go all day and that bright, clean white tee would stay bright, clean white.

Mel didn't even bother to look down at her coveralls, already filthy from just a quick maintenance check on the Cessna. "What's the problem?"

Over the steam of her herbal tea and the faint smoke from the incense she'd lit, Dimi shot Mel a wry smile.

Right. What *wasn't* a problem was a more likely question.

The two of them went back a long ways. As teens, Mel had swept and assisted in the maintenance department, and Dimi had answered phones. Each had been far more at home here than either of their decidedly not *Leave It to Beaver* homes.

Sally Wells, a woman with more dream than cash, had taken them under her wing—Sally, who'd lived as she wanted, wild and free with men and fun aplenty. As their first real role model, Mel and Dimi had both worshipped the ground Sally walked on; Mel appreciating Sally's directness, the way she ran her own show and the world be damned, but for Dimi the worship had gone deeper. She'd wanted to *be* Sally.

Unfortunately, Sally had been unavailable to them for a long time now, and without her around, there was no one for Mel to share the stress of holding all this up with. No one except Dimi. "Tell me," she said to Dimi now. "Believe me, the day can't get worse."

Dimi put her hand over Mel's. "You look tired. You're not drinking that tea I gave you."

"I hate tea. And it's just stress."

"You only hate tea because I tell you it has healing abilities and you think that's a crock of shit." She sighed. "Money's tight again."

"You mean *still.* Money's tight still."

"That's all right." Dimi stood and, primping a little, played with the hem of her skirt, adjusted her top. "We have a couple of hot ones coming in today."

"Hot ones" being Dimi-code for cute, *rich* customers.

"What we have is an unscheduled," Mel said. "I've gotta get out there and do tie-down because God knows where Ritchie or Kellan is."

Dimi pulled out a compact and checked her gloss, ran her tongue over her teeth. "I'll do it."

"Uh-huh." Mel eyed the short, short skirt, which at every move flirted with revealing Dimi's crotch. "You're going to go get your hands dirty, risk that manicure, and tie down a plane? In *that?*"

Dimi smiled. "Should get me a big tip, don't you think?"

"That's not even funny."

"Hey, I'm going to hit on them anyway, might as well get something for it."

"Stop it." Mel knew Dimi was only kidding. Or half-kidding anyway. Dimi enjoyed men the way some women enjoy breathing. "I have enough to worry about."

Dimi sighed and stroked a long, wayward strand of hair from Mel's face. "We'll be fine, hon. You'll come up with something, you always do."

Right. She'd just wave her magic wand and figure it all out. And while she was at it, she'd conjure up a happily ever after for all of them as well. "The oven's down, the gas pump is acting up, and morale's getting low."

"They need a phone call from Sally."

Their gazes met for a long beat.

"You do it this time," Dimi whispered.

"Actually, I was hoping you could, from—" Mel broke off when Ernest appeared out of nowhere, shuffling past the desk, pulling his noisy cart stacked haphazardly with tools and the ever-present jar for liberating spiders.

Mel didn't know how many times she'd asked him not to walk through the lobby like that, to instead go around the outside of the hangar, where customers wouldn't have to see him, but he never listened. At least not to the stuff she wanted him to. "Ernest?"

He'd stopped to stand in front of the vending machine next to the wall map, scratching his head as he contemplated rows of candy bars. "Yeah?"

"Did you by any chance ever clean out that maintenance hangar, the one Danny wants to stock new parts in?"

"Not yet. Busy, you know."

Right. He looked really busy. She and Dimi waited until he'd made his selection, shoved the candy bar into his pocket next to his spider book, and left.

"I hate the secrets," Dimi whispered.

Yeah, and Mel just loved them. *Not*. She looked at the time. "I gotta go meet that flight. Then I have a flight myself, to LA."

"You're changing your clothes first, right?"

"Yes," Mel said with irritation. "Of course."

"You say that like you don't regularly forget to change from mechanic to pilot. Daily."

Mel rolled her eyes. "I'll be back by two."

Dimi nodded, looked wistfully out the window. "You're so lucky."

"Lucky?" Mel laughed in disbelief. "How exactly?"

"You get to get out of here."

"But you hate to fly," Mel reminded her. "You throw up every time."

"I know, I didn't mean . . ." Dimi searched for words. "Look, don't you ever . . . just want to get in the plane and, I don't know, fly off into the sunset?"

Mel just stared at her incredulously. "Never to return?"

"Well . . . yeah."

North Beach was Mel's home, her *life,* and no, she'd never ever thought about going away and never coming back, and she'd always figured Dimi felt just the same. "Okay, what's wrong?"

Dimi lifted a stack of mail. "Just the usual. Here's your in-coming pile. Bills and more bills, if you're wondering, though what's the point of opening them, we still can't pay last month's."

"Officially no one can even bug us until . . ." She glanced at the desk calendar. July ninth. "Tomorrow, the tenth." Oh, God.

"Also we need fuel for the pump, and they won't deliver it without their bill being paid." Dimi leaned over and lit the three candles lining the front of her reception desk. The crystals on her wrists jangled, as did the ones dangling from her ears. The scent of vanilla began to fill the air, joining the incense she'd already lit on the credenza behind her.

"You're going to make people hungry," Mel said. "And the oven's down."

"I'm going to make people feel warm and cozy and at home," Dimi corrected, and smoothed her skirt. "Helps our karma."

Mel wanted to say that she didn't believe in karma or fate, that they each made their own, but the sound of a plane coming in ended the conversation. "They're early." She understood early, she herself was always compulsively early, but it meant she had to run through the lobby, grabbing an extra orange vest off a hook as she went, slipping into the lineman's gear as she moved quickly across the tarmac to greet the plane.

The Gulfstream was a beauty, and her pilot's heart gave one vivacious kick of envy as the plane swept in for a honey of a landing, perfectly controlled by a pilot who was clearly a master of his craft.

When the engine shut off, Mel moved in, squinting against the early chill and wind, using the tie-down blocks to hold the plane steady, her mind wandering as she worked. The oven had gone out twice this month. She needed to look into the cost of a new one. The linemen clearly needed another ass chewing regarding responsibilities, specifically theirs. And then there was the little matter of fuel. She'd have to find a way to pay that bill pronto.

God, her brain hurt.

Finished with the tie-down, she straightened, patted the sleek side of the airplane just for the pleasure of touching it, and blew a stray strand of hair out of her face, wishing she had put on an extra layer of insulation beneath her coveralls because despite its being summer, the early-morning wind off the Pacific cut right through her.

From the other side of the aircraft, the door opened. A set of stairs released. A moment later, two long legs emerged, clad in dark blue trousers, clean work boots, and topped by a most excellent ass. Not averse to enjoying a good view, Mel stayed in place, watching as the rest of the man was revealed. White button-down shirt, sleeves shoved up above his elbows, tawny hair past his collar, blowing in the wind.

Yep, there were a few perks to this job, one of them catering right to Mel's soft spot.

Pilots. This one looked more like a movie star pretending

to be a pilot, but you wouldn't hear her complaining. And just like that, from the inside out, she began to warm up nicely.

The man held a clipboard, which he was looking at as he turned, ducking beneath the nose of the plane to come toe to toe with her, a lock of tawny hair falling carelessly over his forehead, his eyes shaded behind aviator sunglasses.

And right then and there, every single lust-filled thought drained out of Mel's head to make room for one hollow, horror-filled one.

No.

It couldn't be. After all this time, he wouldn't *dare* show his face.

His only concession to the surprise was a raised brow as he lifted his sunglasses, his sea-green gaze taking its sweet time, touching over her own battered work boots, the dirty coveralls, the fiery, uncontrollable red hair she'd piled on top of her head without thought to her appearance. "Look at you," he murmured. "All grown up. G'day, Mel."

Yeah, he'd grown up, too. He was bigger, broader, and taller than the last time she'd seen him, but she couldn't mistake the smile—of pure, devilish, wicked trouble.

Australian accent, check.

Heart-stopping green eyes and long lashes to match the long, thick tumble of light brown hair falling in said eyes, check and check.

Curved mouth that could invoke huge waves of passion or fury . . . *CHECK*. "Bo Black," she whispered, getting cold all over again.

Cocking his head, he let out a slow smile. "In the flesh, darlin'. Miss me?"

Miss him? Yeah, she'd missed him. Like one might miss a close call with a hand grenade. "Get off my property."

As if he had all the time in the damn world, he leaned back against his plane, slapping the clipboard lightly against his thigh. "No can do, mate."

"Oh, yes you can." Staggering at a strong gust of wind,

she planted her feet more firmly as she pointed to his plane. "You just get your Aussie ass back inside that heap of junk and fly it the hell out of here."

"Heap of junk?" Instead of being insulted, he laughed good over that, the sound scraping at her belly because it'd been a long time since she'd heard it.

Of course, she hadn't seen him in ten years, and the last time she had, he'd been eighteen to her sixteen, all long and lanky, not yet grown into his body.

He was grown into it now, damn him, and how. Reaching back, he lovingly stroked the steel of the plane, making the entirely inappropriate thought take root in her brain: *did he stroke a woman like that?*

Clearly she needed caffeine.

And a smack upside the head.

"You know exactly what kind of plane this is," he noted easily. "And how valuable."

"Fine," she granted. "Your toy is bigger than mine, you win. *Now* you can go."

Tossing his head back, he laughed again, and she made no mistake—he was laughing *at* her.

Nothing new.

The first time she'd ever laid eyes on him, he'd been swaggering through the lobby, having arrived in town with his father, Eddie Black, an antique plane restorer and dealer. Tall and teenage rangy, Bo had smiled at Mel and said, "Hello, mate," and she'd fallen—both figuratively and literally—as hard as her tender sixteen-year-old heart could, tripping over her own two feet, landing in a potted palm, amusing everyone in the lobby but her.

The second time she'd seen him had been when she'd opened a stock closet to grab something for maintenance, and had found him in there, leaning back against a shelving unit, a pretty blonde customer wrapped around him like a pretzel, straddling his hips. Bo had had his hand beneath her short skirt, doing things Mel had only been able to imagine.

In fact, she'd done just that for many, many uncomfortably sweaty nights afterward.

He'd been so cool, so typically laid-back. When she'd only stood there at the storage door, frozen in shock, Bo had lazily lifted his head, eyes heavy and sexy-lidded as he'd smiled that killer smile. "No worries. Just lock the door for me, darlin'?"

No worries. Right. She'd just lock the door. Only everything inside her head wanted to stay, wanted to beg, *"Can I be next?"*

That had so shocked her, the unexpected longing, that she'd lost it.

Completely.

Lost.

It.

Which was her only explanation for why she'd blindly reached out, grabbed the first thing her fingers closed over— an air filter off a shelf—and . . . and beaned him on the head with it.

Not her proudest moment, but she blamed her red hair and the temperament that went with it. Dimi had always been warning her that someday the temper would catch up to the fire in her hair and that she was going to piss off the wrong person.

Only Bo hadn't gotten pissed, he'd laughed.

Laughed.

Which in turn had made her feel stupid. God, she resented that.

The last time she'd seen him had been several months later, on the day his thieving, conning father had vanished.

The day her life had changed forever.

"Get out," she said now.

That sexy little smile still in place, Bo slowly pulled out a folded piece of paper from the breast pocket of his white shirt.

She tried to read it but he held the document just out of

reach, forcing her to lean in. As close as she was now, she could see his eyes weren't a solid sea green, but flecked with gold specks. This close she could draw in the scent of him— one hundred percent male. This close she could read the paper:

Quit Deed.

A quit deed to North Beach. Her stomach dropped. "How did you—"

"I recently found a box of my father's things, with a safe deposit box key." His eyes were no longer smiling. "This was in there."

"My God."

He nodded curtly. "Yeah, that's right, Mel. North Beach, and everything in it, is mine. Guess that means you, too."

Chapter 2

Bo watched the very watchable Mel Anderson fume. This involved cinnamon eyes flashing, lush mouth frowning, emotions racing across her face, with fury heading the pack.

"Sally did not deed the airport over," she said.

"Ah, but she did." Bo rocked back on his heels. Waited.

Mel crossed her arms over her chest, which was a shame, but the action did plump up her breasts nicely. Even in those coveralls she was quite the unit. Mel had grown up and grown out, in all the right places.

"You forged this," she accused.

Some of his amusement over seeing her again vanished. "Nope."

"Prove it."

Now the last remnants of friendliness went as well. "How am I supposed to do that, Mel?"

"I don't know. But I prefer you do it from far, far away."

Given that he'd just found out that his father had been royally screwed right before he'd died, Bo wasn't going anywhere. "I want to talk to Sally."

Mel's eyes iced over. "She's not here."

"I'll wait."

"I'll call you."

Clearly, she wanted him gone. Too bad for her. "Where is she, Mel?"

She rolled her lips inward, her eyes suggesting she'd like to see him in hell. Too bad he was already there. But her attitude did give him some pause because he knew bugger well why *he* was pissed. He just honestly had no clue why *she'd* be. He'd have thought she'd be a bit more welcoming, actually, even offer to help him out, especially when she heard what he had to say.

But she did not want to hear anything from him. In fact, she snatched the deed out of his hands, then whirled off.

"Oh, *hell no* you don't." Entangling his fingers in the back of her coveralls, he tugged her back.

"Don't touch me."

But he wanted answers, and he wanted them now, so he held good and tight, clearly infuriating her. She was stronger than he remembered, and in the ensuing struggle, her hair fell from its precarious hold, smacking him in the eyes and mouth. She smelled like some complicated mix of shampoo and plane oil, and he shook his head to clear the silky strands from his vision, firmly taking her arms in his hands.

"Back off," she snarled, struggling against him in a way that had him enjoying this little tussle far more than he should. "Let go, or I'll kick your balls into next week."

"Easy, now," he murmured, just barely managing to hold on to her. "I kick back." Wrapping an arm firmly around her, he held her squirming body close while with utmost care he pried the deed out of her fingers. "I'll just take this."

With a muffled growl, she yanked free of his grasp, the radio and phone at her hip clinking, as well as the various tools she had in her pockets.

Always prepared, Mel was, and it amused him some that so little had changed. Then he watched her nicely rounded ass as it sashayed off. He took a second to appreciate the view, thinking too bad he was here for one thing and one thing only, because she might be fun.

That is if she'd ever learned the meaning of fun, which he seriously doubted.

He followed her from the tarmac into the lobby, nearly losing his nose in the door that she tried to shut on him. "Look at that," he said in her ear. "As sweet as ever."

The only sign she'd heard him was her hand curling into a fist at her side.

She wanted to deck him. Seems Little Miss Hot-Head was still quite . . . well, hot-headed.

Not to mention, just plain hot.

Thrusting her nose high enough into the air as to actually endanger her to a nosebleed, she strutted her stuff across the lobby floor toward the front door, tools clinking.

Once upon a time she'd barely come up to his shoulder, and had been a cute thing with guarded eyes and a slow-to-surface smile. She was still barely up to his shoulder, and he watched with appreciation as she quickly and efficiently moved across the floor with enough attitude for ten women, those coveralls hugging her hips and legs, the radio on one hip and a cell phone hanging off the other, and a wrench in her back pocket, slapping against her ass as she moved . . .

He rubbed his jaw as she stalked right up to the reception desk, perched a hip on the corner and leaned over the beautiful woman sitting there, whispering something in her ear.

The woman immediately swiveled her head and leveled a shocked gaze on Bo.

Bo recognized her, and could tell by the effort it took her to even out her expression that she recognized him as well. By the time he got over there, Dimi was staring at him with cool eyes that gave nothing away. "Bo Black," she said as if his name left a bad taste on her tongue.

He hadn't expected a red-carpet welcome, but this hostility was getting old bugger quick. "Okay," he said easily. "Let's get this out in the open."

Twin glares.

"I don't have a beef with either of you," he tried calmly. "I just want to see Sally." Or wrap his fingers around her neck and squeeze . . .

"Sally isn't available," Dimi said.

Mel had one leg swinging jerkily from her perch, revealing her irritation. As if he couldn't see it all over her face.

Irritated himself, Bo put his hands on the desk and leaned in closer. "When *will* she be available? Tomorrow?"

Mel blinked once, slow as an owl, and didn't answer.

Dimi stared down at her fingers, which were fisted and white-knuckled.

"In a week?" he asked with what he thought was great patience.

Nothing.

Shit. He took a deep breath. "A month?"

Neither woman moved, just Mel's leg swinging, swinging, swinging. He eyed them both a long moment, then forced himself to relax, because he had two things on his side. One, a boatload of patience, and two, nothing else was more important than this. "I can wait as long as it takes," he warned.

"You don't have a job?" Mel asked.

"At the moment, I'm doing a bit of chartering."

"With the Gulfstream."

"Yep. And I'm getting back into antique-aircraft restoration."

"Like Eddie."

The mention of his father's name never failed to deliver a rush of memories and nostalgia, and now was no different. Bo found his voice softer when he answered this time. "Like my father, yes."

Dimi bit her lower lip, looked at Mel. Mel gave her a slight shake of her head, telling Bo what he needed to know.

Mel was the one in charge.

"So what are you going to do?" Mel asked. "Stand around and watch us run the place until Sally shows up?"

Bo made a show of looking around, at the decided lack of customers, at the slightly shabby look to the interior of the lobby, at the nerves leaping off of the two of them that could together provide enough electricity to run a small Third World country. "Seems to me you could use some help around here."

"We're fine," Mel said tightly.

"Fine? Maybe. But who's got the deed, Mel?"

Myriad emotions crossed their faces at that: horror, dismay, frustration.

"Yeah, think about that," he suggested, then whistling beneath his breath, he straightened and walked away.

Mel stared at his strong, sleek back as he headed across the lobby toward the hallway that led to the private offices in the back, and felt her stomach sink.

"What is he doing here?" Dimi hissed.

Mel leaned in and grabbed the phone. "You heard him." Her gaze was still locked on Bo as she punched in the number she'd memorized years ago: Sally's cell. "He wants to talk to Sally. He's not sure the deed is authentic any more than I am." While she waited, listening to the phone ring God knew where, Ernest walked by again, sans cart this time. Mel felt like growling at him, but that would serve little purpose other than to tweak his curiosity, so she managed to control herself.

Sally didn't pick up the phone, but then again, she rarely did. In fact, it had been nearly a year since they'd last talked, not that anyone knew that, because Mel and Dimi had perpetuated the image that they'd talked to Sally a lot more often. It kept the calm, and Mel liked calm.

She got Sally's voice mail. "Sally," Mel said at the beep. "Call me."

Dimi shook her head. "Is he going to tell everyone?"

"Not if I have a say."

"How did he get that deed in his name?"

"It wasn't in his name. It was in his father's."

"Eddie Black."

The man never failed to thrust Mel back in time, to the summer after freshman year. She'd been learning her way around an airplane engine, thanks to Sally and her mechanic at the time, Don, a cantankerous old guy with a cigarette always hanging out one corner of his mouth and a beer at the ready. For whatever reason, he'd taken to Mel, maybe because she'd made it her business to know the difference between a Beech and a Piper, and he liked that in a kid.

Dimi had filed and answered phones in between flirting with the linemen and any customer who happened to possess a penis. She and Mel hadn't exactly been friends, Mel having come from the trailer park across the tracks, while Dimi ran with her rich-bitch crowd. But that summer they'd shared one catastrophic event that had changed things forever: Mel's mother running off with Dimi's father. The remaining parents soon vacated as well, each by different means. Dimi's mom had chosen prescription meds, which ended up killing her. Mel's father's escape of choice . . . booze.

And so the unlikely alliance of Mel and Dimi had begun. Not sisters, not friends . . . just two very different girls stuck together by happenstance.

Not so oddly, Sally's world had become their world. Sally, with her big smile, bigger heart, a magnet for men, usually the *wrong* men. Every year had been a different guy, but that year it'd been Eddie Black.

Something had seemed off to Mel and Dimi from the start, though it hadn't been until later that they'd figured the Aussie for what he was—a con man. And they included in that his laid-back, sweet-talking, sexy-as-hell teenage son, Bo.

Eddie and Bo had parked it at North Beach all that long, hot, lazy summer, and by September's end, Sally had been stupid-in-love, with Eddie calling the shots.

Then something had happened, and Eddie and Bo had gone back to Australia. And Sally had vanished.

She'd called the next week to let Mel and Dimi know she was on a road trip looking for Eddie because—the girls had been right—he'd conned her.

What they didn't know until later was that all Sally's accounts had been emptied, leaving North Beach in a world of hurt. Mel and Dimi had stayed on, running the show for Sally, trying to keep things afloat for when she came back.

Only she hadn't come back. Eddie had driven his van off a bridge and died. Whether devastated or just furious, Sally had stayed gone, letting the girls send her money as they could, mere kids trying so hard to be grown-up.

Sally's calls slowed, coming less and less frequently, then hardly at all. In fact, the past two times they'd sent her money, she'd not even responded, though they pretended otherwise.

In retrospect, with the 20/20 hindsight of dubious maturity, Mel and Dimi probably shouldn't have ever pretended to be in constant contact with Sally, but it had kept the calm then, and the status quo. Besides, dwelling wasn't Mel's style. Nor were regrets. She'd lived with the decisions they'd made back then.

Now Bo would have to do the same. "If that deed's legit," Mel said, "as Eddie's only child, Bo is his heir."

"*God.* I need more tea." Dimi started going through her basket of tea bags, bracelets jangling. "Something calming."

It'd take a planeload of good meds for Mel to feel calm. "It's going to be okay, Dimi."

Dimi shot her a wry glance. "Really? How?" She shook her head. "No, don't answer. There is no answer for that. But it'd sure help if he was ugly, you know?"

Yeah. Mel knew.

"Seriously. Before I realized who he was, I could have just gobbled him right up."

"You gobble up all men."

"Hey." Dimi caught a glimpse of her perfect self in the reflection of the mirror, and laughed. "Look, I realize you're programmed differently than me, and that you actually think before you act, but try and tell me your every hormone didn't stand up and do a tap dance at the sight of him, gorgeous as sin. And that sexy accent—"

"The accent is no big deal."

"You really suck at lying, you know that?" Dimi studied her with a knowing smirk. "Your eyes go all squinty . . ."

"Fine," Mel said, trying to relax her eye muscles. "He looks . . . fine. Okay?"

"Honey, fine would be a nice glass of Chardonnay. Fine is a pretty blue sky. That man is so far off the charts from fine you can't even *see* fine."

Mel tossed up her hands. "And we're having this conversation why?"

"Right." Dimi sat back down, waved her away, crystals tinkling together. "Listen, go kick his Aussie ass out of here, this place is ours."

Mel found a way to smile. "I thought you dreamed of walking away from this place."

"I'll walk away because I want to, not because some bastard takes over."

That was Dimi. Stubborn to a beautiful fault.

"Unfortunately, he's not going anywhere. At least not until he talks to Sally."

"But that's not going to happen. We can't—"

"We have to."

They stared at each other for a long, uncomfortable beat.

"You really think you can con a con?" Dimi finally whispered.

"We have to," Mel repeated.

Dimi leaned close. "You and I both know, he's the son of the very best, he's—"

"Yeah." Mel hopped off the desk and tossed back her shoulders and the stray strands of hair from her face. "I know what he is. Now let's find out what he isn't."

"Mel."

"Wish me luck."

"Luck. You're going to need it." Dimi jumped up and hugged her hard, then pulled back, hands on Mel's face. "We're bad. We're tough. We own our world."

Mel found a smile. It was their old motto, from when they'd been young, scared, and on their own. They were still on their own, but not so young.

And maybe only a little scared.

"Do whatever you have to," Dimi said quietly. "Just get him out of here."

Yeah.

Whatever she had to . . .

At the thought of what that might entail, goose bumps rose on Mel's skin, and not necessarily the bad kind.

Chapter 3

Mel headed across the lobby, mind occupied by her singular mission: *Get rid of Bo Black*.

She passed by the café. Charlene stood behind the counter, scrubbing down the scarred tile, singing along to Metallica. "Mel!" she cried, gesturing her close, looking around them before whispering conspiratorially, "So?"

"So . . . what?"

"Who's the cutie? A business meeting? New client? Old friend?" She drawled out this last word in her Southern voice, making the word ten syllables.

"Uh . . . yeah. Sort of."

"Sort of which?"

"Oh, hey . . ." Desperate subject change. "Did Ernest get the oven going yet?"

"No, not yet." Char bit her lip and looked at the oven, effectively sidetracked. The café was hers and Al's livelihood, at least until he sold more paintings, and since their kids had left last year, the café was also her baby. Char would have rather put her energy into another real-live baby, but Al had talked her out of that insanity. "Ernest just left to go get a part. So, about the guy—"

"Yeah, I've got a call—" She began to walk. Fast.

"I need my gossip fix!" Char called after her. "You know I do!"

Mel loved Char, but telling the woman anything was the equivalent of broadcasting it to the entire world. Following the path Bo had taken, Mel entered the long hallway off the lobby.

The first office was hers. She just *knew* he was in there, waiting for round two. For a moment she stood outside the door, drawing in a deep, calming breath, which didn't tame the butterflies suddenly leaping like crazy in her stomach.

So long. It'd been so long since she'd had to face any of this.

Or him.

Lifting her chin high—a habit she'd adopted to make her feel taller—she pushed open her office door.

And, yep, there he was, sprawled in her chair, boots up on her desk, hands folded behind his head as he sat there, contemplating the universe.

Her universe.

He'd asked for Sally, which made no sense. Did he really not know Sally had never come back here? Did she really have that unexpected advantage?

"G'day," he said when she walked in, a charming smile on his lips, his eyes half-lowered, his fawn-colored hair fashionably shaggy. "Ready to talk, are you?"

She took one look at the long, lean, hard length of him and shut the door behind her. No need for everyone to hear the unavoidable argument heading her way. "Get out of my chair."

A smile quirked about his lips. She was amusing him. "Ah, now that's not very sweet."

She put her hands on her hips, daring him to take a good look. "Do I look sweet to you?"

His eyes heated suggestively as he ran them over her. She was covered from head to toe, for God's sake, but he made her feel . . . naked.

"Well, actually—"

"Never mind!" she said crossly. "Just get out of my office."

"*Your* office?" He looked around, the leather of her chair crinkling with his weight. "That's funny. I remember this as Sally's office."

Crap. "I'm using it in her absence."

"So where is she, on vacation? Swindling or conning her latest victim out of his money?"

She couldn't tell him Sally wasn't around. With that deed, he might feel like taking over right here and now.

If it was legit.

She thought of Dimi, of Char and Al, Ritchie and Kellan, Danny, their mechanic . . . all like family to her. She couldn't lose the reins now and let anything happen to the life they'd all built here.

Then what he said slowly sank in. "Sally never swindled or conned a soul in her life. Apparently, she left that to your father."

Had his eyes been sleepy and sexy only a moment ago? They went cold as ice as he slowly uncoiled and rose to his full height, coming around the desk toward her, six feet plus of pure rough-and-tumble attitude. "Leave my father out of this," he said very quietly.

She dug in her heels and refused to back up. Which put them in each other's breathing space. He was at least a head taller than she, smelled warm and sexy, and seemed to be built entirely of perfectly toned muscle.

And yet it wasn't any of that that stopped her, but the fierce, protective look in his eyes. This wasn't the rangy, trouble-filled, wickedly smiling Bo who'd been caught with his hands up a woman's skirt, but a man with passion and a deep capacity for emotion. *Leave his father out of this?* How was that possible? It had been Eddie Black who set in motion a chain of events they were still dealing with all these years later.

"Then let's leave Sally out of it."

He was already shaking his head. "No can do, darlin'."

"That deed is fake."

"Sally will tell you the truth."

Oh, God. Sally wasn't going to show up to tell her anything. Which meant he was going to hang out here forever. "How about I call you when she arrives?"

"How about I'm not budging until I talk to her?" He took one more step, putting them toe to toe. "And while we're at it, who's running the show without her?"

"Me." She had to tip her head up to look into his eyes, damn him. She raised her gaze past his broad shoulders, past his throat, past his jaw, which hadn't seen a razor today and maybe not yesterday, either, to those mesmerizing green eyes that promised he was up to no good. "*I'm* running the show. Why?"

"Because you're doing a shitty job of it. Your café should be filled with locals but the oven isn't running. Your fuel pump's a mess, you're lucky you haven't been shut down by the EPA. You have bill collectors calling—"

"*What?* How did you—"

He put a finger over her lips, then had the balls to smile. "Let's establish some ground rules here," he said. "One, I'm staying until I talk to Sally. Two, I don't expect your lovely office, but I do have a business to run so I'll need a place to hole up and work while I'm here, with a computer, phone, and radio equipment, of course." His eyes went steely. "And three . . . Don't underestimate me. Something's going on, Mel, and I will figure out what."

She grabbed his wrist and tried to toss his hand aside, but

the man, solid as a rock, couldn't be budged, and she had to settle for a withering stare. "You're not staying long enough to need an office."

"Why, is Sally showing up today?" He cocked a brow at her silence. "Tomorrow? No? Then get used to seeing this face, Mel."

Something popped inside her head. She was fairly certain it was her brain matter coming to a boil. "I don't want you freaking everyone out."

"I don't plan to do any such thing. I just want to talk to Sally."

"I don't see the need for you to park yourself *here*," she said. "Take your fancy plane somewhere and I'll call you." She spun on her heels, opening the door, but a big hand reached over her head and shut it, then held it closed.

This left her crowded up against the wood, with his body not quite brushing the back of hers, though she felt surrounded by him all the same. He was as hard as he looked, all tough muscle and bone, not an ounce of softness to him. *Damn, genius, now what?* She didn't know, but it was hard to think in this close proximity. She stared down at his boots, one on either side of hers.

"No can do on the leaving thing," he murmured, his voice like a caress up her spine, making her shiver. "Nothing personal, Mel, but I don't trust you."

"You're in my space." She said this from between her teeth, caught in some inexplicable place between fury and pure, unadulterated lust.

Unbelievably, he put his mouth to the sensitive spot just beneath her ear. "Yeah. But it's such a nice space." His breath whispered over her flesh, and just like that, rendered her stupid.

And furious. "Get out of here, Bo."

"Why don't you tell me just why it is you panicked when you saw the deed in my father's name?"

She closed her eyes against his voice, which turned out to be a big mistake because with her eyes closed, their position felt even more intimate. "No reason really. Just surprise."

His exhale fanned her temple, and she heard the humorless smile in his voice. "Can't bullshit a bullshitter, darlin'."

She realized she was squinting her eyes. *You squint your eyes when you lie*. She opened them wide. "I'm not."

"So you're asking me to believe Sally left you completely out of the loop on this one."

"No." Mel put her forehead to the door, a very weak part of her wanting to press her bottom back snug to his crotch, which was crazy. *Crazy.* "Yes."

"Which is it?"

"No." She had to tell him this much, he was going to find out anyway. And if she gave this freely, maybe he'd trust her enough to tell her what it was he needed with Sally. "Yes, I knew the deed wasn't in the safe. No, I didn't know why. I had just hoped it'd been misplaced, that's all. And . . ."

"And . . ."

She let out a breath. "People might think the deed is still here. In Sally's name."

"People?"

"Employees."

He went very still in surprise. "So no one knows what Sally did all those years ago? For ten years you thought you were working for her? Do you know how unbelievable that is?"

Yes. Yes, she did. "If your deed is real."

"Oh, it's real." He spun her around, then held her still, looking at her for a long moment. "But what I want to know is, how a smart woman like you didn't see through the crap."

Wasn't that just the question. Maybe because she'd been too busy keeping them afloat. Everyone here had counted on her. Still did. They were her family. And then there was the fact that she'd believed she'd been doing Sally a favor, Sally who'd given her everything. "The deed should have been here. We had no indication otherwise. And if your deed is legit, what took you ten years to show up?"

"You know my father died."

"Yes." The day Sally went after him, as a matter of fact. Bo would have been just eighteen. And alone. And, she thought, remembering how close he'd been with his father, undoubtedly devastated. "I was very sorry to hear it."

His gaze met hers. "Despite what you thought of him?"

"I wanted him gone, not dead. What about your mother?"

"I'd been with Eddie since I was young." There were memories in his gaze, unhappy ones, and her heart squeezed because she of all people understood unhappy memories.

He'd been alone. Eighteen and alone. She didn't want to think about that, or how it softened her, not when she stood so close she could breathe him in, feel the strength of him in his every line. "What did you do?"

"I went into the military, and then to college. It wasn't until I finally went home that I realized what had happened."

"Which was?"

"That my father's 1944 Beechcraft was gone, and so was his savings."

Leaving him with nothing. She didn't want to think about that, either. "And you assume Sally took both?"

"Not took. Conned."

"Sally said your father conned her."

"I'm going to be able to prove my story," he said. "Can you?"

No. No, she couldn't. "You have the quit deed. Possibly forged."

"Not forged," he said tightly. "And in any case, it's not worth anything close to the Beechcraft and the half a mil savings." He looked around derisively. "From what I see, this place is worth a fraction of what I lost."

"So what do you plan to do?" she asked, feeling a bit wary.

"Oh, no," he said. "Now you. Where's Sally, Mel?"

She shook her head, reaching behind her for the handle. But he followed her out into the hall, and naturally, Ernest chose that moment to come back through with his damn cart, slowing at the midway point, watching them curiously.

At a long look from Mel, he sighed and kept moving, cart clanking. *God*. She had to get Bo out of here before he started waving that deed around. In spite of his saying otherwise, she didn't trust him not to claim to own everything and everyone, inciting a general panic.

But the minute Ernest vanished around the corner, Al appeared, and by the look on his face, Mel knew Charlene had sent him to eavesdrop.

Damn it. North Beach Airport gossip could rival any small town in the country for fast-traveling news. Clearly, an APB had been put out. *Get news on the stranger*. With a frustrated sigh, she put her hands on Bo's chest to shove him back into her office.

But as she already knew, the man couldn't be budged unless he chose to be. Trying to choose for him was like trying to move a two-ton bull. A damned stubborn one. "In here," she said with another useless push, exceedingly aware of the heat and hard strength of him beneath her palms as she listened to Ernest's cart coming their way again. *Crap.* "Hurry—"

"Why, darlin'," Bo murmured, bending his head so that his jaw brushed hers. "All you had to do was ask."

Yeah, yeah. She followed him back into the office, watching over her shoulder to see who was looking, shutting the door to give them some privacy. "Now." But one look at Bo had the words falling right out of her head.

He was unbuttoning his shirt.

"What are you doing?" she asked weakly.

"You said hurry." A wedge of sinewy, tanned skin appeared. He shrugged the shirt off his shoulders, exposing his chest, the defined pecs, the correlated ridges of his ribs, his belly—

"No." She loved that spot on a man, so hard with strength yet so vulnerable, loved to put her mouth there—No. *Concentrate!* "Bo, I didn't mean—"

His hands went to the buttons on his Levi's.

Pop.

Pop.

"W-wait!" She forced her gaze up, up into his. "Seriously. I didn't mean—" But at the laughter in his eyes she trailed off, her eye twitching. *He was messing with her*. And doing a damn fine job of it, too, standing there looking like sin on a stick. She was torn between the urge to kill him and wanting, with sudden, shocking violence, to gobble him up in one bite. It was so unfair that he looked as good as he did, that he sounded so yummy with that accent, that when he smiled, he looked even better. *Where was the justice in that?* She slapped her hands over her eyes. "Get your clothes back on!"

He let out another soft laugh that had her every erogenous zone doing a tap dance. But she had great control, and she waited until she heard rustling before lowering her hands, telling herself she was relieved that he'd gotten his shirt back on. Yep, very relieved. "And whatever you do, don't be waving that deed around again!"

In the act of buttoning his shirt, he went still, then stepped close.

It was wrong, but all Mel could think about was his Levi's. And how they were still undone. She let her gaze fall to his chest, his belly, trying to see—

"Mel."

She closed her eyes, a defense mechanism.

"Mel."

Reluctantly, she looked at him.

"Yeah, there you go," he said in a tone that made her forget the Levi's and want to kick him again. "The fact is I'm here." His eyes were determined, hair tousled, mouth half-curved, his big body far too close. "I'm staying. And because I happen to hold the deed and you do not, *I'll* be doling out the rules now. *My* rules."

Chapter 4

Bo had an interesting day. He had no idea what Mel told everyone before she left on her charter flight, but he kept his end of the bargain. He didn't freak anyone out by revealing the deed. At this point all he really wanted was to straighten this out with Sally.

Privately.

In any case, he was left alone to wander around the airport, in and out of the different hangars, refamiliarizing himself with how the place ran.

Just being here brought back memories; of coming here with his father, high on the purchase of the '44 Beechcraft. They'd planned on a complete renovation, then selling the RC-455 at a huge profit to start all over again.

And then Eddie had met Sally.

Sally's smile had transfixed his father into a love-struck fool, and Bo could do nothing but helplessly watch as Sally broke his father's heart so much that he'd lost concentration and driven off a bridge, plunging to his death.

Bo had been left all alone and devastated and, yeah, he'd acted impulsively by going into the military. But it had turned out to be a good thing for him. He'd gotten his business degree and had become a pilot, and by the time he'd gotten out, he'd gone from boy to man. Then the man had been destroyed all over again when he'd finally gone through his father's things and discovered Sally had done more than broken Eddie's heart.

She'd somehow conned him out of the Beechcraft and the cash, leaving nothing but the deed to the decidedly less-valuable North Beach.

Why had Eddie made that deal? What could he possibly have been thinking as he'd signed their life over? Bo didn't know, and he probably never would.

As the day went on, a few private jets came and went, but with North Beach's fuel pump down for the day, many customers bypassed the place entirely, which meant a huge loss of income.

It boggled Bo's business-oriented mind. Ernest was still working on fixing the pump, and supposedly they had another guy coming out tomorrow or the next day. Bo himself could have probably lent a hand to the efforts, but as no one had exactly welcomed him or tried to even talk to him, he figured fuck it. Sure this place was his now, but damn it, it wasn't what he wanted. What he wanted was the Beechcraft his father had loved. The money would have been welcome as well.

To get either, he also needed Sally. *Where was she?*

And what was pretty Mel hiding? He knew it was something, because things were not adding up. She couldn't talk to him. Odd, since he didn't have a beef with her. Though he was beginning to understand she had a beef with him.

Something else that didn't add up . . .

Each of the employees here was interesting, to say the least. Not a one eager to make friends.

Bo didn't care, but he'd hoped for some answers. And yet they were an incredibly tight-lipped, loyal bunch.

He'd thought he'd start with Dimi, but she threw him such

a fulminating look, he just kept walking, instead trying Danny. The mechanic was quiet but steady as a rock, and knowledgeable as hell for someone with flip-flops on his feet and the surf report blaring on his radio. He warmed up a bit when Bo revealed his love for all things aircraft, but was careful not to take the bait with any of Bo's careful probing, giving nothing away of Mel or Sally or anyone here.

Bo tried again with Kellan and Ritchie in the employee break room. They were playing darts, and after awhile, seemed to forget Bo was there, which scored him all sorts of interesting but useless gossip; such as the fact that Dimi serial-dated men, and Mel rarely dated at all.

Must be that cheer and sweetness she had in spades.

Later he tried the café. Char cooked him an orgasmically good burger while singing along to an old STYX song, although singing was a debatable word. She was clearly curious about him but managed to restrain herself from answering any questions.

It was seriously starting to piss him off.

Ernest came next. He was an odd bloke who muttered to himself and spent a lot of time looking at spiderwebs, and was definitely not going to warm up to Bo enough to give him any valuable information.

A bust. The whole day had been a bust, with the exception of the one piece of knowledge he'd gained about the people here: they shared a deep, abiding, unwavering love for this place, and an even deeper one for Mel.

He told himself he didn't care. He was on a mission, and he'd only just also realized that the mission was going to have to include something he hadn't expected: clearing his father's name. Because no matter what happened, whether Bo got the Beechcraft or the money back, Eddie Black did not deserve to be remembered as a con artist, and the thought that it could happen started a slow burn in his gut. Eddie had once saved the young Bo's life, then had raised him while trying to get his own dream off the ground, and as far as Bo was concerned, Eddie had been a fucking hero, and by the time this was over, everyone else here would sure as hell know it.

Mel came back in the late afternoon. Bo watched as she connected with everyone there, making sure all was okay.

Like a mother cat checking on her kittens.

Actually, he thought, it was probably a lot more like a wild tigress checking on her feral cubs. She'd apparently had a long layover and had gone shopping. She'd brought Dimi some crystals. She had a book of old prints for Al, something that made him grin from ear to ear. For Char she'd bought a vintage Warrant T-shirt that made the woman squeal, her maroon hair bouncing as she ran to kiss Mel right on the lips. Kellan and Ritchie scored a new bunny calendar for the employee break room, and not the furry kind of bunny, either. Even Danny got something, a special wax for his surfboard that made him pull Mel in for a warm hug.

Bo himself got diddly squat, unless he counted the cool glances she kept throwing his way.

By six o'clock, the staff began to vacate, and by six fifteen, North Beach was a ghost town.

Bo was waiting. His plan: search the place up and down and sideways for some clues as to what Sally had done with the Beechcraft and/or the money.

A long shot, sure, but Bo had always been a gambling man. He'd already begun to check out the leased hangars on the premises. All but two were longtime rentals, and locked up tight. He'd been through the unleased two today when he'd lifted the master key from Mel's office.

Both had been empty. No worries. Somehow he'd get himself into the other twelve, but that was for another day. For now he made his way through the maintenance hangar. He was checking out the planes kept there, considering where exactly to begin snooping, when Mel found him.

She was wearing her coveralls again, unbuttoned, the arms off and tied around her waist, exposing a black tank top and a pretty pink bra strap peeking out on each shoulder. So apparently, beneath all the tough swagger and talk there was a girlie girl in there somewhere. In another time and place Bo might have tried to draw that woman out, but he was frustrated and tired, and blamed a good part of that—fair or not—on the woman staring at him.

"I'm leaving for the night," she said evenly. "And so are you."

"What, you don't trust me in here? Shock." And because he'd noticed that she didn't like it, he shifted closer.

He had to hand it to her. She remained cool, except for the slight widening of her pupils, which even she couldn't control.

Or the hardening of her nipples.

Yeah, now *that* reaction he really liked.

She crossed her arms over her chest. "Fine. Stay the night for all I care, I have nothing to hide."

"Now, see," he murmured, running a finger over the strong line of her jaw, her skin smooth and softer than he expected, "that I doubt."

She smacked his hand away, but not before he saw the leap in the pulse at the base of her neck.

Fascinating. Suddenly all those answers he wanted included something new—knowing more about her.

"I called my attorney about the deed," she said. "Greg's going to check it out."

"Good." He considered her. "So do you always live and breathe your work, Mel? Or is there more to you than the job? You've never done anything else, right?"

"What else should I be doing?"

"I don't know. Have you looked in the mirror? Hell, you could get a job just standing there and smiling."

She scoffed at that idea. "Don't tell me you're so sexist that you think I'd be better suited for modeling than flying."

He was quiet a moment as the picture of her modeling—maybe modeling absolutely nothing but her birthday suit—took root. "Shit," he finally said a little gruffly, realizing she'd said something that he'd missed. "That picture pretty much took over my brain for a sec, sorry."

"You are disgustingly male."

"Guilty as charged."

"I'm so not doing this." She stalked toward the door.

"Ah, don't go away mad." *Just go away*. But he couldn't help the curiosity. All he'd ever seen of her had been here at North Beach. "What do you do when you're not flying? Or thinking about flying? You all work and no play, Mel?"

She pulled open the door.

"Okaaaaaay, I'll take that as a yes," he said, mouth quirking as she threw a universal sign involving only her middle finger over her shoulder.

"Your momma know you do that?" he called after her.

"My momma taught me."

He laughed, but arched a brow when she whirled back on him. "And what about *your* momma?" she demanded. "She know her son is the son of a con man?"

"My momma taught me," he said softly, echoing her words. But whether Mel had meant it or not, Bo certainly did. His mother *had* taught him—she'd taught him to be quick on his feet so as to dodge the back of her hand, or whatever she had handy.

Mel stared at the door, then turned back. "Look, I'm sorry. I'm just tired." She blew out a breath. "And maybe irritable."

He felt his mouth twitch. "Maybe?"

Her hands went to her hips. "Trying to meet you halfway here, Black." She had delicate purple smudges beneath her eyes, he realized, and her shoulders seemed to carry the weight of her world.

"Go home," he said, tired of the both of them. "We can go at this again tomorrow."

She nodded. "Night."

"G'day, Mel."

She left, muttering something he couldn't quite catch, something about his accent not being nearly as charming as everyone seemed to think. He followed more slowly, taking his time, his gaze searching the hangar thoroughly as he moved.

Because he couldn't stop wondering.

Where would Sally have hidden a plane? And then there was the money. Had she spent it? No way had she put it in a bank to wave a red flag to the government about her conning.

Nope, she'd stashed both. Here? He just had a feeling . . . or maybe that was the itch between his shoulder blades telling him he was being lied to.

Above him, the lights shifted to low. Not exactly subtle, his Mel. Apparently he was to leave now, too. He made his way back to the main hangar, just as the lights there lowered as well. Squinting through the now darkened lobby, he saw two shadows making their way to the front desk.

"I'm worried about her, she works too hard." The soft, Southern accent was Charlene's.

"She's fine, she thrives on stress, our Mel," Al answered.

"Well, I don't."

"Oh, I know that, baby." At the door now, Al stopped to nuzzle at his wife's neck, making her giggle. "I have just the thing to help you unwind."

"Oh, no you don't. I tried to get a little at lunch, and you were too into your silly football game on the radio. You told me to hush."

"It was baseball, and all I said was please, whenever possible, talk during the commercials."

Char huffed but Al was persistent, and she ended up angling her head to give him better access. "Is there a game on tonight?" she drawled a little breathlessly.

"No, ma'am."

"Well, then what are you waiting for? Take me home, big guy."

The front door shut on Al's soft laugh.

Bo moved through the dark lobby, stopping at the sight of another shadow directly across from him.

"Looking for something?" Mel asked in that low, slightly husky voice that always, however inappropriately, brought to mind hot sex.

"You know I am."

"But I still don't know what."

"Sally," he said. "I'm looking for Sally."

"She's—"

"Not here. I know. Thanks."

"Yeah." She studied him a moment, then pulled out her keys, started toward the door.

"Char's right," he said. "You're stressed."

"How do you know?"

"It's in your walk."

"And how is that?"

"Well, you move like you have a poker shoved up your—"

She turned back, her mouth tight. "I do not."

He just smiled.

A frustrated growl escaped her. "I'm *not* stressed. I love it here and I walk just fine."

How the woman managed to work all day and still smell good was beyond him, but she did, and that being a turn-on as well, he wiggled his nose trying to get another sniff.

"And to answer your earlier question," she huffed. "Flying is what I do. It's who I am. It's everything to me. I'd have thought you'd understand that."

"Yes, but I do it good enough that I'm not strapped for cash on a daily basis."

"I'm not that hard up. Just in a slump, is all."

"Darling, you're in more than a slump. This place needs an overhaul. And Anderson Air needs more passenger conveniences, more attention to the little details—"

"My bare-bones service is what makes me the cheapest choice."

"People with Lear jets don't want cheap, mate." He chucked her beneath the chin just for the excuse of touching her and decided not to worry about what that meant. "There's more to this business than flying." He shifted closer, which had the predictable benefit of annoying her, then used the opportunity to inhale as deeply as he could without pressing his damn face into her neck. "You need help."

"If you're offering, I already said no thanks."

"Actually, you never said thanks at all."

She choked out a laugh. The sound had a hint of desperation in it, and he got the feeling she was on the very edge. He tugged on a strand of her wayward, gorgeous hair. "Maybe you need some of Al's stress relief, Bo style."

"Go away, Bo."

"Yeah, I'll go, but I'll be back."

And she'd have to deal with that.

Unfortunately, they both would.

Chapter 5

The next day Mel woke up from a disturbingly erotic dream about Bo, of all people. She sat straight up, panting at the image that had implanted itself in her brain, that of him slowly pulling off her clothing one piece at a time, kissing each inch he revealed.

She had to laugh at herself in the light of day, because— wow, Bo? *So* not going to happen.

Her cell rang. "Did you hear from Sally yet?" Dimi asked.

Mel fell back onto the bed.

Long silence. "How 'bout the deed?" Dimi finally asked, slurring her words.

"Hey, have you been up all night?"

"Sleeping's overrated."

No doubt she'd stayed out all night trying to party away the stress. It wasn't the first time, but for Mel, the worry never ceased. "Dimi—"

"Did you hear from Greg on the deed?"

"Too early for the attorney to call me," Mel said slowly. "Look, take the morning off." Sober up. "Or you'll be dead on your feet."

"Yeah. Okay."

"And don't worry. We're going to be okay."

"I know." But Dimi didn't sound as if she believed it, and Mel had to admit, she didn't, either. She drove into the airport on pins and needles, still a little off balance from her dream. *Get it together,* she ordered herself. *Because if you don't, he'll be able to see it.*

But it was still on her mind all the way to North Beach until she sat at her desk and brought up her e-mail, where she received yet another unpleasant shock. She had an e-mail from LeaveItAlone at an Internet server she didn't recognize, and nothing in the subject or body of the e-mail.

LeaveItAlone?

Mel forwarded the thing to Ernest. *Who sent this?* she typed in her e-mail, and wasn't surprised to get an immediate response, which meant he was in the maintenance hangar on the computer scrolling through porn sites again instead of working.

Someone who thinks you're a pain in the ass, he answered.

Mel sighed, rolled her eyes, and read the rest of his response.

But I'll see what I can find out. In the meantime, stop pissing people off.

Yeah, yeah. *Leave it alone.*

What the hell did that mean? She'd received plenty of ambiguous mail over the years. Each and every time she raised their fuel prices, for instance. Or when she'd had to cut back North Beach's hours of operation from 24/7 to six AM until five PM. Or when she'd once refused a rich client service for his five jets because he'd wanted her to arrange for prostitutes for all his crew.

But none of those had been anonymous threats. So who? Bo?

No. He wouldn't go the anonymous route, he had no need to do so.

Still, the coincidence seemed too much to ignore . . .

Leave it alone. Leave *what* alone? The airport? The questionable deed in Bo's hands? She closed her e-mail program and put the e-mail out of her mind. She had a long charter to Tuscon and back, a flight that would keep her away from North Beach until late, and it was time to put her head there. On the way out for her preflight check, she stopped at the café, where Char was working on something that smelled like pure heaven.

"White Trash Casserole, straight from my momma's box of favorite recipes," Char drawled over KISS screeching on the radio. Her purple hair was piled on top of her head, precariously held there by what looked like two pencils. She wore another pair of short shorts, and today's T-shirt said: TAKE A BITE OF ME. PLEASE.

"Lord, it's going to be a hot one today," Char said. "Or maybe I'm just getting hot flashes." She fanned herself with the hem of her shirt. "Anyway, got a late start this morning, sorry. This won't be ready in time for you but I've got donuts."

If Mel was compulsively early, Charlene was compulsively late, but she loaded Mel up with a bag of the mouthwatering donuts, and all was forgiven. "You need an alarm clock," Mel said.

"Oh, it's not that. Al and I—"

"Stop right there if this story ends with the two of you having sex."

"Well . . ." Char giggled.

Mel grabbed her bag of donuts. "I've got my fingers in my ears, I can't hear you—"

"We just—"

"Lalalalalalala," Mel sang over Char's laugh, and went out onto the tarmac.

Three men stood next to a Piper Mirage in the early-morning sun: Danny, the customer who owned the Piper, and Bo. Danny wore his coveralls and was consulting a clipboard, his long blond hair still damp from his early surf. Their customer was in a pricey-looking suit. Bo wore cargo shorts, a sweat-shirt, and clean work boots, his legs looking long and tanned. All three men, different as night and day, were laughing about something, carefree and easygoing.

Mel hadn't felt carefree and easygoing in so long; money issues, stress . . . And she resented that Bo could show up here, turn her world upside down, and laugh. Damn it, he was integrating himself, making himself right at home. In *her* home.

LeaveItAlone . . .

Had he? Would he?

No, she reminded herself, even if the man made her teeth gnash together, he wouldn't. Not his style.

He lifted his sunglasses to the top of his head and met her gaze. In his she saw the ready humor and the unasked question. *What now, Mel?*

She'd like to show him "what now" right now. But it'd sure be easier if he didn't look like a million bucks standing there, if he wasn't street smart and sharp as a tack, capable of running her world without problem, maybe even better than she . . .

Extra grateful for the bag of donuts in her hand, she stalked to her plane and began her own preflight check. She was in a crouch, writing on her clipboard when two work boots appeared in her peripheral, topped by a set of tanned, toned legs. Bracing herself, she straightened.

Bo eyed Char's goodie bag. "Smells good."

"The donuts are mine."

"Maybe I meant you."

Unbelievably, her nipples hardened. "I smell like oil and gasoline."

Leaning in, he sniffed exaggeratedly, his nose wriggling just beneath her ear, causing a sort of chain reaction from her nipples to ground zero between her thighs. "Mmmm," he said. "Two of my favorite scents."

That they were also her favorite scents would *not* budge her.

"Want to know another favorite scent?" he murmured.

"*No*."

"An aroused woman."

She crossed her arms and stepped back, making him laugh softly. "Yeah, sexy as hell, that scent." He smiled, something that threw her off, then hooked his finger into the bag she clutched to her chest, peering in. "Look at that. You have extra."

"One. You can have one."

He nabbed a large, old-fashioned chocolate glaze, sinking strong white teeth into it and letting out a rough sound of pure pleasure that might have curled her toes, though she'd have to be under the threat of a slow, tortuous death to admit it.

"Have a safe flight," he said around a mouthful.

Damn, just when she thought he was a complete loss to the human race, he had to go and say something nice. "I have no idea how to take you," she said, baffled. "No idea at all."

He shrugged a broad shoulder. "Then just take me."

A laugh escaped her before she could stop herself. "Do those lines ever really work for you?"

He just grinned, and her toes curled some more. Yeah, they worked for him, and it left Mel shaking her head at the entire female population, including herself.

Mel's charter to Arizona went smoothly. Once she'd landed in Tucson, she called Dimi. "Everything okay?"

"As okay as it gets."

There was a lot in Dimi's voice, and Mel felt gray hairs kicking in. Dimi handled her stress badly. That was fact. She downward spiraled in tough times, and it wasn't pretty. Mel wanted to prevent Dimi from falling into that pit again, but how?

Get Bo the hell out of there, that was how. "Hang in there," Mel demanded, and hung up. While waiting for a re-fuel, standing in the blazing sun, she tried Sally's cell again, and this time got an extremely unwelcome surprise instead of Sally's voice mail: the number was no longer in service.

Mel blinked. Stared at her cell phone. Redialed.

Same thing.

She slowly shut the phone, shock crashing over her, wave after wave.

What the hell was happening to her universe?

Late that afternoon, Dimi walked through the lobby of North Beach on autopilot as she closed shop for the day, for once not enjoying the gorgeous view of the lush green hills of the Santa Ynez Mountains or the scalloped coastline, or the fact that the tarmac had three planes on it, which meant paying customers.

She was too wigged out about Bo's return, about Sally's vanishing act, about the deed . . . She could hardly even breathe.

All this worry was bad for her. It made her hair lank, made her stomach hurt. Made her feel like she was playing catch with steak knives.

She blew out her candles, shut down her computer. The café was still hopping but that was Char's deal, so she went into the employee break room for her things and found the lights still on.

Danny stood there, playing darts by himself. He wore board shorts, a loose tank, and no shoes. He threw his last dart, his lower lip between his teeth as he concentrated, and when the dart hit double thirteen, he turned to her and smiled, teeth flashing white, his eyes looking startlingly blue in his tanned face. "Play me."

"Can't." God, couldn't he see she felt so on edge, so tense she thought she might shatter at the slightest provocation?

"Come on, I'm on a roll," he coaxed. "And you look like you could use a little fun."

Fun. Yeah, she needed fun. Mindless fun, and not the platonic kind she always had with Danny, but the kind of fun she could get only with a man who didn't know her, who couldn't look into her eyes and see the pain, or if they did, wouldn't comment on it.

Danny wasn't that guy. He knew her too well, knew all her dark secrets. In fact, even now his smile faded, and he looked at her in that way he had of seeing right into her. If she turned away, he'd just pull her back around.

So she lifted her chin, stalked to the board in her pink miniskirt and polka-dotted halter top, and grabbed a set of darts. Tossing him a long, level look, she managed a smile. "What are we playing for?"

For a beat, his eyes darkened. Then he shrugged it off and smiled that easy smile, making her wonder if she was seeing things. "Name it."

"Such power," she teased.

"Name it," he said again, softly now.

She would—except he couldn't give it to her. She wanted oblivion, faceless oblivion. "Winner gets breakfast for the rest of the week," she said. "Delivered right to their—"

"Bed?"

She laughed. "Desk."

He turned to get his own darts, not showing his face for a long moment. "Deal," he finally said, turning around. "You first."

Suited her. She threw a dart, and unbelievably, missed the board entirely. This was so shocking, she just stood there staring at the dart still quivering in the wall.

Danny, knowing she was usually unbeatable, pulled her around to face him. "Okay, talk to me."

She stared up into his familiar face and felt her throat tighten. God, she was so sick of herself. "I'm good."

"Dimi—"

"No, really. I'm fantastic, actually."

"You're so full of shit your eyes are brown."

"Fine, things are out of control, all right?" She backed away. "*I'm* out of control!"

"Why?"

She couldn't explain, couldn't tell him Bo had the deed and the world she and Mel had created might have never even existed. "It's complicated."

"Most things are, Deem."

"Look, all I know is that tea isn't working, crystals aren't working, nothing's working."

He touched her jaw. "How about breathing? Have you tried that?"

He wasn't teasing her, he was serious and she could have loved him for that alone. She gulped in air and shot him a wry glance. "I am now."

"Good." He kissed her cheek. "Keep doing that." For a moment he stayed close, his tall, lean body supporting hers. "You can tell me, you know. You can tell me anything."

Not this, she couldn't. "Danny. Don't you ever get tired of feeling sorry for me?"

"I don't feel sorry for you. You're too ornery to feel sorry for."

"Good." She went to the line, gripping her darts with new determination. "Prepare to lose." Backing up the words, she threw.

Double twenty.

Her game was back.

Or so he let her think for a few minutes, before he proceeded to kick it into gear and beat her by three points.

"I could use breakfast now," he said, putting the darts away.

"It's dinnertime."

"So?"

She just rolled her eyes and headed to the door before he

could say anything else, before he could see her tension had really only mounted . . .

It was her own fault. She'd gotten complacent. She'd fallen into a false sense of security, and she'd forgotten the pretense. She was good at forgetting. She'd spent most of her childhood forgetting about her father's wandering ways, her mother's drugs . . .

What if it all fell apart again, her entire world? If she lost this job, what would happen to her? She had no talent for anything other than sleeping with men, and even there she hadn't been all that successful or she'd have a diamond ring and a minivan by now.

Nibbling on a nail, she made her way through Sunshine Café, which was still suitably filled. A handful of women sat at one table. They'd flown in on a private jet owned by the husband of one of the women. Dressed in designer gear, they looked like a million bucks, all with expensive bags at their feet, most likely filled with the afternoon's shopping spoils. They probably had perfect lives, beautiful homes, complete with minivans.

At another table sat a couple. The man was in his sixties and now retired, but he had been a Hollywood movie star for years, and had developed an expensive plane habit that North Beach was all too happy to satisfy. The woman dripped bling.

It was the third table to catch her interest: five men, ranging from twentysomething into their forties, rowdy and noisy, all toasting themselves over one deal or another.

Maybe they'd gone to the track and had won big. Maybe they were in town for a convention. Dimi didn't know, but all that really mattered was that they stopped talking as she walked past them and up to Char's counter.

She could almost hear the collective male sigh and smiled inwardly as she waved at Al. "A beer," she said, needing a drink bad and wishing they had the hard stuff. "Make it two," she decided.

"Hey, Sexy. Is this seat taken?"

Dimi looked up into a tall, dark, and gorgeous stranger's face—one of the rowdy men behind her—and because he was the youngest and the best looking, she smiled. "Only by you," she purred, thinking *there,* she'd just found herself exactly what she needed: her mindless oblivion.

Chapter 6

That night Mel tried to call Dimi, but couldn't reach her. Sitting in her small beach bungalow, Mel hung up the phone and stared out at the churning ocean, hating that she knew Dimi was out somewhere, trying to lose herself.

Finally she turned to her laptop and checked her e-mail, gingerly, braced for another message from LeaveItAlone, but nothing.

She didn't know what she'd expected, but answers would have been nice. Was it Sally, asking her to leave it alone?

And if that was true, why hadn't Sally just come out and asked Mel herself? Surely she knew Mel would have done anything for her, if asked.

Unable to think anymore, she climbed into bed and slept surprisingly hard, dreaming even harder. Again a pair of green eyes followed her into dreamland, laughing sea green eyes in a strong, tanned face, with an Aussie voice and a smile that could melt a woman's panties right off at fifty paces.

She woke up to the sun stabbing her in the face and decided she hated green eyes and sexy smiles, no matter who they belonged to. Still in bed, her gaze locked on the picture on her dresser: Sally in the cockpit of the Hawker, her head tossed back in laughter, as it so often had been.

God, Mel missed her. *Still*.

There was also a pic of Mel and Dimi at age sixteen, the day Mel had gotten her pilot's license. They were high-fiving each other, with Mel proudly displaying the license in her free hand.

The best day of her life because of Sally.

Climbing out of bed, Mel moved to her bedroom window, devoid of window coverings because she loved the unencumbered view of the craggy sandstone outcroppings of the Santa Ynez Mountains rising so close to the water. The terrain was rugged. Lots of mornings she got up before dawn to climb. It was great exercise and she loved the dramatic view from the top of the sheer rock faces and massive boulders and overhangs.

But this morning she just let herself stand there watching the day, soothed by the sounds of the sea before she hit the shower and drove into work.

North Beach Airport's day typically began at six A.M. The linemen came in, Char opened the café, the doors on the outside hangars rose, all in preparation for the morning flights. They usually had three to five planes come in to fuel up before nine o'clock. Some of those remained on the tarmac while their rich patrons went into Santa Barbara for their business. Some were towed into the maintenance hangar for work needed, and others simply used the airport as a fuel stop and moved on.

But as they typically did every morning before their day began, the staff and crew gathered at the counter of the Sunshine Café, mooching coffee from Charlene, standing around for the early-morning gossip session.

Mel, who was usually first into the airport, stood in the middle of it now, sucking down caffeine, humming an old Ratt song, which was coming from the ever-faithful boom box. Dimi was nowhere in sight, as usual. The woman was going to be late to her own funeral.

Ritchie was the front lineman today, and Kellan the rear, both inhaling donuts along with Danny and Ernest. Ritchie was talking, using his hands, his big gestures matching the grin on his face. ". . . And then I said, if you won't dress like a Victoria's Secret model, then don't expect me to act like a soap opera guy—"

Kellan laughed. "Oh, yeah, I bet that got you laid."

"Hey, I was just being honest." Ritchie looked at the others. "It's best to be honest. Right?"

The ones with a penis vehemently shook their heads.

Mel sighed. "More donuts," she said to Char. "We need more donuts."

"Got 'em." Charlene came forward to plop down a tray, and it was like feeding piranhas, hands moved that fast. Mel managed to fight her way in and get a cinnamon twist, and had just taken a heavenly bite when Al nudged her. "So what's up with that Bo guy?"

Mel choked on a bite. "Um . . . What do you mean?"

"Just wondering why he's hanging around."

Everyone looked at her, interested. Of course they were, it was *her* own business, which made it front-page news.

Where the hell was Dimi? Mel thought frantically. Dimi would lick the sugar off her fingers or something and suitably distract attention away from this issue. Mel glanced at Ernest, the only person here who'd been around when Eddie and Bo had shown up the first time all those years ago, but he was looking right back at her, no expression.

Was it possible Ernest didn't remember Bo? "Bo's an old acquaintance," she finally said, hoping they'd all leave it at that. "And I'm letting him use some office space."

"What's the story with you two?" Danny asked, perceptive as always.

"No story," she said. "There's no story."

The entire staff shot her a collective gaze that told her she'd have to do better. But until she heard back about the deed—and how it was falsified—she wasn't saying a word.

"Is this guy hassling you or something?" This from Kellan, with all the toughness his twenty-one years afforded him. He set down his donut and puffed up a bit. "Cuz I can talk to him for ya."

"Me, too," Ritchie said, now also resembling a puffer fish.

Silly. Stupidly male.

But they meant it. Everyone else nodded, too, and Mel's throat went tight. These guys, her friends, her *family,* would do anything for her. Anything except the one thing she needed: turn back time. "No one's hassling me," she said. "He's just . . . visiting." She tried to smile reassuringly but suddenly the whole thing felt like a big, fat elephant sitting on her shoulder.

"You sure?" Danny asked her quietly, watching her with those steady eyes. "Because I have a weird feeling you're not telling us everything."

If he only knew . . . But they weren't going to let it go. Of course they weren't going to let it go, that would have been easy. So what could she say? *Look guys, he's saying Sally screwed us years ago and I never knew it. He's holding the deed and none of us are safe.* She couldn't say those things, not until she knew for sure. Should she say that he was a friend? Or how about an ex? "He's an ex," she tried.

"Of Dimi's?" Char asked in surprise, because of course Mel wouldn't have an ex.

Yeah, they'd buy Bo being Dimi's ex, since Dimi had dated just about every single guy in California. And also in Nevada. And Arizona. Why not Australia, too?

Beside her, Danny went utterly, unhappily still. And damn it, she just couldn't do it.

"Actually, he's *my* ex," she said on a pained sigh.

Charlene's jaw dropped. "Yours? But . . ."

"But you never even date," Al finished for his wife.

"Hey, I do so, just . . . just not very often."

"So what happened?" Char asked. "Because damn, girl, he's *hot*." She caught Al's long look. "Well, he is."

"We didn't work out, that's all. He . . ." Mel wracked her brain for a plausible reason to have dumped Bo, and caught a movement out of the corner of her eye. Her heart kicked hard.

Bo himself.

Was he also enjoying her discomfort? Oh, yeah, no doubt. "He, uh, had this habit."

"Drugs?" Charlene whispered, horrified.

Mel couldn't see Bo's face, but felt the heat of his silent challenge. She squirmed but reminded herself that really, this was all his fault. "He hummed during sex."

Silence.

"I could have lived with that," Charlene finally said.

"Yeah, Mel, that's not nearly a good enough reason to dump a guy," Ritchie told her.

Bo came to a stop right behind Mel, and everyone's eyes widened. Cornered, she pretended not to see him, and did as she always did with her back to the wall—came out swinging. "He also had a teeny, tiny—"

Bo cleared his throat. She knew he'd leaned in close because she could smell him, some complicated mix of soap and man, and then he said silkily in her ear, "You want to start telling secrets now? Really?"

No. No, she didn't. Unable to pretend any longer, she turned. Damn it, Char was right. He was hot. Very hot. He stood there wearing a pair of faded-to-perfection Levi's and a soft-looking chambray blue button-down, opened over a white tee. Same boots as yesterday. Her heart bumped involuntarily against her ribs, both irritating and a little embarrassing. He still hadn't shaved, which created the thought before she could stop it: what would that rough jaw feel like scraping over her skin?

She didn't care! she reminded herself. He was the equivalent of the big bad wolf, here to blow down her house of straw. His hair, wavy to just past his collar, was doing its own thing today, which meant a long lock fell over his forehead. She supposed most would say the color of the strands was brown but there was blond and red in it, too. A lion's pelt. She figured Bo would enjoy that analogy. He certainly had the watchful ways for such a comparison, and a graceful, easy way of moving that utterly belied how in control he was at all times. His eyes, as they landed on hers, were clear and fathomless as the sea, giving nothing away, except maybe a tad bit of disbelief at her "teeny tiny" comment.

"There you are," she said with a bright smile. "We were just, um, having a discussion."

In fact, all gazes had swiveled to the "part" they'd been discussing—his crotch.

"G'day," Bo said, keeping his gaze level on Mel. "I need to talk to you."

"Yeah, uh, we're in the middle of a staff meeting. An important staff meeting."

Rocking back on his heels, hands in his pockets, he shot her a smile that wasn't quite friendly. "And in these staff meetings you always discuss the size of your ex-boyfriends' d—"

"We were just warming up with some watercooler talk," Mel said quickly. "Harmless tradition. Anyway, no one but staff allowed, so you should probably . . ." She waggled her fingers to suggest he scoot along. "You don't mind, do you?"

His eyes said that he did, very much, and in them was also a promised retribution, making her wonder at the stupidity of baiting him.

"How about this," he said calmly. "You give me a minute of your time, or we talk in public, right here at your *staff* meeting."

Damn it. He'd do it, too. "I suppose I can give you a minute." She purposely looked at her watch, sighed, then headed through the lobby toward her office.

Bo followed, of course. She could feel his gaze watching her every move. It wasn't often that she thought about being feminine, and it sure as hell wasn't often she wondered if she passed muster, so the normally unconscious movement of walking across the room suddenly became awkward. She felt exceedingly aware that her hair was wild, that she'd thrown on coveralls with little to no concern that they made her look like a short box, that her radio and cell clanked together loudly . . .

Completely unaware of—or ignoring—her discomfort, Bo leaned in ahead of her and pushed open her office door.

The unexpected gesture of chivalry caught her by surprise, and she tripped over her own two feet as she looked up into his enigmatic gaze.

"In," he said, lending his hands to the cause, pushing her into her office, not exactly gently, negating the chivalrous gesture he'd just made. He shut the door, then turned to face her as he rolled up his sleeves. "Now," he said, and locked the door, the sound of it clicking into place, making her pulse skip.

"Uh, there's really no need to lock it," she said.

"Right. So your band of merry men can barge in here to save you when you start screaming. No, thank you."

She reached behind her to grip the desk as she leaned back in a false show of calm and relaxation. Her fingers touched her metal envelope opener and, in reflex, closed over it. "Why would I scream?"

"I don't know, why would you stand around the watercooler discussing the size of your ex's dick?"

"You're not my ex."

"Ah, but you let them think I was. Which means they all think that we've had wild, screaming sex."

"But we haven't."

"No." He smiled, and it wasn't a nice one. "But we're going to."

Her knees wobbled, and it wasn't exactly in fear. In spite of herself, she craned her neck and eyed the neat desk behind her, picturing him shoving her phone and blotter to the floor, pushing her onto the flat surface, then stepping between her legs to take her fast and hard and well. She cleared her throat. "I am not having sex with you just to make my story of you being my ex real."

"How about to prove I don't have a teeny, tiny—"

"Yeah, about that." She grimaced. "I'm sorry, it just popped out of my mouth."

"You're not sorry."

"Okay, not so much, no."

He looked exasperated. "Why didn't you tell them why I'm really here? Waiting to talk to Sally?"

Wasn't that just the question of the day? "Because . . ." Because it would hurt them to know she'd let them believe they were secure when they weren't. Because she'd have to watch them wonder whether Sally had really done the things Bo said she'd done. "Because . . ."

"Because you're a liar," he said softly, and took a step toward her. "Because you've been lying to them for a long time, haven't you?"

Another step, and she felt the hard wood of the desk at her hips, and the harder body of Bo Black at her front. The cool steel of the letter opener remained a comforting weight in her palm.

"Because you know if you admit it," he said, "they'll stop thinking the sun rises and falls on your shoulders."

No. She shook her head in denial of that. Having them admire and look up to her was absolutely not why she ran this place for Sally.

She did it because the place was home, the only real home she'd ever had.

Well, okay, on second thought, damn it, yes, and because they looked up to her and admired her. It gave her a sense of worth. Was that really such a crime? Could he really not understand at all?

Of course he couldn't. He was confident to the point of complete obnoxiousness. He didn't care what people thought of him, it would never even occur to him to wonder. He'd probably never doubted himself, not once.

"What's going on in here, Mel?" he asked, gently tapping her temple. "You've left me. To think about what else you're hiding?"

Hard to think, much less talk, with his body so close to hers, and she resented that he probably knew it. "You didn't by any chance e-mail me the other day, did you?"

His eyes narrowed. "No. Why?"

"Just . . . wondering."

"You get a strange e-mail?"

No, just a threatening one.

His gaze dropped to her mouth. His eyes darkened. "Stubborn to a beautiful fault. That's okay, I'll figure it out." Caging her in by putting a hand on either side of her hips, he shifted closer still, forcing her to tip her head back to keep looking into his eyes. "You could just tell me and save us both a lot of time and frustration."

She tightened her mouth, making him laugh. "No worries, mate. So . . . back to ex-lovers?"

She licked her lips nervously. "It's not so unreasonable a story. It's obvious we're on edge around each other. We . . . had a falling out. It was for the best, with you being an ass and all."

He ran the pad of his finger over the base of her throat, and something warm and delicious and utterly dangerous slid into her belly. "If I'm so off-putting," he murmured, "you're going to want to work on this, then."

"On what?"

Again a swipe of his thumb over her wild pulse. "On how bad you want me."

She slapped his hand away but in a lightning-quick move, he snagged her wrist, and then her other, the one that held the letter opener. He eyed the steel point with curious amusement, then squeezed until it clattered from her fingers to the floor. "You might want to work on that, too. That temper you clearly have smoldering for me." He tsked. "Dead giveaway on that wanting-me-bad thing."

"You are delusional."

"Why?" His gaze met hers. "Are you taken?"

"Taken?"

"Committed."

"No. Not committed." Not that she had anything against the idea in theory, but though she'd had lovers here and there over the years, she'd always discovered some fatal flaw and broken things off before anything too serious began. Char called the phenomenon the Anderson Chronicles. Dimi called it pathetic.

Closing the gap between them, Bo pressed his body to hers. Her nipples had gone hard at the beginning of this little discussion, and now they bore into his chest. Could he feel them? She thought maybe by the look on his face that he could.

"So you don't want me," he said a little hoarsely. "Not even a little."

She had to clear her throat to talk. "Not even a little."

"Prove it," he whispered, lowering his head so that their mouths were only a fraction apart.

"I don't have to prove anything—"

He clucked like a chicken.

"This is so juvenile." Her hands came up between them, her palms open on his chest. To push him away, she told herself, only she didn't push so much as hold on like he was her lifesaver and she was going down. "I am not going to kiss you just to prove I don't want you—"

"Shut up and do it, darlin'."

"You know what? *Fine.*" Grabbing his ears, she yanked his face closer and laid one on him. Only the joke was on her because the moment she felt his warm, delicious mouth touch hers she forgot that this was supposed to be about making her point and instead got sucked into the hot wave of lust that washed over her, drowning out all good sense.

His good sense, too, apparently, because she got much more than she bargained for. He met her halfway, kissing her hungrily, possessively, then deeper still, pushing her back against the desk, his thigh pressing up between hers, his hands—God, his hands.

She might have let him do whatever he wanted, possibly even have stripped her naked and begged him to touch bare flesh this time, because she was lost in the sensations, one hundred percent lost.

But then the radio crackled, and Charlene's voice filled the air. "Mel? Bo's got an incoming. He still in there?"

Her heart pounding, pounding, pounding, nipples hard, thighs quivery, damp between them, Mel stared up at Bo.

He was breathing just as heavily as she was. "It's, uh, about a vintage Stearman PT-13D I'm thinking of buying."

Mel nodded, cleared her throat again, then lifted the radio to her mouth. "Thanks, Char, I'll tell him."

Bo, having apparently proved his point, gave Mel one last long look filled with heat and some other stuff that made breathing difficult, then simply walked out.

She let out a long breath. *Well*. If that wasn't the cruelest thing he'd done so far, making her like him, making her want him. With a shaking hand, she stroked the hair from her face. One of them wasn't going to survive this, and at the moment, body humming, buzzing, *aching*, she wasn't sure who'd be left standing in the end. She sagged back against the desk, thankful for its durability, because, wow.

Just wow.

Seemed she wanted more than for Bo to simply go far, far away. She wanted him to do her first. Which solved it, really. She wasn't lost, she'd merely left reality and had driven right into insanity.

Chapter 7

Dimi woke up on a plane. Now if it had been in the air, she'd have freaked and needed serious aromatherapy, but all was still and quiet, and she relaxed.

It wasn't the first time she'd woken confused . . . There'd been many nights hanging out with the guys until late, drinking with them, getting a little too toasted to drive home. She'd always just made herself comfortable in one of the planes they stored for people who had too much money.

But as she sat up and put a hand to her reeling head, she realized this wasn't just any plane but a Lear Jet, luxurious and plush and gorgeous.

Oh, and bigger surprise, she wasn't alone.

A muscled forearm was wrapped around her waist. Then a pair of lips pressed to her shoulder as a husky, sleepy male voice whispered, "Morning, Sexy."

Before she could get her wits together, she was turned over into his arms. With a sexy smile, he slid a thigh between hers, bent his head, and sucked her bare breast into his mouth.

Right. She remembered now. Gorgeous Guy from Sun-

shine Café. Brother of the owner of the plane she was currently butt-ass naked in. He'd ditched his buddies and his
brother on their night on the town to be with her, and she'd
made it worth his while.

And he'd made it worth hers, taking her mind off the fact
that Bo Black held the key to her livelihood. A brutal reality
that thrust her back into insecure, desperate, fearful mode, a
feeling she hated and resented with all her heart.

Gorgeous Guy nibbled his way to her other breast, rocking an impressive morning erection between her legs as she
tried for a graceful escape. "So." She cleared her throat.
"Anyone here remember last night?"

He lifted his head. "You don't?"

She shrugged. "Well, we did get fairly toasted—" There'd
been plenty of alcohol in the wet bar right behind them.
"Everything's a bit of a blur."

His smile faded. So did Mr. Impressive between her legs.
"You don't remember any of it?"

Ah, hell. A sensitive one. Furtively, she tried to get a look
at his watch without further insulting him but his jaw went
tight. "It's five forty-five," he said gruffly.

Oh, shit. She wriggled, trying to get free. "Move, Sugar,
I've got to get up."

He pulled back, still looking shocked.

Galvanized into action, she hopped off the buttery soft
leather double recliner and winced at the hangover rattling
her head. Ignoring the opulent interior all around her, she
began searching for her clothes. She found her panties dangling off a window shade and pulled them on, getting a flash-
back of the man behind her yanking them off her last night,
inadvertently scratching her tender inner thigh in his hurry.
"The crew signs on in fifteen minutes," she said. "They're
probably already gathered in the café, listening to AC/DC
and mooching off Charlene. You've got to be gone."

"We're not taking off until ten." He reached for her, slipping his fingers between her legs. "Let's have breakfast."

"I can't!" She batted him away. "I have to work."

"Come on," he cajoled, pulling her back against him. "We clicked so well last night, let's continue the fun."

How much clicking could there have been if all she remembered was him scratching her? "Sorry. Breakfast isn't my style." Her bra was in his loafer. She shimmied into that and began the hunt for her skirt and top—there, on the back of the pilot's seat. "Where do you usually go when you tie down here for the night?"

"A hotel, but—"

"Good. Great. Take the rental car I arranged for you yesterday and come back in a few hours."

He came up behind her, again tried to hold her. "I had fun," he whispered, nuzzling her jaw.

The sun had come up, and for all Dimi's worldliness, she never had sex in the light of day. *Never*.

"We have a connection," he said.

Uh-huh. A connection. He couldn't be more than twenty-four, and she knew men. At that age, the biggest connection they had was to their own penis. Mostly, she figured, he just wanted to get lucky again. "Get dressed."

He pulled on his pants, his shirt, and began hunting for his shoes. "How about next weekend? Are you—"

"No." She softened her voice. "I'm sorry, no." She put her hands on his shoulders and tried to turn him toward the door to shove him out, because damn it, if Mel caught her with one of the clients, she was going to skin her alive. "Go," she said.

"This first." He leaned in to kiss her but she shifted, giving him her cheek instead.

"Hey, I want a kiss."

"Well, I don't." She never kissed her lovers. Like getting naked in the light of day, it seemed too intimate, too real. Putting her hand to her head, which was threatening to leap off her shoulders, she tried to smile. "Look, I'll call you, okay?" Standard line, of course, used only to avoid a scene.

He saw right through her, and went from pout to something else, something darker and much closer to anger. "You don't have my number."

From the radio in her skirt pocket she heard Kellan say something. *Shit.* Indeed, the crew had arrived, probably all in the lobby snacking on donuts, hangover free. Damn it.

Danny would look at her with that combination of disappointment and regret, like it was *her* fault she sometimes tended to use sex as her Prozac, and Dimi would feel like crap. "I've got to run—"

But Gorgeous Guy grabbed her arm and held on with a shocking strength. Just last night that strength had been incredibly arousing. Now, not so much. "Let go of me," she said very carefully.

"You can't just run out on me."

She went from guilty to mad without passing GO. "Look, I can do anything I want."

"So that's it?" he asked, eyes narrowed, definitely annoyed. "You got off and now you're done with me?"

She looked down at the hand still wrapped around her arm, at his fingers digging into her skin, and felt a frisson of unease. "Let go of me. *Now.*" To ensure he did, she shoved him back and then hopped down from the plane, racing out of the hangar.

Asshole. Why did men have to be assholes who ruined everything?

The bright morning sun nearly blinding her, the cool air burning her lungs, she turned toward the lobby. With any luck, she wouldn't see a soul, and indeed luck appeared to be on her side as she entered the side lobby door and found the room empty.

Even the café was quiet, which meant that everyone had dispersed and gone off to begin their day. Whew. Bypassing her desk, she headed straight for the restroom to freshen up, thinking *ha*! she'd made it, she was in the clear—

"*Dimi!*"

Previously Gorgeous Guy. Yelling for her, damn it. With a wince, she turned back, and from across the expanse of the lobby, saw him heading right for her. Gone was any trace of the soft, sexy smile he'd exhibited last night, and in its place was a determination to have a scene.

Yep, she was still a jerk magnet. Good to know. She debated about just dodging into the bathroom and letting him pound on the door, but before she could, he was right there in front of her. Okay, no problem. She'd just knee him in the nads if it came to it, then drag him back to his plane and leave him there for his friends to find—

"Don't walk away from me." His brows were furrowed together, assuring her that she wasn't the only one feeling the effects of a pounding hangover. "Don't ever walk away from me."

Was he kidding? She opened her mouth to blast him, but someone stepped in front of her.

Danny; tall, rangy, and lanky, with his blond surfer-dude hair sticking out of his baseball cap, falling to his shoulders. Not handsome, not even take-another-look cute, but he had a pair of clear blue eyes that could cut right through a soul, which she hoped they were doing right now to Previously Gorgeous Guy. Danny held a wrench in one hand, a cup of coffee in the other, which he casually lifted to his lips to blow away the steam before taking a sip. "Problem?"

"Do you mind?" Previously Gorgeous Guy gestured to Dimi. "I'm trying to have a conversation here."

Not budging—in fact still blocking the view of Dimi entirely—Danny bent his head and took another sip of his coffee. "Oh, yeah," he sighed. "Charlene can make a cup of coffee. Want one?"

"No," Previously Gorgeous Guy said through his teeth. "I don't. I want to talk to *her*." He pointed to Dimi with one jerky motion.

Danny nodded, then slowly shook his head. "Unfortunately for you, she doesn't seem to be that interested in having a conversation." Without taking his eyes off him, Danny cocked his head. "Dimi?"

"No," she said to Danny's back. "I'm not interested in having a conversation."

Danny nodded and spoke in the same easy voice, though she could hear unbendable steel beneath it. "You okay?"

"Fantastic." She'd never stood behind Danny before. He was bigger than she'd thought, sturdier. He had himself a set of broad shoulders, and buns of steel, too. All that surfing, she supposed—

"Dimi."

Lifting her gaze, she realized Danny had craned his neck to look at her. "Give us a moment?"

He was telling her to go into the restroom, that he'd take care of the issue, meaning he'd escort the guy out of the lobby and either back to his plane or off the premises. "Right," she said, and gratefully made her escape.

Inside the bathroom, she caught a look at herself in the mirror, and stared. Her hair had gone on a party without her permission, she wore no makeup, both an absolute crime in her book. She was pale enough to scare herself, but worse, her skirt and top were wrinkled. She also had four paw-print bruises on her arm where the guy had grabbed her, not to mention a scratch on her inner thigh.

She definitely looked a little rough around the edges, like she'd been ridden hard and put away wet, like she didn't care about herself and where she'd been.

And as that sank in, her eyes filled. *Idiot.* What she'd done last night had been stupid and careless and dangerous. And it could have had an extremely unpleasant ending.

Yet she'd known all that and had done it anyway.

The restroom door opened and she turned her head, expecting Danny, expecting to have to put a smile on her face and pretend all was well, that she was "fantastic" as always, knowing she needed to thank him.

But it wasn't Danny at all. Mel stormed in, and Dimi prepared for a lecture, to be berated about her bad choices, to feel an inch tall.

But Mel didn't even glance at Dimi. She went straight to a sink, cranked on the cold water and bent. Dimi watched in surprise as Mel closed her eyes and slapped water on her cheeks. "Mel? What's the matter?"

She didn't answer for so long that Dimi thought maybe she wouldn't. Finally, she straightened, water dripping off her nose. "Men suck."

Dimi laughed. "Well, I agree with you there."

Mel stared at herself in the mirror, then at Dimi. And it was a huge testament to how upset she must be that she didn't mention Dimi was still wearing yesterday's clothing and looked like shit. "It's possible I'm going to kill him."

Dimi blinked. "Who?"

"Bo Black. Who else?"

Dimi pushed Previously Gorgeous Guy far out of her head and went from pissed to panic. Again. "What did he do now?"

"You mean besides being born?" Mel closed her eyes. "He kissed me."

This was so far from what Dimi had expected, it took her a moment to process. Mel hadn't kicked Bo Black's most excellent ass out, but she'd kissed him. "Okay, you win the bad-morning award."

"Gee, thanks." But Mel didn't look like it'd been bad at all, and Dimi took a closer look. "You really let him kiss you?"

"It wasn't a planned thing, believe me. It started out this stupid dare—"

"*What?* He got you on a dare? Jesus, Mel, the guy wants to take over our world and you let him goad you into—"

"Did I start out this story with 'hey, a great thing happened to me this morning'?" Sounding extremely grumpy, Mel reached for a few paper towels to dry her face. "And anyway, he's busy now, looking at some Stearman."

"He's got the money for that?"

Mel shrugged. "I have no idea."

"So . . ." Dimi had to ask. "Are the old rumors true? Can he make a woman orgasm with a single touch?"

Instead of laughing, as Dimi had expected, Mel turned away. "It was just a kiss."

Which didn't answer the question, Dimi noted. More panic. It jangled inside her belly. "You going to turn into *me* now, Mel, and fall for the wrong guy?"

"Okay, repeat after me," Mel snapped. "Just. A. Kiss. And believe me, it won't be repeated."

"I don't know . . ." Dimi watched her oldest friend pace, which didn't make her feel any better. "They say that once he kisses you, it's like a drug. You have to have him again. And again."

"Whoever 'they' are, they're wrong."

"Good, because he's a *Black,* Mel."

"Yeah." Mel rubbed her temples. "I know."

"He's been making himself at home, working from here." She let some of her panic show. "Acting like he has the right. He really believes that deed is real."

"I know." Mel closed her eyes. "He has got to go far, far away." She tossed the paper towels into the trash.

If Dimi had had herself together, she'd have opened her purse and offered moisturizer, but as things were, she didn't have either her purse or her wits.

"Okay, let's try this again." In the way that Dimi had admired for years, Mel drew herself up straight and tall.

"Try what again exactly?"

"The whole damn day. And trust me, if Bo so much as looks at me, he'll regret it." With that, Mel stormed out of the bathroom in much the same way she'd stormed in.

Dimi looked in the mirror. "She's going to need you," she told herself. "Which means you have to be the strong one for once."

Her reflection looked worried.

* * *

Mel worked her tail off, struggling to stay one step ahead of North Beach's needs, their customers' needs, her employees' needs.

Of Bo Black.

But everywhere she turned, things seemed to go wrong. The morning after the kiss—she refused to think in plurals when it came to the incident, though it had been plural kisses, heavenly plural kisses she'd dreamed about all night long—she came into work and found the front door of North Beach unlocked. Dropping her things, she rushed through the airport, but nothing looked touched. Nothing missing. Nothing bothered.

And yet later, sitting at her desk eating a donut from Char, she'd have sworn someone had been through her things.

Paranoia?

Or reality?

With nothing missing, she had no idea. And still nothing from her attorney on the deed.

At least her e-mail box remained empty of vague threats.

The next morning, the fourth since Bo had shown up, they had a scheduled five thirty AM incoming. Mel had come in early—tired from *still* dreaming of Bo's body buried in hers—only to find herself devoid of linemen. Pissed, Mel called Ritchie, and got no answer. She dialed Kellan.

"Yo, dude," he said groggily. "This'd better be good."

"Yo, *dude,*" she shot back, with some sarcasm added in because it was early and she hadn't had any caffeine yet. "There's an incoming, and you're not."

"Ah, shit." This was followed by a rustling noise, probably the kid falling out of bed. *"Shit,"* he said again, breathless.

"Shit on your own time."

"Yeah, Mel— I'm sorry—"

She hung up. He was sorry, and so was she because she could hear the plane now. Once again she dropped her own job and found herself racing through the lobby, grabbing an orange vest and directing the aircraft herself, a beauty of a Raytheon King Air. She handled the tie-down, greeted the pilot and his guests, then stayed on the tarmac for a moment, enjoying the sun rising in the chilly, purple-blue dawn.

"So do you do every job in this place by yourself?"

She turned and faced the outline of a man as he came toward her, the sun in her face. Didn't matter. She'd have recognized him from the way he walked, confident, of course, with a carefully banked bad-assness in every line of his tough body, a body he'd pressed against hers. The taste of his kiss came back in a flash, hot and sweet. The feel of his hands on the skin of her back, where he'd skimmed beneath her shirt and—

Stop. Don't think about it . . . Try not to think about it every living moment of every single day . . .

Was he thinking about it, too?

Unable to see Bo's expression, she lifted her hand to block her eyes and watched his long, sleek shadow move closer. His face seemed to have as many strong lines and angles as the rest of his tough, lean form. His hair had been finger-combed at best. Against the early chill, he wore jeans, and a soft, worn leather jacket, and looked a little rough, a little edgy.

And a whole lot sexy.

"You work too hard," he said gruffly. "And half the time, it isn't necessary. You have linemen."

Nope, he was definitely not thinking about The Kiss. "Kellan overslept."

"Slacking off," he said and shook his head. "You should have his ass for breakfast."

A little flicker of panic. If the deed turned out to be real, would he fire all of them? Sell? "It was a mistake, Bo. We all make them."

"Like yours?"

"What are you talking about?"

He crossed his arms and looked down at her. "The lie you told me."

Oh, God.

"Trying to remember which lie, aren't you?" he asked very softly.

Now, see, she hated that he was right nearly as much as she did the twist in her gut.

"This place is sinking," he said. "You're a great pilot, but business clearly isn't your strength."

True enough, but how would he know unless . . . "So it *was* you. Snooping through my files."

He frowned. "What? No. Ernest likes to talk."

"Ernest? Are you kidding me?"

"I saved a spider, and now I have a friend for life. That's how it works, Mel, a little give and take." He ran a finger over her hairline. "So you ready for the big reveal? Because *I* am. You know, where you tell me what's going on."

She stared into the gorgeous morning, feeling the fist around her heart tighten a bit more. "I called Sally."

His eyes met hers for a long moment, a little intense, a little intimidating, and a whole lot exciting, giving nothing away. "Is that right?" He stepped closer, so that now they were nose to nose. Or her nose to his fabulous chest. "What did she say?" He'd shaved, the scent of his shaving lotion or soap floating to her on the breeze. Citrusy. Woodsy. Inherently male.

His eyes held hers prisoner, and there were things in them, a barely banked heat, and . . . yep, the memories of their kiss.

He *was* thinking about it.

And right there in the morning chill, she began to overheat from the inside out. "She's swamped."

"Ah. Too swamped to talk to me, right?"

She couldn't do this. It was one thing to lie when she believed one hundred percent in the cause, when she was doing what was right, in the only way she could. But it was another entirely when she felt lost and alone and afraid, very afraid. She turned away, but he pulled her back around, putting his hands on her arms as if he had a right, as if he was comfortable enough with her to do whatever he wished.

In defense, her hands came up and settled on his chest, where she could feel the rock-hard strength of him—just in case she hadn't seen it along with sheer determination blazing from his gaze.

He wasn't going to just go away. He couldn't. And he wasn't going to take her word for anything.

He wasn't ever going to give up.

"Just talk to me," he said. "It's all I'm asking."

"Maybe it's not any of your business."

"It was my father's business. With him gone, it became mine."

"Your father didn't earn that deed fairly."

His jaw tightened. His eyes went to ice. "You don't have any proof of that."

"And neither do you."

He stared at her. "One of these days you're going to eat those words."

"Take your hands off me."

"Funny, that's not what you said the other day."

Shoving free, she took a step backward. And then another, because with him, she needed distance, lots of it. Whenever he looked at her, strange things happened; she could feel the sexual pull, like a relentless, unchanging tide, and damn if she didn't actually feel a hint of that old painful, unrequited crush she'd once had on him.

Pathetic.

She moved away, into the lobby and into her office, where she settled in to the stacks of bills and files she needed to work on.

One of these days you're going to eat those words . . .

He believed in his cause, with his whole heart. It was

even more disturbing than the fact that he'd turned her upside down and upside right, not to mention *on*.

And for the first time, she wasn't sure she was doing the right thing. Wasn't sure of anything at all.

God, she hated that.

Chapter 8

Dimi had a tradition when it came to entering the book-keeping information for North Beach. The first half of the month, she sat at her desk and pretended to work while she actually read a book. The second half of the month she raced to catch up.

Unfortunately, it was the second half of the month. Even more unfortunately, she was in the middle of a good book. But she needed to get on top of things before Mel crawled up her ass about it, wanting to see the accounting printouts.

First she sorted the mail into piles, then opened her stacks and sent each to the correct in-box. Then she went through Mel's mail, which was how she found herself staring down at a letter that read nothing more than:

Leave. It. Alone.

Dimi grabbed the envelope it'd come in. The postal stamp was dated five days ago, the place it'd come from so smeared she couldn't read it.

At that moment, Bo happened to walk by, heading toward the tarmac. He took one look at her face and stopped. "Dimi?"

Clearly she had her feelings all over her face, which she changed into a scowl to reflect her feelings for him. "What do you want?"

"You okay?"

"I'd be better if you were back in Australia."

With a sigh, he began walking again, and when he was gone, she picked up the phone to dial Mel's office. "You've got a letter here you're going to want to see."

One minute later they were both staring down at the plain white piece of paper with the plain Courier 12-point computer font.

"Matches that e-mail I received," Mel finally said. "Friendly, huh?"

"You do have a way with people."

"I try."

They stared at the letter some more.

"Bo?" Dimi asked.

Mel shook her head. "No, he wants the opposite of leaving it alone."

They were silent another minute, then Dimi shook her head. "Not Sally—"

"She'd call," Mel agreed.

But why hadn't she?

"Hell," Mel said heavily, and took the envelope and note with her, vanishing back into her office.

Dimi went to work entering the receivables. Not exactly rewarding work. In fact, she could have saved Mel the trouble of reading all these worksheets and simply told her it was same as always—that is, shaky—but she never had the heart to break Mel's.

Mel, who tried so hard to keep them all together, Mel for whom this place meant everything, Mel who kept Dimi on the straight-and-narrow path.

Mostly.

Dimi thought about her little transgression with Previously Gorgeous Guy, and sighed. So she still made the occasional bad decision. Sue her. A leopard couldn't change its stripes. Or spots. Or whatever it was.

Bottom line, she wasn't perfect.

And neither, she thought, as she watched the pretty flickering vanilla candle on the corner of her desk, was Mel. Mel could have, *should* have, kicked Bo's excellent ass for touching her. But she hadn't.

Interesting. And telling.

Dimi could see Bo on the tarmac now, looking over an aircraft that belonged to a customer he'd brought in. Since he'd gotten here, he'd been bringing people, helping customers, booking them charter flights . . . generally upping their business without effort.

Damn, he was good. *Bastard*.

A mug was set down on the desk before her, and then a lemon muffin—her favorite. She looked up.

"You were talking to yourself," Danny said. "Maybe sugar and caffeine will help."

It wasn't often she felt self-conscious with men, or revisited past actions, but ever since Danny had had to intervene with that idiot, she'd had a hard time looking him in the eye.

It wasn't as if he'd said a word about it, either. In fact, Danny was a man of very few words, but she felt off her footing nonetheless. "Thanks."

Perching a hip against her desk, he sipped at his own mug. He wore another baseball cap today, on backward, his blond surfer-dude hair brushing his shoulders, which were encased in his mechanic's overalls. The sleeves were shoved up, revealing corded strength in his forearms from all the heavy lifting and work he did. On his left wrist were two black leather bands. He had clean hands for a mechanic. Work roughened, but clean.

"You okay?" he asked quietly, bringing her gaze up to his.

They'd been friends forever, but this was something she

couldn't talk to him about. "Are you kidding?" She busied herself with the paperwork spread before her. "I'm fantastic."

"Yeah." He shook his head. "Don't you ever get tired of lying through those pretty teeth of yours?"

She went still but refused to look at him, instead started hitting keys on her computer, which brought the screen to life. Unfortunately the last thing she'd been doing was playing Solitaire, and it started beeping at her, and she got herself good and flustered before she managed to lower the volume. "Maybe I *am* always fantastic."

"Uh-huh, and I'd buy it off your looks alone," he agreed. "But I'm not much of an exterior kind of guy."

Again she lifted her head and found her eyes locked on his dark, melting ones. "What does that mean?"

"It means I'm more interested in what you have going on in here." Reaching out, he touched her temple. "And here." Shocking her with his nerve, he tapped her chest, just above her left breast.

She caught his hand and pushed it away. "Don't."

"Don't what?"

Don't . . . hell, she didn't know, but her heart was doing some funny jumping thing, and she stood up. "Look, I'm really busy here."

"Right." A single nudge of his finger and the file covering her book fell to the side. The cover revealed a guy wearing a loincloth with a woman on her knees in front of him in a ragged ball gown.

Dimi's dirty little secret—exposed. She devoured historical romance novels, the sexier the better. As for why . . . Well, it didn't take a shrink to figure that out. She knew exactly what drew her, and it wasn't just the fabulous, amazing, jaw-dropping sex—but the happily ever after.

But so what? Everyone was entitled to their occasional vice.

Or three.

Danny cocked his head. "Interesting work."

She shoved the book in the drawer. "Listen, if you don't have something you need done, beat it."

"Oh, I need something done."

She felt herself flinch at the sexual innuendo, and faced him, jaw jumping, head high, eyes oddly burning because this was Danny, and she'd not expected it of him. "Look, just because I slept with that idiot," she said tightly, "and just because I read romance, does not mean I'm easy—"

"Whoa." His smile faded as he rose to his feet. "I don't think that. I've never thought that."

Her heart was still pounding, her eyes hot with embarrassment. She didn't want to do this. God, she didn't. In fact, she needed a drink. Now. "Go away, Danny. Just go."

He stared at her for a long beat before letting out a jagged, frustrated breath.

"Please."

Clearly unhappy about it, he turned away.

Dimi let out a sigh of relief, but it backed up in her throat when he suddenly pivoted back, hunkering down at her side so that she had no choice but to look right at him.

"What?" she asked with the haughty tone that had sent lesser men running.

"You're keeping a dangerous pace, Deem."

"Yeah? And what would you know about that?"

His eyes held secrets. "Plenty."

She closed her eyes, then heard a twin-engine plane approaching right before the radio crackled, and felt shamefully grateful for the diversion. "I've got to—"

"Yeah." He held her gaze another moment, then rose and walked away.

Damn it. To give herself a minute, she sniffed at the mug he'd left her.

Earl Grey. Not quite the alcohol she craved but instead, her favorite tea. She swallowed past the odd lump in her throat and sipped as she watched him go, that long rangy form moving with the ease and confidence she imagined he'd honed from years and years on the waves.

To have even *half* of that belief in herself . . . with a sigh, she reached for the radio. The incoming customer was Wayne White. Wayne had a woman in every port in the world, and as Dimi sipped her tea, she opened her purse and checked her reflection in a small compact.

Because—something no one else knew—Wayne had a woman in this port as well.

Her.

It'd been going on and off for years, since the day she'd turned eighteen and he'd bought her a gold and diamond tennis bracelet to celebrate. Now as his plane circled and lowered, she wondered if he was alone.

You're keeping a dangerous pace, Danny had said.

No doubt. But it was that pace that made her feel alive.

"We got it under control?" Mel's voice asked Dimi via radio.

"It's covered," Dimi assured her, applying lip gloss as she watched the tarmac. "Ritchie's out there right now."

Still holding her radio, Mel stuck her head out of her office and looked at Dimi from across the expanse of the lobby. "Why are you primping?"

"I always primp."

"There might be passengers with Wayne."

"So?"

"So . . . Maybe one of them is a wife."

Yeah, Wayne had a habit of collecting those. "Let me repeat myself. So . . . ?"

"So a new wife is going to take one look at you and be jealous as hell. We want him to loiter, buy gas, maybe some maintenance hours . . ."

Dimi tossed her compact aside. "I hear you."

"Do you really?"

"Don't worry, Mel. I don't *have* to act impulsively."

"Huh. Didn't know that."

"Funny. I'll make sure he keeps his pants on, okay? Does that make you happy?"

"I'm dancing in the hallway," Mel said.

"Fine."

"*Fine.*"

"Killjoy," Dimi muttered, and sipped her tea.

"Yeah, I live to kill your joy," Mel muttered back.

That night Mel stayed late catching up on paperwork, and when she was finished being unable to pay all the bills, she walked through the lobby, restless. She ended up in the employee break room, eyeing the dart board. If only she'd been able to talk to Sally, if she'd heard from Greg on the legitimacy of the deed, if, if, if . . . she'd feel better. Or at least not tense enough to shatter if someone so much as looked at her cross-eyed. She reached for the darts, thinking maybe a game with herself was just what she needed.

"You any good?"

God damn it. Why was that man always where she didn't want him? She pulled out her darts, then turned and eyed Bo, who was propping up the doorway with a broad shoulder, an easy but daring smile on that mouth of his. It made her want to smack him.

Or kiss him.

Where that thought came from, she had no idea. She weighed the darts in her hand. "I'm okay."

"Yeah?" He didn't believe her, it was in his voice.

Spoiling for trouble, she balanced, aimed, and threw the first dart.

Bull's-eye.

He arched a brow. "Better than okay, I'd say. How about a game?"

"You any good?" she asked him, mocking him.

A slow smile curved his lips and stirred the butterflies in her belly. "I'm okay," he said.

She handed him her darts but he shook his head. "Oh, no.

Ladies first," he said politely. "Three darts. How about highest score wins?"

Hmmm, should be no problem for her, she'd been playing darts since before she could fly. "Wins what?"

His eyes heated and darkened. "Winner's choice."

Staring at him, she experienced a frisson of unease. "Um . . ."

"What's the matter, Mel, you afraid I'll win?"

"No." Ha. Bastard. "*I'm* going to win."

"Then you're afraid of what you'd pick as winner's choice." He shrugged. "No worries, if you're afraid. We don't have to play."

"Bite me."

"When and where?"

Her belly quivered again, damn him. Ignoring his soft laugh, she moved to the board to pull out the one dart she'd thrown, extremely aware of him behind her, tall, watchful, quiet now. Back at the line, she took a deep breath and threw.

Her first dart hit the triple twenty, and a confident smile returned to her mouth. Her game was still on. Smirking seemed unsportsmanlike so she bit her lip to keep it back and threw her next dart.

Double twelve. Hmmm. A little off.

"Worried?" he asked, from right behind her now.

He stood at her shoulder. She could feel the heat of him, the strength. And if she closed her eyes she could almost feel his breath at her temple—

No. No closing her eyes. Because then she could smell him, just soap and all man. "Back up, you're in my breathing space."

He grinned, a flash of white teeth and pure trouble. "You're worried."

"Are you kidding me? I'm never worried."

He just kept grinning.

She threw her last dart. She knew better than to throw when mad, to throw when she hadn't taken a deep breath and gotten him out of her system.

She landed a three. Straight up, no double, no triple.

"Eighty-seven," he said, and winced. "Ouch."

"You think you can do better?"

"Let's see." He made sure to brush against her as he went for the darts, pulling them from the board, arm raised, biceps straining at the sleeve of his T-shirt.

He caught her looking at him and winked.

She ground her teeth and backed up to give him room.

He eyed the dartboard, aiming with his tongue between his teeth, gaze narrowed in concentration. Then he let the dart fly.

Like a pro.

Triple goddamn twenty. Catching her jaw hanging open, he smiled. "I've seen a guy do this once or twice."

Oh, boy. Had she really agreed the winner could pick the prize?

Was she insane?

She forced a yawn. "Man. I'm awfully tired."

"Not falling for that one, mate," he said, and threw his second dart.

Double fifteen.

She stared into his green eyes and saw the humor spiked there amongst the flames. He was playing with her.

Crossing her arms, she took a big step back and waited for him to throw the third dart, but she knew without looking he'd beaten her score.

"Another triple twenty," he said very softly, and came up behind her, his legs brushing the backs of hers. "I win."

His hands settled on her shoulders and turned her around, his smile positively wicked, eyes flashing.

In spite of herself, her heart caught. Her nipples tightened. *Bad* nipples. "I'm not sleeping with you because you won."

He laughed. "Darlin', trust me, if that was my prize, I wouldn't waste our time sleeping."

The growl began low in her throat, and he laughed again.

"But as lovely as your body is . . ." His gaze swept over it from head to toe and back again, stopping at all the points that tingled and burned. "I think I'm going to pass."

Wait a minute. He was going to pass? She didn't know whether to be giddy with relief or insulted.

"It's information I'm looking for," he said very quietly now. "And you have it."

She crossed her arms. "I don't know where Sally is."

"Swear it."

"I swear it." She held her breath, expecting him to call her a liar. Or demand another prize.

He did neither. He just stared at her, as if assessing her for honesty, then nodded once and walked away.

Chapter 9

The next morning, Mel braced herself and checked her e-mail, but found nothing odd. When the early North Beach rush faded, she took the leave-it-alone letter and envelope to the post office to see if they could read the return stamp for her. She waited twenty minutes in line only to be told that the return stamp couldn't be read, too blurred.

But the barcode . . . another thing entirely. They could trace that. If the right guy was in, that is, which he wasn't. They told her to come back tomorrow. The joys of rural routing.

Mel got back to North Beach and had a charter to fly to Santa Cruz, which took her until midafternoon. Finally back at her desk, she called her attorney. He was sorry for the delay, he'd been out of town, he'd get back to her regarding the deed first thing tomorrow.

Warning: another sleepless night ahead.

But she still had the rest of the afternoon to face. She changed into her coveralls to put some time in on the Hawker. Char caught her heading to the main hangar and called to her over the sound of Motley Crue on the boom box, rattling the windows. "Come eat before I close up."

Mel shook her head. "Thanks, but I've still got to—"

"Eat," Char said in that Southern voice of steel. "You probably skipped lunch, didn't you?" She was fanning her shiny face with an oven mitt, looking flushed. "I've been talking to men all day and I need an estrogen fix. Please? I know you're swamped but just leave it alone and keep me company for a few."

Mel went still. *Leave it alone.* The three little innocuous words that had been ringing in her head for days. Coincidence? She took a good look at Char, who was clearly over-heated and quite possibly the sweetest woman Mel had ever met. There didn't seem to be any way that Char could have anything to do with the e-mail. For one thing, she and Al hadn't come to North Beach until after Sally had left the country. They'd never even met her. "You look hot, Char."

"Damn hot flashes! I just stripped down in the kitchen and hosed myself off with the handheld faucet in the sink and it didn't help! Look here, I've got five-cheese lasagna. The best in the state."

Al poked his head out of the kitchen. "In the whole coun-try, babe."

"Oh, you. You're just trying to get lucky again. But I'm too DAMN hot, so back off."

Al lifted his hands and backed off.

Char blew a strand of hair from her head as her gaze swiveled to Mel. "Now I mean it. Get over here and eat."

"I'd do it," Al called out. "She's PMSing."

"If by PMSing you mean sick of men," Char yelled back, "then, yeah, I'm PMSing!"

Al ducked back into the kitchen, but not before Char snapped him in the ass with her towel.

"Jesus, woman!" He grabbed himself. "Watch the parts!"

"I was nowhere near the parts. And just because I didn't

want to have sex with you this morning doesn't mean I'm PMSing."

Mel covered her ears but sat obediently. She was no idiot, Char's lasagna *was* the best in the country.

"What, if you hear sex talk, your ears fall off?" Al asked Mel.

"What's with the sex talk? There's no sex talk," Char said.

"Sure there is," Al said. "I'm not getting any, we're going to talk."

"One morning! I had a headache one morning!"

"I could have solved your headache." Al accompanied this with a wild wag of a brow.

Char rolled her eyes.

Al winked at Mel.

Mel dug into the huge plate of lasagna Char set in front of her. "I can't hear you over the roar of my brain matter as it spontaneously combusts." She swallowed her first bite, then moaned. "God, this is heaven."

Char beamed with pleasure.

"Ah, look at that." Al pulled her in and kissed her neck. "You look so pretty when you smile." He nibbled. "And you taste even better than your lasagna."

Char shoved him away but, softened now, she smiled, and so sweetly Mel actually had to look away.

"I'm sorry I snapped at you," Char murmured. "I'm just tired. These hot flashes are a bitch."

"I know, baby. I'll give you a foot massage when we get home, no sex talk, I promise."

"Oh, no, that's okay. Maybe we can incorporate something cold, that's all. *Ice* cold. Like . . . ice cubes . . ."

Al laughed softly. "You're on."

Mel kept eating, but her heart sighed. The two of them might fight big, but they loved bigger, loved through thick and PMSy moods, and though she didn't always understand it, there was no denying the power of such emotion, and sometimes looking at it reminded her of what she didn't have.

When she finished overloading her arteries, she thanked Char and made her way to the maintenance hangar. Danny was in the air with a customer, diagnosing a problem with a plane. Mel flipped on the back lights, working her way through the huge, yawning open space, back to where she kept her thirty-year-old baby, the Hawker. "Hi, honey, I'm home." She pulled over her tool cart, and also the large tub of cleaning fluid. Then she got out her three-step ladder and buried herself in the engine compartment.

Over the years, she'd slowly replaced this and that on the aircraft as she got the extra cash, hoping one day to fly the thing again. Now she was working on the spar strap, a task that required poking and prodding and wrenching and hammering, a good thing actually, because she began to feel some of the anxiety and tension that had been gripping her all week finally fade away.

She was tired. And it was no wonder. For nights now she'd done little more than toss and turn on tangled sheets, thinking about Bo; about the episode in her office, about what would have happened if she hadn't come to her senses, about how sometimes she even wished she hadn't come to her senses at all, that instead she'd let him strip her and then himself, and work his magic on more than just her mouth.

Or about when he'd beaten her at darts last night, how a small part of her, the secretly lonely and apparently horny part, had waited for him to claim her as the prize.

Lord, she had it bad.

He'd known it, too. He'd known what he did to her so effortlessly, and he liked it. He'd been liking it ever since, and telling her so with his gaze.

Rat fink bastard.

God, she wanted him. But she had enough to worry about without adding stupid, ridiculous irresponsible sex to the mix.

She needed a bigger wrench. Grabbing one off the tool cart behind her, she went back to work. She was close, closer than she'd ever been, to getting the Hawker in flying shape, which was good because she could fetch a pretty penny for it.

Not that she'd be able to sell, given its sentimental value. She'd acquired the Hawker from Sally, who'd actually meant to have the plane tossed into a metal heap and salvaged for scrap.

But Mel could never do it. This plane held a lot of firsts for her. Her first aircraft. Her first real possession that had been worth anything. Her first 'I love you,' which had been right in the cockpit, too, though that had come from an amused, touched Sally on the night she'd handed the keys over to Mel.

Mel knew it was silly not to sell, silly and sappy, but at least she'd managed to keep that sappiness from most of the world, all of whom believed her to be one tough cookie.

And she was that, too. Tough to the core, a real fighter. She cranked on the wrench and thought of the fight with Bo yet ahead of her. Yeah, that was going to be her toughest battle yet, and she needed to keep in sharp shape for it.

She heard the heels clicking long before she could actually see anyone, but Dimi was the only one who'd wear heels out here. Then she appeared in a white lacy sundress that played peek-a-boo with her toned, tanned, perfect body, as usual by some miracle completely spotless.

Dimi took a moment to glance at the mess around her—tools, cleaning fluid, parts, old plane . . . and wrinkled her nose. "Couple of problems. One, you have a few calls."

"Anything I want to take?"

"Hell, no." Dimi studied her pretty pink nails. "They're all on hold."

"How many?"

"Three."

They had only three lines. Which meant that with all

three lines tied up, no one else could call in. Mel opened her mouth to point that out, then shook her head at the amusement in Dimi's gaze. "Looking to cut out of here, huh?"

"Actually, I was looking to get you out of here." Dimi leaned over the tool bench and blew out a breath. Dust flew. "Disgusting."

"You could have radioed me instead of risking yourself."

Dimi pulled a new rag from a box, spread it over the bench, and carefully sat. Then she removed a chocolate bar from her pocket.

As junk food was usually banned from Dimi's body, this was the same as a scream of frustration and/or stress. "What's up?"

"Pretty much our entire future," Dimi said. "No biggee." Tearing open the wrapper, she offered half to Mel.

Mel took a bite and the chocolate burst in her mouth, making her moan.

"Not quite as good as an orgasm, but close enough, I'd say." Dimi chewed for a moment. "They're all bill collectors threatening your hide, by the way. On the phone. And as I'm rather fond of your grumpy-ass hide—" She cocked her head and studied Mel's filthy coveralls. "I don't want anything to happen to it."

"Thanks. I think."

"Don't thank me yet. Second problem."

"Starting to feel like Job here."

"Yeah, but at least this one doesn't have anything to do with Bo trying to talk us into hating Sally."

Mel opened her mouth to say that wasn't what he was doing, but decided it'd sound like she was siding with the enemy so she said nothing.

"Someone's here to see you. Bill Watkins."

Bill Watkins held the note on Mel's Cessna. He was a man's man who believed women belonged at home, pregnant and barefoot. He hadn't wanted to sell Mel the plane two years ago but she'd convinced him to take a chance on her. She'd made payments for fourteen months before being two days late on a payment because she'd gotten grounded in New Mexico due to storms, and he'd come unglued, threatening legal action. Dimi had gone and had drinks with him, talking him out of said action, gaining Mel an extra week.

She'd paid. She'd paid other months when she'd had to eat mac and cheese for two weeks, but she'd always paid.

Anderson Air had grown since then, and she was doing better. In fact, her payment wasn't even due for two days but Bill had taken to showing up every month to get his check in person.

"He wants to *see* you," Dimi said. "I told him you were on a flight."

"And he believed you?"

"Yeah, until he saw the Cessna on the tarmac. He's currently in your office. God, he's such a first-class prick."

Mel took another large bite of chocolate but it didn't give her as much joy this time. Just like a man to ruin even that small pleasure. "I'll have the money." She was just waiting for yesterday's deposit to clear. "But he can damn well wait the two days."

"Then I'd stay here and hide if I was you. Just to avoid having to see him twice. I'll see what I can do."

"Thanks."

Dimi got up, brushed off her still-spotless butt. "Just doing my job. For once."

"Dimi?" She hesitated. "Regarding Bill. Don't go solving this one yourself, okay? I can handle him."

"You handle everything."

"It's the analness in me." Mel knew that despite Dimi's come-what-may attitude, she'd fight to the death for this place, and the people in it, and would do anything to keep the status quo.

Anything.

Mel intended to make sure she didn't have to. "It's going to be all right."

Dimi's eyes went shiny, but she nodded. "I know." Then she was gone.

Mel dropped her forehead to her plane, closing her eyes for a moment to draw a deep breath. She'd just made yet another promise that she intended to keep with her whole heart, but a small part of her wasn't sure she could.

With no time for a pity party, not right now, she dove back into the Hawker, even though, truth be told, she was a little out of her league at the moment. She couldn't get the strap free to save her life. She could call Danny, but she wanted to do this on her own. In any case, she climbed back into the engine compartment, having to really lean her body inside to reach—"*Ouch.*" She eyed her knuckle as blood welled to the surface of her new scrape. Oh, yeah, that was going to burn in a minute—

She heard a footstep and went still. Damn it. Ducking down behind the plane, she froze on the ladder, hopefully just out of sight.

The footsteps came close, heading directly for her, which couldn't be, no one had seen her. She held her breath and wiped her bloody knuckle on the thigh of her coveralls, then grimaced at the burn.

The footsteps stopped.

Utter silence reigned, the kind that was too quiet. Awkward.

Unable to stand the suspense, she lifted her head.

And locked gazes with a set of sea green, amused eyes. "Problem?" Bo asked.

Argh! "You. You're my problem!" She stopped trying to make herself invisible, though there was something to be said for invisible. She knew what she looked like—hair wild, grease and blood smeared across her coveralls, no makeup— and she wished he'd stop looking at her. Wished she didn't care that he was looking at her. "I'm pretty busy," she said, in open invitation for him to leave.

"Working?"

That was better than admitting to hiding. "Yep. Lots of work, so—"

"Cuz it looked like maybe you were hiding."

"Why would I do that?"

"No reason—"

"Good. Because I'm not."

". . . Except the man in the office wanting his payment for the plane he sold you."

Damn it. "Fine. I'm hiding, all right? But I'm not late on that payment, he's just an—"

"Asshole."

She stared at him. "What?"

Bo shrugged. "I don't like it when blokes with too much money harass people doing the best they can."

"You—you think I'm doing the best I can?"

"Let's just say I know you're trying, although you need to get on North Beach's receivables. You have too much out-standing."

"And you know that why?"

"Because I'm holding the deed."

"How do you know what's going on in the books, Bo?"

He lifted a shoulder. "Dimi spent some time in the stock closet with the parts delivery guy the other day, and I sat at her desk and answered phones. And maybe perused a bit."

"You are a shifty bastard."

"Yeah, I probably resemble that remark. Anyway, it's not looking good. Not bad, but not good."

Mel didn't need him to say so, she'd felt the noose tight-ening around her neck all on her own, and it was getting tighter every single day. "Some months we do just fine," she said, chin up. It was the other months, the slow ones, that killed them.

Her.

But even those months they survived. They loved it here,

she loved it here, and that love had kept Sally's memory alive. Sally, who'd begun North Beach with nothing more than her own wits and a big grin—who'd kept it going on those wits.

And now, Bo wanted her to believe that for ten years, it'd all been an illusion.

As if reading her thoughts, he sighed, seeming to wrestle with himself over something. Probably the urge to strangle her. Putting his hands on her arms, he hauled her down off the ladder in one swift, economical movement, setting her on the floor right in front of him as if she weighed no more than a sack of potatoes.

The touch felt predatory, and just aggressive enough to have her pushing him away from her, but once again her hands hit the solid wall of his chest. She didn't, couldn't, budge him. "I really hate that," she said.

"What, that there's someone stronger than you? You can't always be the queen bee, Mel."

"You want to be the queen?"

He smirked, then lifted her bloody knuckle. "You need to clean this."

"Yeah, I know—" Her breath clogged her throat when he pressed his mouth to her fingers. Her pulse leapt into high gear, pounding like a steady drumbeat at each pulse point, making her head swim, her body feel like her clothes were too tight, like she needed to strip down to skin and have him do the same.

All because of his lips on her fingers. "What are you doing?"

"Kissing it all better." He lifted his gaze to hers. "Did it work?"

If he only knew.

Chapter 10

Mel yanked her hand free, sending a glare in Bo's general direction without looking right into his eyes. Looking into his eyes was bad, very bad, as she tended to see things there that couldn't really be there, things like desire, heat . . . affection.

An illusion, of course. He was here to get back what he thought Sally had stolen.

"Touchy," he said as she pulled away.

"Just keep your grimy paws off me."

He arched a brow at that, clearly noting that only one of them was grimy, and it was certainly not him. Watching her, he leaned against the hull of the plane, crossing his arms over his chest as he got comfortable. "Bill's gone, by the way. You can relax."

Yeah. Except she couldn't, not with him this close. "How do you know he's gone?"

"Because I told him to come back when the payment was due."

Well, if that didn't throw her off balance. But hell, she'd

been off balance for five days now, ever since Bo had landed here and flashed that deed.

A deed that had her world upside down.

God, it all made no sense, no sense at all, and her brain hurt sorting through it all.

"Are you trying to come up with a thank you?" he asked, looking amused again.

"Thank you," she said, just a little bit grudgingly.

He ran a finger over her chin. "You know, I think you just might be the most stubborn woman on the planet."

"Don't touch me," she said, and slapped his hand away. "I can't seem to think when you do."

His gaze ran over her features. "Giving information to the enemy, Mel?"

"You're holding a deed that puts the most important thing in my life at risk. Like it or not, you're not my enemy, you're in my camp."

He said nothing to that for a long beat, but relaxed, letting out a slow smile that made her knees wobble.

"Stop that," she demanded, pointing at him.

The grin spread, and she shook her head, baffled, and admittedly aroused. Good God, he was potent. "Bo . . . What do you want from me?"

"Interesting question." He peered into the engine compartment, while she peered at him. He wore jeans, cargo styled, loose and low on his hips, but leaving no doubt that beneath the denim was a Class A body in prime condition. His T-shirt was black, half tucked in and half not. Carefree, laid-back, sexy.

Dangerous.

At least to her own peace of mind. "You buy that plane you were looking at?"

"I'm thinking about it. With a little work, I could make a sweet profit off it. I saw another the other day, too. A '38 Spartan, you see it?" He glanced back at her, his eyes shiny, his smile easy.

She hadn't seen him excited about something before, she realized. He was happy, and damn it, it looked good on him. "I saw it."

"You have a beauty right here as well." He stroked a hand over the Hawker, peering into the engine. "Ah," he said, and pointed to the casing. "Bad bolt, it's all rusted, see? No worries, mate. Hand me a wrench."

She narrowed her eyes. "Why?"

"Because I can get it off for you."

"I'll do it myself, thanks." She'd been trying for days.

"I'm standing right here, and I've got better leverage than you." He cocked his head and gave her that smile, which she was sure had charmed the panties off too many women to count. "You're afraid to let me help you."

"I'm afraid of what you'll want in return."

"Just a tiny little thing, really."

She crossed her arms. "I told you, I don't know where Sally is."

"Yeah, yeah. Old news. I figure one of these days you'll either cave or she'll show."

Her gut tightened. "Why wouldn't she?"

"Why don't you tell me?"

He sounded . . . confident. As if he knew something, which of course, he didn't.

Did he? "Why would you hang around?" she pressed. "Why don't you just go home and I'll call you—"

"Ah, but will you?" He smiled, a challenging light in his eyes. "Nah, I think I'm better off sticking around, thanks. Plus there's the added bonus, of course."

More than her gut tightened now. "What's that?"

"Bothering you."

"You don't get to me."

"Is that right?" He took a step toward her, bringing them entirely too close, so close that she could see those mesmerizing flecks of gold dancing in the green of his eyes. So close that she could smell him, that complicated, glorious scent of a far-too-sexy man. So close she could do nothing but soak him up. "Yeah, I get to you plenty," he said.

She waited until she could be sure her voice would be even. "You really think you can get that bolt off?"

"Sure."

"Is it going to cost me?"

He just looked at her, eyes hot.

Her belly quivered. Her everything quivered. To hide it, she laughed. "Men." She whirled back to the plane. "I'll fix it myself."

"Suit yourself." With another shrug, he went back to holding up the hull with his butt and back, all casual and laid-back as he watched her from eyes at half-mast.

Sort of the way a sleeping lion might watch its prey.

Mel decided to put him out of her mind as she dove into her toolbox. She got a bigger wrench and went back for the bolt, wielding the tool as hard as she could—until her fingers slipped, scraping yet another knuckle. *"Damn it."*

"Need me to kiss that one, too?"

Yes, begged her body. *"No!"* She wiped the blood off on her coveralls. "It's just a little nick."

He agreed with a low laugh. "Yeah, and you've had more than your fair share of knocks."

"It's called shit happens."

"Yeah." His smile faded. "Neither of us have lived a walk in the park, have we?"

Her eyes met his, saw the understanding there, and sighed. "Ah, hell, Bo. Do we really want to do this?"

"Do what?"

"You know. *Talk.*"

He smiled. "Afraid of a little chitchat? No worries. Charlene and Al already told me all about you."

"They did not."

"Oh, yes they did. I sang along to a Twisted Sister song on the radio and Char melted on the spot. She was worried you broke my heart. I told her I'd recovered."

"Yeah, I'll bet." She put her head back in the engine compartment. Recovered, her ass. They both knew only one of them would get hurt here. Damn, if only she really could get that bolt off by herself . . .

"Oh, and I might have mentioned . . ." He arched a brow. "That I intended to get you back."

At this, she dropped the wrench. It landed right on her toe. Hopping up and down, she glared at him. *"What?"*

"You heard me."

She gritted past the throbbing radiating up her leg. "Get me back. Ha! And why aren't you taken, anyway?"

He choked out a laugh. "A personal question, Mel?"

She actually felt herself blush. "Forget it."

"No, you're curious." He smiled. "It's cute."

"Maybe I just wanted to see how hard up you are."

"Pretty damn hard up."

Her gaze flew to his, wondering if he meant the words as hot and erotic as he'd said them.

His eyes were burning up.

Oh, God.

"You going to offer to help me get un-hard-up?" he asked.

"No! And this isn't funny," she said when he laughed.

"Well, actually, it is a little."

She wouldn't look at him as she looked down at her feet, because her toe hurt like a son-of-a-bitch.

Again he pushed away from the plane and came close, too close. "Char thinks I'm still carrying a torch for you."

"She has a heart of gold and you took advantage of her to get information."

"She does have a heart of gold," he agreed, not denying the charge. "But I have a feeling you're the real heart bleeder here."

"What does that mean?"

"I've seen you; working late, working your ass off and your knuckles to the bone. Literally." He smiled when she rolled her eyes. "I've seen you mother Kellan and Ritchie, and listen to Ernest give you yet another reason why he can't clean that damn closet you want him to clean. You help Charlene when she gets busy, you get Al photography work with a customer . . . face it. You love these guys, all of them, and you treat them like family because your own failed you so badly."

"Leave my past out of this." At least he hadn't figured out that her bleeding-heart syndrome didn't extend to her social life, and that she hadn't had sex in—

"I would, but then Char told me how you don't date much." He tipped her chin. "You hard up, too, Mel?"

She pointed her wrench at him, put it to his chest to make sure he kept his distance. "Not that hard up."

"I don't know, you nearly went off like a rocket when I kissed you—"

"Hey, there were *two* of us going off like rockets, thank you very much!"

He grinned. "Me thinks the lady protest too much."

"You are impossible!"

"Yeah, I've heard that one before." As she spun to limp away, he caught her, pulling her back around. "What do you suppose it says about me that your snarling attitude turns me on?" He put his other hand on her arm, holding her. "Stand still, darlin', I want to look at you."

"You are one sick man."

"I meant your toe." Crouching down, he lifted up the pants leg on her coveralls.

Oh, God, had she shaved in the past week? "I'm fine," she said, trying to pull away.

He looked up, his hair falling across his forehead, his eyes now level with her belly. An undeniably erotic position. "Yeah, you are," he said softly.

She stepped back, putting some space between them, turning away while he straightened.

"This place," he said to her back. "It really means a lot to you."

She closed her eyes, struggled to keep her voice even. "You shouldn't believe everything Charlene says. She's working with cooking sherry."

"Are you denying you care deeply about North Beach, that you put everything of yourself into it?"

To this, she said nothing. She couldn't, or she'd give herself away.

"Odd that you'd do so much for just a job," he continued, and she could feel him watching her. "Why, when Sally knew this place wasn't hers."

"I don't know that." Not yet.

"Why would I lie?"

She turned back to him. "After what your father did to Sally . . . ?"

In a blink, all hints of heat and amusement vanished, leaving in their place a cold, tough, impenetrable hostility.

"I just don't see how Sally could be the bad guy," she murmured, willing him to try to understand. "*You're* holding the deed. If Sally swindled your father, as you say, then where's the money? The plane?"

"Where's Sally?" he countered.

They stared at each other, at an impasse. Finally, Mel conceded, and buried her head back in the engine compartment, going back to the only sure thing in her life: work.

Chapter 11

Bo watched Mel busy herself in the plane again, and decided she had the sweetest ass he'd ever seen in a set of grungy brown coveralls.

But as he stood there watching her work on the Hawker, he was filled with so much frustration he didn't know what to do with himself.

She didn't believe him.

No one believed him that Sally had stolen from his father, that his father had been a good, kind man who couldn't have conned a fly—much less a woman.

Putting his fist through a wall sounded good. So did dragging Mel down to the floor and stripping off those coveralls to find the soft, warm woman he knew hid in there somewhere. Oh, yeah, getting her to whimper and pant his name in hungry desperate need would go a long way toward dissolving his temper, that was for damn sure.

But chances were she wouldn't go easy. She'd probably fight and claw and bite, and though that might be fun another time, he wasn't in the mood for that kind of thing at the moment. At the moment, he wanted a soft, warm, willing woman, one who'd wrap him in her arms and offer to kiss his hurt away.

As if she'd ever do that. Because it turned out she was holding a grudge against him for his father's sins.

Sins his father hadn't even committed.

Damn, he was tired. Tired of the battle. He'd come here with some half-baked idea of getting his justice, of selling out from beneath Sally's feet. But now he was thinking of something else entirely.

This woman, the most troublesome, annoying, frustrating woman he'd ever met. "Mel."

She didn't bother to answer. She still had her head buried in the Hawker. She was filthy, smelled like fuel and oil, and God, he must have hit his head at some point this morning because she *still* revved his engine.

"Shit on a stick," she muttered.

He stuck his head in next to hers, surveyed both the situation and the spot of grease on Mel's nose—wisely not mentioning the latter—and said, "I can get the bolt off."

She turned her head and leveled those icy eyes on him. "Yeah, but it'll cost me."

He wished he understood the female mind better because he had no idea what she was thinking other than wishing he was far, far away, preferably dead.

"Ratchet, please." She jerked her head toward the toolbox.

Willing to play along, he backed out of the engine and peered into the toolbox. "Not here."

"Try the parts closet, there's a box of tools there on the floor."

He turned toward the closet, opened the door.

"Sorry, there are no blondes in there," Mel called out.

"What?"

"You don't remember the second time I ever saw you?" she asked. "Right there in that closet, banging some blonde?"

He looked at the shelves. He didn't often think about the past. It was filled with memories best forgotten. His mother's cold voice and colder heart. Eddie's plane habit, which caused frequent moves from one small airport to another . . .

Then, Sally, the woman Eddie had lost his head and then his heart to, despite the fact that *she* didn't possess one.

A heart, that is. Brains, Sally had in spades, and it hadn't taken her long to sink her hungry claws into the love-struck Eddie, or his bank account.

Buh-bye savings account.

Buh-bye hopes and dreams.

And then, finally, buh-bye Eddie.

Bo's jaw tightened as he looked inside the closet. Hell, yeah, he remembered being here, missing home, worrying about his dad, burying all that stress into the one thing a male teenager couldn't stop thinking about.

Sex.

It hadn't been too difficult, not when American girls had flocked to him, drawn by his accent and, as he'd discovered, his earthy nature and athletic body. Yeah, he'd gotten quite the education here in the States. "I had a good time in this very closet *several* times, if I remember correctly."

Mel had pulled her head out of the engine and was watching him with her own memories all over her face. "I only found you in there the once."

"You stood right there," he said. "Mouth hanging open, soaking up the sights."

She bristled. "I couldn't help but see the sights! You didn't bother to try to hide a thing!"

Ah, he was getting an interesting vibe here. "Admit it. You wanted the same thing the blonde was getting."

"Did not," she said hotly. Too hotly.

"Liar."

Oh, yeah, *there* was that steam coming out her ears again. Damn, she was something all riled up, but a part of him wanted to see the other Mel; the soft, sweet Mel she showed everyone else. But never him. "I can't believe you're going to be so stubborn about me helping you fix that plane."

"I don't trust you."

Odd how, given everything he'd been through, it was that that hurt him. "It's a fucking bolt, Mel."

"Fine." She tossed down her wrench. "What do you want in return?"

He'd have settled for one of her smiles instead of the frown he seemed to generate at every turn, but that seemed too revealing a request, and besides which, made him feel stupid. "It won't be painful, if that's what you're thinking."

"Tell me."

"A kiss," he said, and shocked the hell out of the both of them.

She looked at him for a long beat, then went back to studying the engine.

And that got him. Had he ever done anything to her? No. Had he ever, in any way, hurt her? Bothered her? Got in her way? *No.* He'd been pretty balls-out patient if you asked him. Now he could help her, and she didn't even want to accept that help.

Or another kiss.

Since he knew damn well she'd nearly gotten off on their last kiss alone, it wasn't a lack of wanting on her part. Which meant it must be fear. Fear of its going too far, of her letting it. *Wanting* it.

Which in turn meant she must like him a helluva lot more than she'd let on, because he'd bet she didn't lose control often.

If ever.

"I can do this myself," she said stubbornly, and bashed yet a third knuckle against the casing. "Shit." She sucked on the offended finger, straightened, and bumped her head. "Shit *shit!*" She had a knuckle in her mouth, her other hand on the top of her head as she backed off the ladder, tripped on a wrench on the floor, and staggered backward.

Before he could nab her, she'd fallen butt first into the large tub behind her filled with cleaning fluid and various parts—industrial-strength cleaner that he knew if he dropped a penny inside, it'd clean it down to shiny copper in two seconds. It would skin her alive. "Jesus, Mel." He reached for her, knowing she had to strip in a hurry. Yanking her out of the tub, he reached for the zipper of her drenched coveralls, one mission in mind: save her skin.

"Hey." She slapped his hands away.

"Mel, that stuff is going to eat your flesh—"

"No kidding!" She was hopping up and down as she kicked off her athletic shoes. "Ouch, ouch . . ." More hopping as she shrugged the coveralls off her shoulders, revealing a white satin bra.

His tongue stuck to the roof of his mouth, but the pained sound she made galvanized him. Tugging the coveralls off her hips, revealing white satin panties, which matched her bra.

Don't look. Don't look. But her skin was already going pink.

"The hose," she gasped, pointing to the hose coiled against the wall, used for washing down the concrete floors. He ran while she shoved the coveralls past her knees and kicked them off.

Yanking the hose from its holder, he cranked it on, trying not to notice how the scraps of silk covered her. Or *didn't* cover her.

"Hurry!"

Adjusting the spray, he nailed her with the water, telling himself he was a pervert for noticing her underwear.

Mel let out a short gasp at the shock of the icy shower, but not another sound as he ran the water from her shoulders to torso to belly to legs and back up again while she slid her hands over herself, hurrying the process along, skimming her arms over her slightly rounded belly—his favorite spot on a woman—her breasts, making his own breath back up in his throat.

Don't think about it.

Yeah, right. Her bra and panties were good and sheer now, her nipples pressing hard against the thin material on top, and on the bottom . . . She was waxed or shaved or something, so the wet satin clung to every fold, every dip, every gorgeous inch, and melted brain cells at an alarming rate.

God. It was like every wet T-shirt contest he'd ever witnessed, only better. More like every hot fantasy he'd ever had. Only better.

Waaaaaay better.

Then she turned, presenting him with her back, her ass, and the hose jerked. So did a singular part of his anatomy. He stood there, running the water over her, watching it race in little rivulets down her body, and he wanted to lap it all up with his tongue. He felt like a voyeur, he felt like a jerk, and he'd never been hotter in his life.

Finally she stepped free of the water, crossed her arms over her chest and glared at him as if this was all his fault. Tossing the hose aside, he stepped toward her as he unbuttoned his own shirt.

"What are you doing?" Taking a step back, she came up against the hull of the plane.

He shrugged out of the shirt.

Gaping at him, she unfolded her arms and put her hand in the middle of his chest to hold him back. "You just stay dressed, Bo Black—"

Cutting her off in midsentence, he lifted her arm and shoved it into the arm of his shirt.

"Oh," she said, and Bo watched humility war with pride as she put her other arm in and hugged the shirt to her. It came to midthigh on her, and she stood there, arms wrapped around herself, staring at his now bare chest. She bit her lower lip, and said nothing.

Was the woman actually tongue-tied? Tongue-tied while looking at his body? Again her gaze flicked over him, lingered.

She was. And he was just male enough to find that incredibly fascinating. "The word is thanks."

She sighed. "Thanks."

She said this so begrudgingly, he had to laugh. "Yeah, don't hurt yourself." Turning to the plane he grabbed the fallen wrench and worked on the bolt himself. It took him a moment, but he did get it, and dropped the thing into her hand.

She stared down at the rusty bolt. "You win."

Due to all his blood still pooled behind the buttons on his Levi's, he was only working on two cylinders and didn't follow. "Huh?"

"You win."

"Just to be clear," he said warily. "I win what?"

He didn't know what he expected, but it sure as hell wasn't that she'd stalk toward him, grip his arms, and slam her mouth over his.

Chapter 12

Mel's kiss left Bo staggered by a barrage of sensations. First, her mouth. God, that mouth. It was the mouth of wet dreams across the land. Warm, eager . . . She tasted like everything missing from his life, things he hadn't even known existed.

So shocked by that, he let out a dark sound, a bit staggering in its neediness, and braced himself as he hauled her up, kissing her hungrily, frantically, unable to stop himself. Her breasts, covered in that wet sheer bra and by his own shirt, smashed into his bare chest. Her thighs entangled with his. Her heart drummed a staccato beat against him, so fast and heavy it was amazing that people didn't come running to see what the racket was. Or maybe that was *his* heart. Hell, he didn't know, and it didn't matter. Then she pulled back, leaving him gasping for air, painfully aroused.

Her cinnamon eyes dropped to his mouth before lifting once again to meet his. In them was a confusion, a heat, and a temper he wanted to snarl right back at. Or soothe . . .

"What the hell *was* that?" she asked, her voice low and husky. "I mean *what the hell?*"

"You're asking me?" Risking life and limb, he fisted one hand at her back, gripping the material of *his* shirt low on her spine. He sank his other hand into her wet hair, tugging her head back, looking into her eyes . . .

"All I know," she said shakily, "is that you need to keep your shirt on always."

"Why?"

"Like you don't know how ripped you are."

"Again," he decided.

"Um . . . what?"

"This. Again." And he kissed *her* this time.

Harder.

Wetter.

Deeper.

He did it to keep her quiet, because damn, he liked her quiet. He liked her just like this actually, mouth fixed to his, little whimpery pants escaping her as if she couldn't get enough. Then she sucked his tongue into her mouth and he couldn't think at all because his heart was going to leap right out of his chest.

Her hands ran up his sides, over his ribs, her fingers sinking into his pecs painfully enough to make him suck in a breath. She tasted hot and sweet and felt even better, and she was wet all over, with a hot little bod he definitely needed more of. He was quite certain there would be a price to pay for this glimpse of pure, unadulterated pleasure, there was always a price, but not caring at the moment, he backed her up to the Hawker, pressed her up against the cool steel and took his mouth on a cruise over her throat. Nudging the shirt off her shoulder wasn't a problem, and the wet, sheer bra wasn't, either. He simply tugged it down, groaning when a breast popped out, her nipple pebbled and thrust upward, as if begging for his attention. "Mmm," rumbled from his chest, and he took it in his mouth.

"Ohmigod." Mel's fingers sank into his hair, fisting it, doing her best to make him bald before he hit middle age.

He didn't care. He sucked hard, then flicked her nipple with his tongue. She gasped, and her head fell back, thunking against the plane, dislodging a few tools she'd set around the opened engine compartment. As they rained to the ground around them, clanging and clattering, Mel jerked, then stared up at him, eyes huge, mouth open as if she needed it that way just to breathe.

God, she looked like heaven standing there, his shirt off her shoulders, caught on her elbows, opened to reveal her breasts, one nipple wet from his mouth. "Mel—"

"This isn't happening," she said. "Is. Not. Happening." Her eyes were dilated, her mouth a little swollen. And he'd left a slight whisker burn on the underside of her jaw that he wanted to press his lips to.

In fact, he did, he leaned in and kissed her there, or tried to, but she slapped a hand to his chest and held him off. "Guess you got another airport quickie," she said. "Only in the hangar this time, not the closet. Oh, and not with a blonde."

Wow. Her opinion of him was even lower than he'd thought, and he had to remind himself that he didn't care. "A quickie implies that I got off."

She stared at him. "I'm a damn idiot," she muttered and brushed past him. Hauling open the closet with more force than necessary, she pulled out another set of coveralls, shoving her legs through one at a time while he eyed the peek-a-boo hints he got of her panties and belly as his shirt rose high on her thighs.

"You have three more rusty bolts," he said. "I could—"

"I can take it from here."

Of course she could. "Because God forbid you actually lean on someone, right?"

"I lean plenty."

"Prove it. I know there's something going on here, Mel. So prove it—lean on me. Let me help."

She hesitated, as if she just might decide to actually trust him, but in the end she slowly shook her head and walked away, leaving him hot, wet, still turned on . . . and disappointed. Extremely disappointed.

Wayne took Dimi out to the fanciest restaurant in town, and then they drank and danced for hours before going to a five-star hotel and roughing up the sheets.

So one would think she'd wake up with a smile on her face, but instead she drove into North Beach feeling hungover and . . . empty.

Intent on getting over herself, she entered the lobby head down, searching through her purse for her favorite lip gloss as she went, then plowed right into Danny. "Oomph," she said, teetering on her heels.

He put his hands on her hips until she gained her balance, then pulled back immediately, leaving her with the oddest sense of loss.

"Someone on your tail again?" he asked.

She looked into his face, void of its usually friendly smile. He smelled like the coconut wax he'd probably used on his surfboard that morning, and the scent was so familiar she felt a little rush of comfort, despite his distant expression. "No. Thanks."

"I was going to ask how you are, but let me guess. You're fantastic, right?"

"Why wouldn't I be?"

He gazed at her for a long moment, as if maybe he wanted to say something, but in the end, he simply nodded and let her pass.

She shrugged off the encounter with a big mug of tea and sat at her desk. Because the afternoon before she'd left off in a great part of her book, she dove right back in, and it was thirty minutes before the phone bothered her. After transferring the call to Mel, she sipped her tea and realized someone had left a small box in her top drawer, wrapped in pretty pink paper.

Lifting her head, she looked around. No one. She opened the box and pulled out a small but beautiful candle, decorated with seashells and scented like a glorious summer day. It put a smile on her face as she searched for a card, a signature . . . nothing.

She looked around again, expecting to see someone watching her—Mel, Char, one of the early-bird customers—but no one was paying her any attention at all.

Hmmm . . . She lit the candle and went to work. But after a few moments, the smile was gone and worry weeded its way through her as she called Mel's office.

"Hey," Mel answered, sounding a little breathless.

Dimi frowned. "What are you doing in there?"

"Eating bonbons and watching *Oprah*. How about you?"

"Funny. I'm going through the billing."

"Yeah? About time—"

"Yeah, yeah. Look, it's a good news–bad news sort of thing. Good news: you've got a message from a few of your receivables, money is coming in the mail for Anderson Air. Bad news: somebody else has been here."

"Customers are good."

"Stick with me, Mel. Somebody has been in my billings for North Beach."

Suddenly she had Mel's full attention. "Doing what?"

"Not sure," Dimi admitted. "But the date these files were last accessed was yesterday morning, and . . ."—she hated to admit this—"I haven't worked on them since the day before yesterday."

"It was Bo. He told me you'd left your accounting up on the screen when he sat at your desk to help with the phones."

"To help with the planes, not help himself to my files! *Bastard*."

"Yeah. But Dimi, Jesus. You must have left your computer on all night. You can't leave that stuff up and available to anyone with two eyes."

"Two eyes, and our deed." Dimi rubbed the tense spot between her eyes. "I'm so sorry. I'm just . . . stressed."

"I know."

"What if he stays?" Dimi asked softly. "What if he fires us? God, Mel, what else could I even do for a job? I'm uniquely suited for nothing!"

"Look, let's not borrow trouble, okay? We don't even know if the deed's legit."

"Right. It isn't. It can't be."

"Exactly."

Dimi drew a deep breath. "Okay, I'll try to maintain. Oh, and thanks for the beautiful candle."

Mel paused. "Uh . . . not me."

Dimi looked at the flickering wick, inhaled the incredibly soothing scent. "No?"

"No."

Dimi shook her head as the phone began to ring. "Gotta go." She switched lines. "North Beach."

"Dimi."

Hmmm, deep, mysterious male voice. So far so good. "Yes," she said. "Can I help you?"

"It's Todd."

Todd. She didn't know a—

"From the other night."

Dimi went still.

"I came in on my brother's jet with some other guys, and we—"

"I remember." Previously Gorgeous Guy.

"Did you like the candle?"

Leaning forward, she blew out the candle, watched the thin line of smoke rise into the air. "I'm hanging up now. Don't call me again."

"Wait— I just wanted to apologize, and—"

"Apology accepted. Good-bye." She clicked off and tossed the candle in the trash. Then, on second thought, pulled it out and left it on the corner of her desk as a reminder that she made bad decisions, and in light of that . . . *no more men*. Not a single one.

Mel sat at her desk and stared at her phone. Today was the day she'd hear from her attorney, and knowing that had her body quivering with a high level of awareness.

Or maybe that was just from yet another long night of sensual dreams in which she'd let Bo strip off more than her coveralls, in a world where he could press her naked up against the Hawker and take her. . . .

Jeez, the porno dreams had to stop! She'd managed to avoid Bo this morning by sheer luck, because he'd flown out early and had stayed out. A good thing because he was so damn potently, outrageously, dangerously sexy, she could hardly stand it.

He had customers waiting for him. Turned out he was a popular guy, and had a lot of connections.

Not only that, but he'd brought business into North Beach, a lot of it. Every day someone new stopped by— someone he'd recommended the place to, for fuel or maintenance . . . or to hire him to find them an antique aircraft. He was single-handedly saving North Beach. She didn't really want to think about that, so instead she went into the café for something bad for her.

Charlene was there, gushing all over one of her customers, a woman with a young baby, both of whom had come in on a flight and were waiting on maintenance. The baby was wailing away, little arms and legs bicycling like crazy, her face bright red from the efforts.

"Wow," Mel said, realizing the kid was actually putting out more decibels than Van Halen on the radio, and that was saying something. "She's got a set of lungs."

The mother, looking a little harassed, blew out a breath. "Got that from her daddy. She likes to listen to herself all night long."

"Give her here." Char cuddled her close. "Ah, look at you," she cooed with a smile. "You're such a pretty thing."

The full-out wail lessened slightly. "Yeah, that's it," Char murmured, stroking her fingers over the baby's forehead. "That's it. You're nearly all done now, aren't you?"

And unbelievably, the crying stopped.

They all stared at the baby, who looked up at Char with huge, soaked eyes and trembly rosebud mouth.

"My God," the mother breathed. "Whatever you're doing, don't stop."

Char smiled down at the baby. "Oh, look at you, you're so precious."

Al came out of the kitchen, saw the baby in his wife's arms, took in the look on her face, and sighed. "Ah, man."

"Isn't she beautiful?" Char asked him.

"Beautiful, now give her back."

Char chuckled. "Isn't he silly?" she asked the baby. "Go away, Al."

"It's that look in your eyes," he said uneasily. "Like you want another."

"Because I do."

Al went pale. "Okay, seriously. Give the baby back, Char."

She just kept cuddling the baby, a secret smile on her face.

"Honey? We're past all this baby stuff, remember," Al said, sounding a little desperate. "No diapers. No midnight interruptions. Life's good, Char, really good. We're in the home stretch, in the clear, you know?"

"I'm just holding her, Al."

"Okay," he said, then nodded. "Okay, then. That's good." He nodded again, hesitated, then went back into the kitchen.

Char smiled at Mel. "Yeah, I'm just holding her." She leaned in. "And wanting another one."

Mel glanced at Al in the kitchen.

"Oh, don't worry about him. I'll promise him sex every night, he'll be fine. He's a great daddy . . ."

Mel's brain had caught and snagged on *sex every night*. She imagined herself with someone, making love every night, and before she could stop the thought, her brain plugged Bo into that equation.

Whoa.

Momentarily struck by that image, she had to shake it off, but it took her an embarrassingly long time to do so.

"Mel? What's the matter?" Char asked.

"Nothing. Nothing's wrong." Mel fanned air in front of her face. *Sheesh*. "Gotta go." And she took herself and her letter to the post office. Unfortunately, it was lunchtime, and the rest of the free world was there, too. She had to park around the block, and by the time she got inside she was panting from the heat, sweating unattractively, and felt like her heart no longer fit inside her chest.

The same guy was behind the counter and he looked as unhappy at his job today as he had yesterday. He glanced at her and sighed. "He's got the flu, lady. You'll have to come back."

"Are you kidding me? No one else can run the machine? How hard can it be?"

"Hard."

"Look, can I see the manager?"

"I am the manager."

Great. Perfect. She drove in the heat back to North Beach and faced yet another unpleasant surprise as she walked in the door.

"Line one," Dimi called out. "Attorney."

Their eyes met. Mel's heart stopped. "I'll take it in the office," she said as if her world hadn't just stopped spinning. She ran down the hall, skidded to a stop in front of her desk, then stared at the phone as if it were a spitting cobra. "Grow up," she told herself, and picked up the phone.

"Got news," Greg said.

Mel couldn't breathe and her legs felt like rubber. "Okay."

"You should probably sit."

Right. She fell into her chair. "Sitting. Go."

"The deed Bo Black has in his possession is legit."

Dimi burst into the office, took one look at Mel's face, and sank to a chair.

"Sally deeded North Beach," Greg continued, "and all its possessions, except for what's in the individually rented hangars, to Eddie Black. When Eddie Black died, everything he owned went to his sole beneficiary—Bo Black."

"How long ago?" Mel asked.

"Ten years."

She'd been working for Bo for ten years. Worse, Sally had known all this time . . . Every time she'd called, she'd known. Every time she'd drained the accounts, she'd known. Every time she'd asked Mel how things were, she'd known . . . "How did you find out?" she asked hoarsely.

"City records. Not that hard to find, actually. In fact, anyone could look this sort of thing up and get answers."

Mel thought of the e-mail note and the letter she'd received. "Can anyone figure out that *I* went looking?"

"These days, with computer trails and such, yes."

Mel nodded, then realized he couldn't see her. "Thanks," she managed, hung up, and thunked her head to the desk. "My God."

"There has to be a reason," Dimi said. "He threatened her. *Something.*"

"Maybe."

"Definitely."

Bo was still away on his flight, but Mel knew she'd have to face him eventually. Knowing it felt like torture. For the next few hours, her pulse beat unevenly, and she kept breaking out into a sweat.

The deed was legit.

Life as she knew it had changed forever, but she was

nothing if not a survivor. She had plenty of smiles in her arsenal, and she pulled them out now, pasting on the "I'm Fine" smile for everyone who looked her way. And she'd leave it there until she knew for sure what the hell had happened, and why.

The next e-mail came in just before closing. Mel stared at it: BackOffOrElse. As before, the body of the e-mail was blank, but this time there was a subject line.

I mean it.

Mel felt the tingle go down her spine and knew she was getting close. To what, she had no clue.

Chapter 13

Mel waited for Bo until 5:30, then couldn't handle it anymore. She grabbed her things and left her office. Dimi was gone, she'd left much earlier, without a word, making Mel's chest tighten with worry. Mel had loved Sally, but Dimi had positively worshipped the woman, and so for her, this would be harder.

Mel's brain had been racing since Greg's call, pounding with what if's—if Bo hadn't gone into the military, if he'd gone through his father's things sooner, if, if, if . . .

In any of those scenarios, she and everyone here would have been gone years ago.

The implications of that staggered her. All this time she'd *never* been in charge, not of her life, not of this place . . .

Ernest was in the parking lot, and as she came out he looked at his watch. "You're punching out early."

"It's five thirty."

"Early for you."

"I wasn't the one who wasted two hours this afternoon napping in the storage closet."

"Maybe you've been napping with your eyes open."

A more real truth had never been spoken. "You ever trace that e-mail?"

He took off his cap, scratched his greasy head, then narrowed his beady eyes on her. "I told you I was working on it. Why?"

"I got another one."

"Hmmm."

"What does that mean?"

"It means I'm glad I'm not you," he said.

"Can you trace it or not?"

"I'll look," he said, and hitching up his pants, moved toward the building. "But it'd be helpful if you stopped doing whatever you're doing to get them mad in the first place."

Yeah, she'd just stop what she was doing—except she didn't know what that was.

Then it hit her—she did know. It was that she was tracing the deed—looking for Sally.

Feeling more fragile than fine china, she got into her car. She picked up a pizza, then drove to Dimi's.

Dimi opened her door, took one look at the box, and blew out a breath. "You know how I feel about carbs."

"It's thin crust."

"Well, all right, then." She made a show of looking around Mel. "At least you didn't bring him."

"Who?"

"*Him*. You know, bastard Bo."

"Dimi—"

"Sorry." But she didn't sound like it.

Dimi wore a pale, pale yellow sundress that revealed her willowy lean form. They sat on the beach, bare toes in the sand, watching the waves pound the surf while they consumed the pizza and a beer each.

Light for Dimi.

Not light for Mel.

Dimi daintily sipped her beer as if this was high tea, the

bracelets on her wrists jangling, a frown on her mouth. She brushed the nonexistent crumbs from her fingers. "Well. The evening is still young. I've got to go live it."

"We should talk about it, Dimi."

"Why?"

"It'd be the mature thing to do."

"Damn. I hate it when you're grown-up." She played her toes in the sand. "I don't get it, Mel. Why would she do this to us and never say a word about it? Why would she let us think everything was status quo?" Her voice thickened with tears. "Hell, we were sending her money. Money that wasn't even *hers*."

Mel shook her head. She felt sick about it, too.

"The only thing I can think is, she somehow lost the deed to him in an unfair bet or something, and by letting us send her money, she was trying to get back what Eddie had stolen from her." Dimi looked up at her, hopeful once more. "That has to be it, Mel."

"Then why didn't she return my call? Why did she change her number?"

Dimi closed her eyes, shook her head stubbornly. "Something's wrong."

"I'm afraid so, yes."

"We have to help her."

Mel made a pained sound. Help Sally? She'd have loved to. Only Sally didn't want their help and they both knew it. "Dimi—"

"Don't say it."

"She crossed the line. She stole money. She had *us* steal money."

"But there's a *reason*." Her voice shook. "I know it."

Mel reached for Dimi's hand. "Listen to me. I don't know what's going on. Like you, I want to believe there's been a mistake. Okay? We're together in that. We're together in all of it. No matter what happens."

Dimi squeezed Mel's fingers. "I know. You're my family, Mel. But things are going to change. It's going to suck. You know that."

"Maybe Bo won't—"

"Honey, you're the smartest woman I know, don't go stupid on me now."

Mel blew out a breath. "I'm going to talk to him."

"Talk to him? Or do him?"

Were Mel's nightly dreams all over her face? It didn't help that she hadn't actually seen Bo since the other night, when she'd had to strip in front of him and let him hose her off. Since she'd let him put his hands all over her . . . *God*. "I'm not doing him."

"Uh-huh. And I'm still a virgin."

"I'm *not*." But she wanted to be. What did that say about her, that she wanted the man who was poised to tear apart her entire world?

"Okay, maybe not yet, you're not doing him," Dimi allowed. "But the signs are there."

Mel pushed up and stalked down to the ocean. "Signs. There are no signs. What signs?"

"Well, that right there," Dimi pointed out dryly. "The defensiveness is a dead giveaway, hon."

Mel kicked the wave at her feet. "Damn it."

"No one can blame you. I mean the guy's a walking, talking fantasy. But honestly, if you're looking to dip your toes into the testosterone pool, then let me help you pick a better one."

"Uh, no offense, but I've seen your choices."

"Yeah." Dimi sighed. "True enough."

"Look, I'm tired." So damned tired. "I'm going home to bed."

"I vote for Madigan's."

Madigan's was the local bar, where no doubt she'd find Kellan and Ritchie, and a whole host of others looking for a good time. Normally Mel would consider it, for no other reason than to keep Dimi out of trouble, but tonight it seemed exhausting. "Not tonight."

"Suit yourself." Dimi picked up the box of pizza.

"Dimi? We're going to be okay."

Dimi's smile didn't meet her eyes. "Yeah, I know."

Mel nodded.

But they were both lying through their teeth.

The next day, Mel brought Bo's shirt into North Beach, washed but not ironed, and went in search of him. *Time to face the music*. She passed Kellan and Ritchie in the employee's break room playing darts, then Danny sprawled on a cart beneath the aircraft tow truck in the maintenance hangar, swearing up a storm.

In the back of that hangar Ernest was talking to a spider in the supply closet.

"Where's Bo?" she asked him.

Ernest carefully coaxed the spider into a jar, which Mel knew he'd take outside. "Tie-down."

Right. He was on the tarmac, either conducting a tie-down or getting ready to. The lingo had been a part of Mel's vocabulary for years, and was second nature. So why she got another image altogether—one of Bo Black physically tied down, possibly naked (okay, definitely naked) shocked her into immobility.

Ernest frowned, peering into her face. "What's with you?"

Her mouth had gone dry. She cleared her throat. "Nothing." Whirling around, she marched to the tarmac.

Bo stood there doing a preflight check on his plane, consulting a clipboard. Taking a deep breath, she refused to note how good he looked in shorts and a clean white T-shirt. She stalked up to him, slapped his other shirt against his chest, then took a big step back and a bigger mental one.

Bo looked down at the shirt in his hand, then back at Mel. "You okay?"

"Yes."

He hooked a finger in the neckline of her top and pulled the neck out to take a peek inside.

"Hey!" She batted at his hand.

He stepped back with a smile. "Just checking your skin. No burns."

"I told you!" In disbelief she felt her nipples harden.

Noticing, he waggled his eyebrows, and still smiling, walked away.

Bastard. "Hey," she called after him.

He turned back.

"There's, um, something else."

"What?"

"I heard from my attorney." God, she hated this. "Your deed is legit."

"I already knew that."

"Yeah." Damn, pride tasted like shit. "So. What now?"

He paused, then walked back to her. "I told you. I want to see Sally. I want to see her face and hear her say she screwed over my father."

She had to ask, but it took her a moment. She stared at his throat, then lifted her gaze. "Are you going to prosecute?"

"You? No."

"The others."

He looked at her for a long moment, making her suffer. "No," he finally said.

"Sally?"

"I want to talk to her," he said, making no promises there. "I'll take it from there."

He still didn't know how long Sally had been gone. Oh, God. "Bo. Since the deed's legit, and you're now holding it, why do we have to do that and drag Sally and her name through the mud?"

"To clear my father's name." He said this in a voice of

steel and arguing against it would be like butting up against a stone wall.

She let out a shaky breath. "We should tell everyone . . ."

"What, that I don't hum when we f—"

"You know what I mean."

"That I don't have a teeny, tiny d—"

"We should tell them that this place is yours now," she grated out. "That you're their boss. *Our* boss. That our fate here is in your hands."

He looked at her for a long moment. Then looked away and let out a long breath. "I just want what was my father's. I'm not trying to hurt anyone here, you know that."

When she didn't say anything, he let out a rough sound and turned and walked off the tarmac.

Yeah, she ought to bottle up these incredible people skills of hers. Blowing out her own breath of frustration, she followed him into the lobby. He'd vanished, and she didn't want to face the necessary staff meeting without him, so she wandered toward the café, needing food.

"Hey, good mail news," Dimi called from her desk, and waved some checks over her head. "I'll run to the bank with the deposit. By tomorrow, Anderson Air will be flush again!"

"Thank God." She went into the café. There were two customers eating there, with Al entertaining them with the stories of his photos as he hung up some newly framed ones.

"Finally," Char drawled as she flipped something at the stovetop. She jabbed a spatula in Al's direction. "I've been asking you to get those up forever. Watch it, that right one's crooked—"

"Yes, dear."

"And that center one should really be on the left—"

"Yes, dear," Al said again.

"And—"

"Babe." Al shot her a laughing glance. "You can either ask a man to do something, or tell him how you want it done. Not both."

"Yes, but—"

"If you already knew how you wanted these arranged, why didn't you do it yourself?"

Char put her hands on her hips. "Because it's the Southern way to simply boss you around."

Al laughed. "Back off or else, woman."

Back off or else . . . Mel blinked as once again an odd sense of déjà vu came over her. Another unfortunate choice of words?

Or something else.

"Fine, I'll just back off," Char said with a laugh, giving Al a smacking kiss on the cheek. She went for his other cheek as well but he turned so she kissed him right on the lips. He hugged her hard, then patted her ass.

Easy affection. No long, furtive looks, nothing to suggest their words were anything other than easy banter, and Mel told herself to shake it off. "Hey, we're having a staff meeting later, okay?"

"Oh?" Char smiled. "Raises?"

They all laughed, but Mel's was hollow. She accepted a sandwich from Char, and though she'd been hungry, now it stuck in her throat.

So did her next bite when she caught sight of Bill Watkins coming in the front door, frown in place, eyes cold.

She'd written his check, it was on Dimi's desk, but that didn't mean she had to see him. She looked up into Char and Al's knowing glances.

"Quick," Char said, pulling Mel through the kitchen. "Out my back door."

Al waggled his brow at Char and murmured in her ear, "I'll take your back door, baby."

Mel rolled her eyes but ducked beneath the counter and through the tiny kitchen toward the door that opened onto an alley behind the row of leased hangars. She blinked into the bright sunny day, running down the alley across the way and into the maintenance hangar, where she stopped to huff and puff for a moment. She really needed to exercise more.

"What are you doing?"

With a gasp, she whirled, and faced Ernest, who stood there with a scowl and a broom.

Great, *now* he was cleaning. "Nothing," she said defensively.

"Ah, Jesus." He took off his baseball cap and scratched his head. "You running from Bill again?"

"No, I—"

"Pathetic," he grumbled, slamming his hat back on. "This never happened when Sally was here."

"Really?" she answered a little hotly, but then again she *was* hot. "Because I remember lots of times having to wait for a paycheck, something you've never had to do with me in charge."

He sighed. "I'm guessing you don't want to be found."

"No," she admitted, expecting him to say "too bad" and call Bill in here, exposing her for the fun of it.

Instead he jerked his head behind him. "Go on."

She blinked at him. "What?"

"You hard of hearing now? I said go."

Didn't need to tell her twice. She took off.

"And don't run like a girl!" he called after her.

She kicked it into gear, heading back outside, straight for the next hangar, where they kept their overnight clients' planes. With no one waiting on their plane, the hangar would be dark, cool, and blessedly empty except for boxes and boxes of old records they kept there, and probably lots of the spiders Ernest loved.

The door was locked. Fumbling with her key ring, she finally got the door open and slid inside, and then carefully locked herself in.

Then she turned to eye the space around her and crashed right into a hard, impenetrable chest.

Chapter 14

Mel opened her mouth to scream but a hand clamped over it. An arm held her immobile. And in that beat of time, she recognized the wall of lean, hard strength, and gritted her teeth.

Bo.

"Well, now, look at what I have here, all nice and breathless for already . . ."

She bit his palm, and with a hiss, he pulled his hand away from her mouth. But he didn't let go of her. With both of the hangar's big rolling doors closed and no lights on, she couldn't see him clearly, couldn't see anything but his tall, solid outline. In the still, musty air, she could smell oil and fuel, and something else. Something just as unfortunately pleasing.

Man. Her face was inches from his throat and she thought about biting him there as well but then he bent his head, putting their mouths a breath apart.

From deep inside her came a quiver, a little hopeful surge as her body said, *Oh, please, let's have him.* "Let me go."

"You sure say that a lot," he noted.

"You have your hands on me a lot."

"Know what I think? I think you like me. In fact, I know it. So let's admit the rest. You want me. And as luck would have it, here I stand, ready and willing to let you take full advantage of my body."

To go with that outrageous statement, he turned them both, pressing her back against the door, holding her there while his hands glided up her sides, grazing her ribs, the outside curves of her breasts, and just as she sputtered with his audacity, he slid his fingers in her hair, palming her head, holding her still as he lowered his mouth.

"Don't," she whispered, still panting, from her run—or so she told herself—grateful now for the dark because he couldn't see her face, and the longing surely plastered all over it. She didn't understand that about herself, how she could want *him* of all people. "Don't even think about it."

"Oh, I'm thinking," he assured her in that honey of an Aussie voice, the voice that even now was coaxing her right out of her comfort zone.

"And more than thinking," he warned her.

She shivered, then locked her knees. "Do anything, and you'll be walking funny tomorrow."

Cocky to the bone, he laughed, then pressed that long, rangy, tough body even closer. "You sound all whispery and needy. Why's that, darlin'?"

"I was running!"

He gave a slight shake of his head and his nose grazed her jaw. "You want me. You want me bad."

She went for a laugh but it sounded more like a moan. Damn it. She locked her weak knees. "You are so delusional."

Now his lips actually skimmed her throat, and goose bumps rose over every inch of her body.

"Admit it," he said.

"I have no idea how you fit inside any door with your big head."

"You think *that* head is big . . ." He nudged his hips

closer, rocking another part of him against her, right in the vee of her thighs.

Oh, God. Her knees wobbled again but she lifted her chin. "You are such a *boy*."

"There is nothing boy about what I've got for you," he assured her. "It's all man."

"And it's all one-sided, you know."

Another soft, knowing laugh. "Okay." Another brush of his lips over her throat, then the spot where her neck met her shoulder. "You keep telling yourself that." He stroked a hand up her ribs and cupped a breast. A thumb rasped over her nipple. A little sound escaped her lips before she could stop it, an unmistakable sound of desire that floated in the air between them.

Lifting his head, he met her gaze.

"I'm cold," she lied.

"It's ninety degrees in here, Mel." His thumb continued to tease her nipple. His other hand glided down her back, cupped her butt, and then dipped between her legs.

Her shocked gasp reverberated in the charged air of the silent hangar.

Echoed.

His fingers pressed on just the right spot and she actually whimpered for more.

"Yeah, you're just cold," he rumbled softly in her ear. "Cold as ice. That's why you're melting into a little pool of longing at my touch." Continuing to nibble along her collar bone, he murmured, "This is bound to happen, you know."

Because she was afraid that was true, she got mad. *"Back off."*

Still holding her with his hands . . . God, those hands . . . He smiled wickedly down at her. "I'm telling you, it's a waste of time to fight it." He stroked his fingers over the seam of her jeans, pressing in just . . . the . . . right . . . spot—

"Oomph," escaped him when she stomped on his foot. "Okay," he muttered, "you *can* fight it."

She made a scramble for the door, then stopped short. *Aw, hell.*

"Just remembered what brought you here in the first place, huh?" he asked, sounding amused. "Who is it, Bill again?"

She put her hand to the door. "Damn it. Yeah."

Turning to face him, she slid down until she could sit on the floor. "Why are *you* here?"

He sat next to her, companionably taking her hand in his as they prepared to wait. "I've told you. I want to know what happened to the Beechcraft and my father's money."

"No, I mean *here*. In the hangar. Why are you here?"

His gaze slid to the boxes of old paperwork, and suddenly, she knew. "You've been snooping."

He shrugged. "A bit."

"Find anything?"

Another shrug of a broad shoulder.

She closed her eyes. "What's going to happen, Bo?"

"I'm going to talk to Sally, and if she can pay me back, she can have her deed and I'll be out of here ASAP. If by some miracle she has the plane, I'll be ecstatic. Either way, little'll change for you."

Her stomach tightened, though she wasn't sure whether that was because she couldn't produce Sally, or because he'd said he'd be out of here ASAP. "We've got to have that staff meeting. Tell them."

He looked at her with shocking gentleness. "If you're ready."

It didn't escape her that this wasn't a power trip for him, he truly didn't care when and if people knew he was holding the deed, and more than her stomach quivered now—her heart as well. "You ever wake up and think, *How did I screw up so badly?*" she whispered.

A half-smile tugged at his mouth. "All the time, mate. All the time."

* * *

They had the staff meeting at the café, where they'd been having their meetings once a month for years. But in all that time, Mel had never felt as nervous as she did now. Palms damp, stomach jangling, she looked around at everyone sitting at the table with her, surrounded by the sunshine-yellow walls, by Al's pics, the tempting scent of fresh cookies on the tray in front of her. "Thanks for staying a few minutes late."

Ritchie looked at his watch. "Is this going to take long? I've got a hot date."

"Yeah, with his own fist," Kellan murmured beneath his breath, making Al crack up and Ritchie punch him in the arm. Danny separated them with a shove.

Ernest wasn't paying any attention, he was entering some notes in his spider book. Char was fussing with the cookies, adding more to the tray.

Dimi met Mel's gaze, drew a deep breath of her own, then put her hand over Char's. "Please," she said softly. "Mel needs your attention."

Mel drew a deep breath of her own and carefully didn't glance at Bo, standing just at her right. He'd been quiet, solemn, surprisingly free of quick wit and sarcasm, even going so far as to ask her if she was okay.

She wasn't.

But that wasn't his responsibility. "I have some things to clear up," she said. "And it might seem confusing and unnerving, but I promise you, I'll do everything I can to make it all okay." Another deep breath. "Bo . . ."—she hitched a shoulder in his direction—"isn't my ex."

All eyes swiveled to Bo.

"Huh," Ernest said.

Al scratched his head. "Makes sense."

Because, naturally, in the real world, Mel wouldn't be able to get a guy like Bo. Great ego boost . . .

Ritchie looked at Bo. "Does this mean you don't hum when you . . . you know."

Bo shook his head.

Char spoke a little breathlessly. "And you don't have a teeny, tiny—"

Again Bo shook his head.

"He's Eddie Black's son," Mel said. "The man Sally fell in love with and went to Australia for ten years ago."

Dimi clasped her fingers and stared down at them as her knuckles went white. Danny shifted closer to her and touched her arm, but she shook her head.

Ritchie and Kellan hadn't been around long enough to know Sally, but she'd been spoken about in such detail they thought of her as a legend. Eddie was definitely the bad guy in their eyes, and their mouths fell open as they stared at Bo.

"Why are you here?" Al asked him.

"I'm getting to that." Mel looked at each of them, the people she'd come to care about and love, as if they were her own blood. "He's here because Sally deeded Eddie the airport before he died. Bo is holding that deed."

Everyone let out a collective gasp.

"If that's true," Al said, "what took ya so long to come here and claim your spoils?"

"The deed has been in my father's things all this time," Bo answered. "But because I was in the military, I just recently found it."

"You're Eddie's beneficiary, then?" Ernest asked.

"Yes."

"What about your mother?"

Bo's mouth was grim, his eyes shadowed as they had been that one other time Mel had heard him discussing his mother.

"She's out of the picture," Bo said.

Silence followed this as everyone digested the meaning of what they'd been told. Mel watched Bo, aware of something in his voice, a carefully banked emotion. He didn't give anything away, though, nor did he say what a disappointment all this had been, or what he'd expected to find: the Blacks's life savings, not to mention an extremely valuable—both monetarily and emotionally—1944 Beechcraft.

Dimi was watching him, too, and Mel knew she was shocked that he hadn't revealed Sally as a possible thief and con.

"How do you know the deed's legit?" Ernest asked.

"I checked," Mel said.

"So you're, like, our boss now?" Ritchie asked.

"Look, I don't know exactly what will happen," Bo told them. "But for now, yes, I hold the deed, and everyone's job stays the same. No one's getting sacked."

"For now," Dimi said faintly, and covered her mouth.

Danny wrapped an arm around her shoulders. "Is Mel still manager?"

Bo looked at Mel. "If she wants to be."

Mel looked at him right back. No, she couldn't just pretend everything was the same. "For now," she said, eyes locked on his, "that might be more of a coposition."

Everyone fell quiet again, a very strained quiet that spoke volumes of everyone's worry about Mel's job.

"Hey, costatus is good enough for me," she told them, trying to lighten the mood. "I can fly more."

Bo's eyes widened slightly, clearly surprised at her unexpected support.

"Maybe we could all get raises," Ernest said slyly.

Bo smiled just as slyly. "Help me increase business, and you got it."

"Increased business sounds good," Al said, obviously trying to help smooth the transition. He squeezed Char's shoulders. "Hon?"

"I'm up for that, too." She lifted the tray of cookies. "Why are there still cookies?"

Everyone dove in and began talking, but the tension remained, and Mel's cookie stuck in her throat.

After the meeting, everyone went their separate ways. Dimi tucked away her latest novel, removing it from beneath her keyboard to her bottom desk drawer. Then she turned off the computer. They'd had more customers today than in a long time, and it had been a good receivables day.

Thanks to Bo.

She gritted her teeth as she headed into the airport bathroom, but fact was fact: Bo might now be ruler of her world, and he was also good for business.

Not that it mattered, her safe, cozy, happy little world was done for.

How long would he keep her?

Her stomach dropped as she stared at herself in the mirror. *God*. She needed a drink, she was shaking for a damn drink.

Ernest stepped out of one of the bathroom stalls, scaring her into a gasp. "All yours," he said, pulling along his cleaning cart.

Dimi glanced in the stall. "You left the seat up."

Ernest craned his scrawny neck and looked back over his shoulder. "So?"

"You're a boy. You're supposed to put it down when you're done."

Ernest switched his chew tobacco from one side of his cheek to the other. "Why? I need it up."

"Yes, but it belongs down."

"Listen, missy, you don't hear us guys complaining about you women leaving it down all the time, do ya?"

"Well, no, but—"

"Humph." With that, he left the bathroom, dragging his cart behind him.

Dimi locked the door behind the impossible man, then stripped and changed for clubbing because she needed out, and needed out now. She put on a glittery, gold stretchy dress that showed off everything and made her feel sexy, and then added five-inch heels because height gave her a feeling of power. She exited the bathroom and strutted across the lobby and back to her desk for her purse. When she straightened, Danny was watching her.

"Oh," she said, startled. The look in his eyes blistered her skin, and encouraged by that, she practiced the smile she was going to use tonight—mysterious, spicy.

The heat in his gaze vanished in a blink. "Nice," he said coolly. "But I like your real one better."

For some reason, that pissed her off. "Maybe this *is* my real one."

He'd come in the side door from the maintenance hangar, and shut the door now, coming closer. She watched him take in her snug, shimmery cocktail dress, the way it plunged nearly to her belly button, and wondered if he thought she looked good.

Then wondered why she wondered. He rested a hip against her desk, long legs sprawled out, arms at his sides, one large hand accidentally brushing hers. "That's not your real smile," he said.

She hated his presumptuousness, that he was judging her. "It's just a smile," she said.

"And will it be just another guy?"

Goddamnit. "What do you want from me?"

"Absolutely nothing." He'd changed to go home, and wore faded Levi's, so white in the stress points she imagined one more washing and they'd disintegrate. The knees were nonexistent, and he had another hole over a thigh. She could see tough muscle and tanned skin peeking through, and it was a shocking reminder that he wasn't just a mechanic.

But a man.

Not her type, though, not at all. And not because of what he did for a living, but because he didn't play the games that she did. No, he was . . . real.

And she didn't know how to be.

Plus, and this was the kicker, although she sensed glimpses of hunger for her, and though she knew he cared about her, he'd never come on to her, not once.

When it came right down to it, he didn't want her.

"Look," he finally said. "Why don't you hang out here tonight?"

Her heart skipped a beat. "What?"

"It's poker night. Char's cooking Mexican. Al's got a jar of dimes just waiting to be won."

She went very still. Was he asking her out? Oh, God. She couldn't do this, not with him, not with someone she cared so much about, someone she'd have to see every day after she managed to screw it all up. Terror warred with excitement.

"You'd be safer," he said.

Nope, not asking her out. Just looking out for her. And just like that, she deflated. "I'll be fine." And with more attitude than she felt, she walked out the door.

That night Bo sat at Danny's desk, sifting through aircraft parts on ebay, waiting for everyone to leave so he could resume his nightly snooping through the old records. He'd spent his first few nights here going through the leased hangars. As he'd already discovered, two had been empty. The others had aircraft in them, one was filled with parts, and one was Ernest's, loaded with boxes and boxes of crap. Not surprising. Footsteps clicked across the floor. Mel's battered boots.

A ghost of a smile curved his lips as she appeared at his side. "Hey."

"I have a question."

"About . . . ?"

He expected her to ask about Sally, about Eddie. About the future. Anything other than what she did ask.

"About your mother," she said softly.

He felt himself tense. "What about her?"

"You're . . . not close."

He choked out a laugh and turned back to the computer

screen, speaking the understatement of the century. "No. Not close."

"Yeah." She nodded. Kicked at the floor. Shoved her hands farther into her pockets.

And didn't go away.

Finally, he sighed and leaned back. "What?"

"I'm not close to my mother, either."

"Maybe that's why we're both so screwed up."

"She left you."

It wasn't worded as a question, but it was definitely a fishing expedition. "No. Eddie took me."

"Why?"

He didn't answer. Didn't want to. But she was staring at him, he could feel it. He played on the computer for a moment, but then she put her hands on his chair and turned him to face her, so he saw the exact second she got it. "She hurt you," she breathed. "But not by leaving. She physically hurt you. Oh, Bo."

At the tone, at the fucking pity, he surged out of the chair, and stalked to the window.

"Bo—"

"Don't," he said, staring hard at a Douglas in maintenance. *God, don't.* "It was a long time ago." Then, because he was an idiot, he looked at her.

Her heart sat in her eyes, a big welling of sorrow and empathy, making him sorry he'd said a word. "Why didn't Eddie take you sooner—"

"They separated before I was even born." He lifted his shoulder again. "She moved around, making it difficult for him to find us unless she needed money. Finally, she showed her hand, and by that I mean put bruises on me where they could be seen, and he got me. End of story."

"And you were eight?"

"Yeah."

"Bo."

She seemed shaken and again he turned away.

"Look, I'm really busy here—"

As if to prove it, Char radioed that he had a call. It was a customer and, his back to Mel, he stretched the phone conversation out, until finally, he heard her boots move away.

Leaving him alone, extremely alone.

Just as he'd wanted.

He waited to make sure everyone had left before going to the storage hangar. As he had before, he helped himself to the boxes there, all old records. The next time he looked up, it was dark outside. There was only one more row of boxes to check, and he shifted those aside so tomorrow night he could remember where he left off, and then stared down at a door in the floor he'd just revealed.

A basement storage area. The trap door was locked. It took him five long moments to run to maintenance and find a crowbar, then five more to pry open the door.

Inside it was pitch black.

Yet another five minutes was lost finding a flashlight, but then he was back. He climbed down the ladder and shined his light over . . . more boxes.

Shit. He reached for the first one, dated the year he'd first come here, and memories rose up and gripped him by the throat.

His father telling him how much he was going to love the States. How he'd fallen for Sally, and that Bo would, too. How they were all going to be so happy. Together.

Bo had believed it, too. He hadn't suspected a damn thing. Sally had gotten past his eighteen-year-old radar, and that still burned.

God, he missed Eddie, so damned much. With a sigh, he opened the box—and hit jackpot: old accounting journals undoubtedly dating from the days when records had been kept by hand. Pages of bank statements, receipts, bills . . . and an unmarked general ledger, which Bo would be willing to bet his last dollar didn't belong with the "official" books of North Beach, because those books were upstairs. He'd seen them.

Two sets of books had been kept.

And possibly still were. Not uncommon, certainly, but what intrigued him most was the list of large deposits.

Deposits unaccounted for, no explanation, not matched to any customer, adding up to close to a million dollars.

A million dollars. Staggering, really. Where had the money come from? Where had it gone? And the biggie—*did Mel know*?

Given that the dates of the deposits ran from before Sally had met Bo's father until right up until the time of Eddie's death, the money could have come from anywhere, but Bo would bet his suddenly highly coveted deed to North Beach that Sally had conned it from someone else's pocket.

Some of it *Eddie's*.

What would Mel say? Would she look at the records, and *still* stand up for Sally? Or would she begin to see that maybe things weren't always as they seemed?

That people weren't always who they seemed?

He gathered some of his find and stepped outside the hangar, onto the tarmac. He eyed Mel's Cessna, the Cessna she worked so hard to buy on her own, and wondered why he cared what she thought. Wondered, even as he was afraid he knew the answer.

But he hadn't come here to the States for *her*. He'd come to claim back what was rightfully his father's. *His* now. And as Mel's plans were in the way of that, he'd be smart to steer clear of her.

Yeah.

Unfortunately, he wasn't always smart . . .

Mel had a simple plan for the evening—relaxation. After a two-mile run on the beach, she called for Chinese to be delivered in an hour, then stripped, stepped into her bathtub, and let out a long sigh. Ah, the power of hot, hot water and bubble bath. She shampooed her hair, added a desperately needed ten-minute deep conditioner, then stuffed her hair beneath a shower cap. She lathered up a leg to shave, and the doorbell rang.

Naturally.

The Chinese food was early. Grumbling, she got out of the tub with one leg still lathered, wrapped her torso in a towel and went to the door. "Thanks," she said as she pulled the door open a crack, then froze.

Not Chinese.

Bo stood there in loose black jeans and a snug black T-shirt, looking darker than sin and just as tempting, a fat file tucked beneath one arm, a look on his face that . . . Well, she couldn't miss the temper, but she could have resisted it. But she couldn't miss or resist the sadness.

She reminded herself that she didn't care. She even tried to shut the door on him but as she already knew, he had the reflexes of a cat, and he simply reached out and slapped a hand on the wood. With heart-stopping trouble in his gaze, he looked her over. "Is it Halloween?"

"What?"

He touched the cap on her head and she remembered. Naked except for her towel and the lovely plastic shower cap on her head.

"Sexy," he said.

She shifted her gaze to the ceiling. *Dear God, are you listening? I know it's been awhile, but if you could open up a huge hole and swallow me up, I'd appreciate it.*

But no big hole gobbled her up. "I'm conditioning my hair."

"Ah," he said with a little smile.

Shaving gel plopped from her unshaved leg to the ground. Bo raised a brow.

"And I'm shaving," she said through her teeth. "Actually, I'm bathing, so if you'll—"

He continued to hold the door open, looking her over slowly, making her squirm. Why was it that this man always managed to see her at her most absolute worst?

"You should see your face," he said, amused.

Yep, this was how she looked while planning murder. *His*.

"Let me in, darlin'."

"I don't think so."

"What if I said I have something you're going to want to see?"

"There is nothing of yours I want to see."

That had his grin spreading, the rat fink bastard. "You are such a liar."

Unfortunately true. She wanted to tell him to go to hell, but his smile had faded, and there was something about his expression now, an utter solemnity, a knowledge . . .

And misery.

And though he was extremely careful to try to hide it, he was also mad.

Oh, God. What now? Could there be more? And what would he say to all she hadn't told him, that though she couldn't hand him Sally's location, or even her phone number, she— or maybe it had been him, or some combination of both— had stirred things up enough that someone was now sending her threatening e-mails and letters . . .

She'd attribute them to spam, but her spam was usually along the lines of "lengthen your penis" or "grow your hair back" . . . not *leave it alone*, or *back off or else* . . .

She tightened her grip on her towel. Wracked her brain for a good reason to turn him away when everything inside her knew she had to face this.

Him.

"You going to let me in, Mel?"

Funny thing was, she'd already let him inside her heart, at least a foot, or two. He just didn't know it. So in the end, she let him all the way in, stepping aside to once again let the big bad wolf into her house of straw.

Chapter 15

With difficulty, Bo tore his gaze off Mel's extremely hot, extremely wet body and closed his mouth so he didn't start noticeably drooling. He stepped over the threshold of her cottage and looked around to distract himself.

Her place was tiny, but well cared for. An overstuffed loveseat faced the small woodstove with a potted fern on either side. There were pictures on the walls, Al's no doubt; some prints, some actual photographs, all of airplanes except the personal photos, though there were few of those. She had one of herself and Dimi mugging for the camera inside a biplane. Another of Charlene and Al painting Sunshine Café, both covered in yellow paint. And yet another of the woman who'd changed Bo's life forever.

Sally. Dark-haired, blue-eyed, smiling, gorgeous, vivacious, suck-'em-in-and-kill-'em Sally. With a tic in his jaw, he turned away. If he was being fair, he could understand that Mel didn't know the real Sally. And in that same fairness, he also understood that once he gave her the proof of the real Sally, she wasn't going to be happy with him for showing her that the only woman who'd ever been there for her, the only positive adult influence she'd had as a child, was a criminal.

Throw rugs dotted the scarred wood floor. There was lace at the windows, which surprised him. She'd made herself a home here away from the airport, probably her first. "Look at that," he murmured. "You have a secret Martha Stewart thing going on."

She rolled her eyes, but it didn't hide her blush.

God, she was sweet. In a sort of porcupine way. And she was also so damned sexy scowling at him, he could hardly stand it.

"Any idiot can go to Target or Wal-Mart," she muttered.

"Don't ruin it for me." He smiled, which was almost unbelievable considering why he'd come. "I like picturing you as a homebody. You pining away for a hubby and kids, Warrior Mel?"

"Shut up." She tightened her towel and stalked toward the bathroom, from which wafted steam and the scent of bubble bath. "I'll be right—Hey!" she squeaked as he snagged her by the back of her towel and slowly but inexorably pulled her back against him.

"Hey yourself," he said softly, enjoying very much the feel of her backside as she wriggled, which had the predictable effect, and when she felt it, she went still as stone.

Oh, yeah, darlin', he thought. That's *exactly* what you think it is. He tossed the file down to the couch to wrap both arms around her, holding her stiff spine to his chest as he put his mouth to the sweet spot on the back of her neck and nuzzled. "You smell good."

"I—" This broke off with a low, sexy moan that escaped her lips when he gently sank his teeth into the side of her throat. "Stop that."

"Okay, I'll stop that." He turned her around and tugged off the ridiculous shower cap, ignoring the shaving gel soaking into the legs of his pants as he ran a finger down between her breasts to loosen her towel.

She slapped at his hand, but weakly, he noted. "Don't look at me. I have conditioner in my hair and I need to shave."

"Call the fashion police," he said. "What's the punishment, do you think? The rest of the night in bed without dinner?" Christ, what was he doing? He'd come for something else entirely but now this was all he wanted. She was all he wanted.

"Bo, stop. I mean, look at me, I'm a mess—"

"I'm looking. I don't see a mess." She was gorgeous. He captured her fingers in his and brought them up to his mouth.

"This is ridiculous," she whispered, then staring at his mouth as he sucked on one of her fingers.

"You didn't think it was stupid the other night."

"It's just some sort of physical thing."

"No kidding, it's physical." He was currently hard enough to pound nails, and she hadn't even touched him. And she smelled like heaven. To get more of it, he bent his head and sniffed at her like a puppy. He dragged his mouth over her bare shoulder, touching her skin with his tongue.

Her fingers dug into his arms as a low but undeniable moan escaped her. Thrilling to the sound, he sank his teeth into her.

"Bo," she hissed.

"Right here."

She lifted her head and for one beat they stared at each other. "Bo," she said again, and moved toward him at the same time that he caught her up, their mouths connecting as if they could inhale each other. Bo certainly meant to inhale her. He freed her towel, leaving her just as he wanted her—nude. Yanking her up and against him, he had one hand in the center of her back, one palming her extremely palmable ass, spreading his fingers to touch as much of her as he could. "Christ. Christ, you're so hot. Why am I still dressed?"

"I don't know." She had both hands fisted in his hair now, once again doing her damnedest to make him bald, but it only turned him on all the more because she was already out of control, panting, writhing against him as if he was the best thing since sliced bread.

And in that moment, here with her, he felt like it. She transcended him, made him feel like Superman, and god-damn if that wasn't the most arousing thing ever.

"Bo." She fastened her mouth on his throat, not exactly gentle, and in return he tugged on her dripping hair until her head fell back enough that he could kiss her again; hard, wet, deep, while his fingers slid between her legs and dipped into her creamy heat, making him stagger, groan, then stagger again, until he fell back with her onto the couch.

Thank God for Target, he thought dimly, sinking into the soft, giving cushions with this unbelievably hot, wet, naked gorgeous woman straddling him.

She was trying to strip him, making little frustrated sounds as she tore at his clothes. Lending his own hands to the cause, together they pulled his shirt over his head. She let out a little hum of pleasure at the sight of his bared torso, then leaned forward and kissed a pec. "I can't even remember why you're here," she whispered, and for a moment, the words brought him out.

Because despite being more turned on than he'd been in a good long time, *he* remembered why he was here. When he told her, when he showed her what he'd brought, she was going to get that cold, distant look in her eyes and not want to see him. Not want to talk to him.

And certainly not want to—oh, God—lick him. He opened his mouth, honesty warring with lust, but then she tugged open his jeans and slipped her hands inside.

And just like that, lust won. He'd been touched plenty but for some reason, her hands felt different, her kisses felt dif-ferent. Gliding his hands up the backs of her thighs, he urged her closer over him as he kissed her again, and again. His fingers still playing in their wet heaven, he dragged his mouth from hers, making his way down to a full curve of a breast. Her nipple was pebbled up tight, going even tighter when he sucked her against his tongue. Pulling back, he blew out a soft breath on the tip as he sank a finger deep inside her.

She cried out, the sound drenched in pleasure. Her head fell back, her hair falling over her shoulders and breasts, which were still wet from his mouth. She looked gorgeous, like a goddamned goddess, and he could only stare up at her, awed, as he added another finger, slowly grazing his thumb over her clit.

Another gasp, the sexiest sound he'd ever heard. *"Bo."*

Had he ever heard his name uttered like that? Like in that moment he was her air, her sustenance, her very life?

He wanted to hear it some more. Lots more. Leaning forward, he put his mouth back on her breast, not losing the rhythm of his thumb on her center, urged on by her rocking hips and soft cries.

"Bo—"

"Come," he said against her nipple. "I want you to."

"I can't—"

"Can." He watched her intently, taking the cues from her pumping hips to see how hard to press, how fast to take her. With another surprised cry, her head fell back again, her throat a lovely arch, her eyes tightly closed.

Beautiful. She was so goddamned beautiful he could hardly stand it. Her hands came down to hold his in the right spot, as if desperate to make sure he finished her off now that she was so close, as if she was afraid he'd disappoint her. But he had no intention of disappointing her, and he carefully tended to her body, groaning at the sight of her straining against him.

And then, with a darkly erotic sound, she burst. She was still shuddering in pleasure, his fingers still deep inside her, when the doorknob on the front door wriggled.

They both froze.

Still breathing hard, dewy from her orgasm, Mel gripped Bo's arms and yanked, and they both fell off the couch to the floor.

"What the hell—"

Before he could finish that thought, Mel slapped a hand over his mouth, holding him down with shocking strength for a completely naked woman who'd just exploded all over him.

"Shh," she hissed, and pushed his head farther down and out of sight.

Which is how he found his mouth an inch from a still-erect nipple. He stared at the beautiful sight as the front door opened all the way.

"Mel?" called a female voice, a Southern female voice.

Char.

She was probably bringing dinner, because Char had more mothering genes in her little pinky than Bo had good sense.

"Honey," she called out. "I brought a plate of chicken enchiladas. Al loved them, so I thought . . . Mel?"

Out of sight, on the floor in front of the couch, Bo turned his head and met Mel's light brown eyes. In them was a promised retribution if he so much as breathed.

Nope, not going to breathe. Instead he opened his mouth and licked her nipple like she was his favorite flavor of lollipop.

She jerked.

The nipple hardened all the more.

And Bo smiled.

"Mel?" Char called. "Damn it, did you go for your run already?"

Mel shot Bo more daggers. Poisoned daggers, by the looks of them. They still lay tangled on the floor, Mel completely naked, him not so much. Given the heat blazing from the woman's gaze, she'd figured out exactly how vulnerable her situation was. To make sure of it, he slid a finger back inside her.

A strangled sound escaped her. In fact, Bo could have sworn her eyes crossed with lust.

Above and behind them, Char let out a long-suffering sigh, set something down on the kitchen table, and exited.

The moment the front door shut, Mel catapulted into action, shoving Bo away, leaping up to her feet. Grabbing her robe, she shoved her arms into it. When she realized the robe was on inside out, she growled.

Bo laughed, and she rounded on him, pointing to the door. "Get out."

"Oh, is the fun over?"

"Yes!"

He pointed to the big, fat file he'd brought, the elephant in the room. The thing was still perched on the edge of the couch, the sexual storm somehow having left it utterly untouched.

Mel stared at him, her hair beginning to dry in long, fiery waves around her face. He could tell by her expression she'd completely forgotten, and that she couldn't quite believe it. "Just tell me."

"I found old accounting records, and—"

"Found?"

"Okay, let's say liberated."

Her mouth went grim but she said nothing.

"I still haven't located records of the Beechcraft, but this set of books was very interesting."

"How so?"

"It's clearly a second set of books for North Beach, and I'm betting it doesn't match the first. Want to take that bet?"

Mel hugged her robe tighter to herself, as if she hadn't just been butt-ass naked in his lap, panting his name as she came. "Lots of people keep two sets of books."

"With huge deposits unaccredited to any source? Deposits that were probably never actually entered into the official set of North Beach's books, or at least into the set the IRS saw? Deposits that add up to a staggering million dollars?"

"What?"

"All dated just before and during the years that my dad was involved with Sally. Which begs the question: if *Sally* is the one who got ripped off in all this, why did all of my father's money vanish, and Sally's bank account swell?"

She frowned, then turned her back to him.

"Oh, no you don't." He pulled her back around. "We're talking about this."

Her jaw hardened and so did her eyes. Beneath that robe she might be naked and still quivering, but on the outside she was the strong-headed, strong-willed woman she'd been from too young an age. "I'd like you to leave now."

"You can't ignore this, it's not going anywhere. *I'm* not going anywhere—"

"Yet."

"What does that mean?"

She licked her lips. "You're not going anywhere yet. But you are eventually. You're going back to your life. While mine, and everyone else's here, will never be the same again."

Her quiet devastation staggered him. Before he could formulate a response, she dropped her forehead to his shoulder, and surprised, he pulled her in, hugging her close for one minute before she gathered herself and stepped away. "I'd like to go through the paperwork."

"Of course."

"By myself," she said.

"Mel—"

"Please."

God, the look in her eyes slayed him.

"Myself," she repeated.

He pulled on his shirt, then moved close, running a finger

over the dark smudges beneath her eyes. She seemed exhausted, and all he wanted to do was tuck her against him and take her to bed. But she'd never allow that now and he knew it. "We need to talk about this. Soon."

She glanced over his shoulder, back toward the couch, where the file sat. Whatever she was feeling, she kept it to herself. "Good-bye, Bo."

"I'll see you tomorrow."

"Good-bye," she said again, and practically shut the door on him as she pushed him out into the night.

The next morning, Bo showed up early at the airport in hopes of catching Mel alone, but she appeared to be a no-show.

In fact, for the first time in the week since he'd been there, the coffee-donut gossip ritual at the café began without her.

Ritchie and Kellan couldn't wait to tell everyone about their double date with twins. "They're athletes," Ritchie reported in awe. *"Gymnasts."*

Al whistled. "Bet they're flexible."

"Oh yeah, we got wild, dude—" Kellan broke off at Char's glare. His wicked smile faded. "I mean, it was tender and respectful. Very tender and respectful."

"Enough." Ernest gestured with his donut toward Danny. "I got a complaint. You need to stop using aerosol anything in maintenance. I found a dead arachnid in there."

"A what?" Danny asked.

"A spider! You're killing them."

Char sighed. "Okay, let's talk about me. I'm cranking down the AC from 78 to 68 degrees, and I don't care how much it costs, I'm too damn hot all the time!"

Al wisely refrained from saying a word, but he looked like he was thinking at least a few.

No one spoke of Mel's absence.

Finally Bo had to ask. "Where's your fearless leader?"

Char looked at Al.

Al looked at Ritchie and Kellan.

Both of whom looked at Danny.

Danny looked at Dimi.

Dimi quietly sipped her herbal tea. "Hmmm? Oh, Mel. She's running a bit late this morning, that's all."

Bo would be willing to bet that Mel had never been late to anything in her entire life. Just as he'd be willing to bet she'd stayed up late going through that file he'd brought her, and was now either still formulating her response to what she'd found, or plotting his murder.

The airport began hopping with its usual morning business. Bo himself had an appointment to look at a Douglas A-24 in Los Angeles, which he reluctantly left for, but not before pulling Dimi aside. "I want to see Mel later," he said. "Tell her I'll only be a few hours."

Dimi smiled at him noncommittally. Bo grated his teeth and piloted his flight to LA and back.

When he returned, Mel *had* come in, but was now on her own charter flight to San Francisco, forcing him to cool his heels for the rest of the day, which he spent tracking down a Piper for a customer.

Dimi kept interrupting him with phone calls—creditors, salespeople, even one person asking if they sold model airplanes.

Finally he called Dimi's desk. "What are you doing?"

"My job," she replied sweetly.

"Do you forward all these kinds of calls to Mel?"

"Not anymore. You're in charge now."

He drew a deep breath, but patience didn't come. "I hope you're finding it therapeutic to take your anger out on me."

"Actually, not as much as I'd hoped."

He sighed. "Do you really give Mel this many phone calls a day?"

"Oh, no. For her, I screen them."

He pinched the bridge of his nose. "Do you think you could screen them for me?"

"Nope," she said with that same cheer.

"Why not?"

"Because I don't like you."

At closing time, when Mel still hadn't come in, Bo went to Dimi yet again.

"Oh, dear," she said with a little smile, bracelets jangling, as she set aside a book—*a book?* "Didn't I tell you? She's going straight from San Francisco to Seattle."

"No," he said through his teeth. "You didn't mention that."

"Sorry." But she didn't look it. "You did ask me to screen your calls, remember?"

Bo slapped his clipboard against his leg while he considered strangling her. But though Dimi had been obnoxious today, she didn't look smug so much as . . . worried. Hell. Had Mel fallen apart at that file he'd left her? "Look, did she say anything about—"

Dimi shook her head. "Not a word about anything."

He was not going to gain an inch here, but that didn't prevent him from trying. "Sally hasn't called yet, has she?"

"Nope."

Really, he might as well just bang his head against the wall. "Thanks. You've been a big help."

Now her smug smile made a flashing appearance. "I try."

The next morning when Mel woke up she did just what she had done the one before: stared at the file Bo had brought. At the thought of what was in it, she groaned and rolled to her back, and had a new thought.

Two days ago, she'd let Bo get her naked, finger her to an

orgasm, and he hadn't so much as lost his pants. As it had ever since, the memory made her by turns hot and achy, and hot and humiliated.

She had to get a grip.

Maybe the trick was simply not to look directly at him. Yeah, she'd try that. It shouldn't be so hard now that she had something new to obsess about.

She stared at the fat file again. *God, Sally, what did you do?*

With a sigh, she got out of bed, showered, dressed, and drove to the airport and, as was the norm—except for yesterday, when she'd needed to be alone—she was the first to arrive. Unlocking the front door, she flipped on the lobby lights. As they flickered to life, she noticed the jar on the front desk. Curious, she moved close, then stopped short.

In it sat a big, fat, hairy, spindly spider. Skin crawling, she grabbed the note next to the jar and took a big step back, reading while the spider stared at her.

Mel,
    Here is proof why I can't clean out the maintenance closet. This spider is a brown recluse, and they do have a bad rep, but they're endangered. We need to preserve their environment for all of mankind.

                                        —Ernest
P.S. Any more wonky e-mails you want to tell me about?

Mel gritted her teeth. No more "wonky" e-mails but the spider was seriously wigging her out. She picked up a pen and gingerly used it to push the jar away so she could check the flight schedule beneath. When she'd looked yesterday morning, there'd been only two flights there; now four were listed as incoming, and it looked like Bo had scheduled two of those himself.

For North Beach, that was booming business.

"It might take awhile to make this place worth what I actually lost," said a male voice. "But apparently I have little choice."

Mel whipped around to face Bo, who'd come in so quietly she hadn't heard him. "What if you don't ever make back what you lost?"

"I can always sell."

The words stopped her heart. "I thought you didn't have plans to do that."

"I don't. Yet." He wore a pair of black Levi's today and a white button-down shirt, with Black Aviation's logo on the pocket, once again half-tucked in, half not, sleeves shoved to his elbows. His hair had been finger-combed at most, falling in untamed waves. His mouth, the one that had kissed her the day before yesterday until she hadn't known her own name, was unsmiling. He watched her with those inscrutable eyes, the ones that gave nothing away, nothing at all.

"Is selling really a possibility?" she asked.

He just looked at her.

Yeah. It was. He could recoup at least a part of his losses and get revenge on Sally in one fell swoop, and they both knew it. Too bad the revenge would be on her, not Sally at all.

"Are we going to talk about it?" he asked. "About what you thought about the records I brought you?"

She thought her heart was breaking, how was that?

"Or maybe we should talk about those—what did Ernest call them?—*wonky* e-mails."

Oh, God.

"What did he mean, Mel? Because it sounds like maybe you've been keeping more secrets, in which case, I'm just shocked."

In the charged silence came the drone of an incoming engine.

Their gazes locked.

"Saved by the plane?" he murmured.

She ran to the door leading to the tarmac.

"You can run," he called out after her. "But you can't hide."

Chapter 16

The day was busy. Mel couldn't believe it but planes came in and out, they fueled up, and Danny had all the work he could want.

At the end of her shift, she and Dimi together looked at the schedule on the computer, and smiled tiredly.

"Like old times," Dimi said. "The advertising you've done has helped."

Some of Mel's smile faded at that, and she slowly shook her head. "It's not the advertising, Dimi."

Dimi's smile faded, too. "Yes, it is."

"No. It's Bo. He's brought in customers. He's got contacts we don't, and connections. He's doing for the airport what Sally used to do with such ease."

Give it life.

She'd tried like hell, but the truth was, all she wanted to do was fly. This day-to-day managing, the handling of the employees, being the end all to everyone, the peacemaker, the mom, the shrink . . . She'd never really even admitted it to herself, but it was getting old. "He's done all this. We should acknowledge that."

"Bite your tongue."

"It's true. And . . . It's a good thing. No matter what we think of him, he's better at this than I am."

"No, he's not! No one's better than you—"

"No. And I just hope he's enjoying it so he keeps at it rather than selling."

Dimi stared at her, eyes bright. "Listen, I've got to get out of here."

Of course she did. She didn't want to talk about this. "Hot date?" Mel asked.

"Nah. I'm tired of hot dates."

Mel laughed.

"I'm serious," she said, and because she actually did sound serious, Mel studied her more closely.

Dimi was dressed today in snug Bermuda shorts and a lace tank top, with a denim jacket open over the ensemble. She looked pretty, but not her usual over-the-top sexy, something Mel should have picked up on earlier. "What's wrong?"

"Can't a woman just be bored with men?"

"Well, you'd think."

Dimi sighed. "I've dated four guys this week and every single one of them had a major flaw."

"Such as they're penis-carrying humans?"

"You're too young to be so cynical."

"It's not cynicism, it's realism," Mel insisted. "Men are fun but they're not everything."

"And planes are?"

Mel winced.

"Sorry," Dimi said quietly. "I didn't mean—"

"It's okay." Mel shut down the computer. "Listen, why don't we do something tonight—"

"You on babysitting duty?"

"Come on, you know you have a tendency to self-destruct when you get stressed—"

"I'm not stressed."

"We're both stressed."

"Okay, I'm stressed," Dimi admitted. "But not self-destructing."

Mel met Dimi's gaze and found nothing assuring. "Dimi—"

"Look, you want me less stressed? Get Bo Black the hell out of here. Make things go back to the way they were."

"Which is what exactly?"

"Easy."

"Honey, nothing about this life has ever been easy."

"Then tell me why the hell we're doing it."

Mel shook her head. "Because we've always loved it."

"You mean because *you've* always loved it."

Mel absorbed that unexpected punch. "Wow," she said, sitting back.

"Damn." Dimi shook her head. "Clearly I need to go to a corner and have a time out." She grabbed her purse. "On second thought, I think my bed, *alone*, will work wonders."

Mel grabbed Dimi's hand. She loved Dimi, she loved her with all her heart, she loved all of them, but she couldn't go on doing this, keeping secrets, walking on eggshells, wondering when it was all going to come crashing down on her. "I'm going to tell him, Deem. I'm going to tell Bo the truth."

Dimi stared at Mel.

"I'm going to tell him we don't know where Sally is. That we've never known."

"Why?"

"I can't hide it anymore."

"You've been stronger than steel all these years, what's changed?"

"He's been honest. I want to do the same."

"It's too late for honesty, it was too late from the moment all those years ago when we decided to take over and run this place in Sally's name. I mean, my God, Mel, you're going to hand over our power, our very livelihood, and all for what? A hard cock?"

Mel slowly stood up. "That's not exactly fair."

"Really? Why not?"

"Because first of all, I'm not sleeping with him."

"But you want to be."

Damn it, that was true enough. "And second of all," she said, ignoring that because she wasn't quite ready to face it. "And this is the biggie. *He has the deed*. He has a right to know everything."

Dimi let out a rough sound that perfectly conveyed her opinion on that. "Eddie forced Sally to give it up."

"Maybe. But Sally won't call me back, so we don't know that."

"Oh, my God. He put his hands on you, and now you believe everything he says, you believe him over Sally."

"Sally hasn't said a word! Don't you get it? We're on our own! We've always been on our own!"

"You're not on your own, you're with Bo."

"Dimi."

"No." Dimi moved to the door. "I don't want to talk about this."

"He brought me some bank statements," Mel called out to her. "Early statements from North Beach."

Dimi turned back.

"They show how much money Sally had over a period of five years, starting the year before Bo and Eddie came to town."

"So? Sally was broke."

"See, that's the thing." Mel didn't know how to do this gently. "She wasn't broke. She had a million dollars in the bank when she vanished."

Dimi's mouth fell open. "What the hell? We've never had anywhere close to that much money. We never had any money at all."

"I know," Mel said grimly. "But it's there in black and white."

"Oh, my God."

"I'm going to find out what's going on, and to do that, I'm going to ask Bo to help me—"

"Mel—"

"He brought me the information, Dimi. He didn't have to do that."

Dimi was shaking her head. "I'm against this. His motive in coming here was to hurt us."

"Sally, maybe. Not us."

"Same thing."

"Why did she have all that money, Deem? She let us think she didn't have any—"

"Are you listening to yourself doubt her? You are truly on his side in this!"

"No, I—"

Dimi pointed at her. "When you get home tonight, look in the mirror. Because I swear to you, it's all over your face."

"Dimi—"

Dimi shook her head. "I can't do this with you, not now." And she walked out.

Mel let out a breath and checked her e-mail before closing down. She was still going over the conversation with Dimi in her mind so the unexpected e-mail hit her like a blow to the belly, from *You'reNotLeavingItAlone*.

Chapter 17

Funny thing about wanting justice and revenge, about being so filled with grief that you couldn't reason—it was hard to maintain that level of fury.

In Bo's case, it turned out he was far more human than he'd thought, and because he was, it was also harder than he'd imagined to look directly into the eyes of the person you planned on hurting.

Especially now that he'd kissed Mel, touched her. Yeah, she was still keeping secrets—a white-hot poker stabbing into his chest—but he dreamed about her. Dreamed about more than just kissing, about what would have happened the other night if they'd *both* been naked, if they hadn't been interrupted. He'd have had her on that soft couch, on the floor, in her bed.

A loud crashing noise woke him. It was the hangar doors sliding open, which sent sharp sunlight slanting across his face, completely eradicating the erotic dreams.

He blinked, realizing he'd fallen asleep the night before while snooping through more boxes in the hidden storage area. Sprawled on the cold floor, he looked up at the outline of a woman above him in the doorway, the obnoxious sun behind her throwing her body in bold relief.

A hot body that kick-started his for the morning.

Mel came down the stairs. He would have known it was her just by the sheer attitude of her boots as they clicked, clicked, clicked toward him.

She came to a stop and stood, hands on her hips. "Still snooping?"

He closed his eyes against the glare and cleared his throat. "Yeah. It's what happens when the people around you keep their thoughts and secrets to themselves."

She muttered something, then vanished, and he lay there, still a little undone by his graphic dreams, and then his not-so-graphic reality.

He was hard.

Then the boots clicked again, and a hot mug of coffee was set before him. He turned his head and stared at it.

Was he dreaming again?

Mel crouched at his side. Her hair was lit like fire as she looked him over from head to toe and back again, her gaze slowing at his thighs, and in between—skidding to a halt there. Her pupils dilated slightly, and unconsciously, or maybe not so unconsciously, she licked her lips. "You find anything else?" she asked a little hoarsely.

It took him a moment to go from thinking about sex to why he was here in the first place. "Not yet. There's a lot to look through."

She nodded, her gaze again landing on the button fly on his jeans as if she couldn't help herself. "Yeah, it's hard— um, tough work." Her face went beet red. "It's tough work going through all this stuff."

He couldn't help it. He grinned. "You said hard."

And she put her hands to her cheeks. "Did not."

"Did."

She whirled away. "I don't know why I try with you."

"Really? You're trying?" With a groan, he rolled to his feet. "I must have missed that part."

She began to walk to the door, but he pulled her back around.

"You're so good at annoying me I nearly missed it," he said, staring into her tight face. "What's wrong?"

She was quiet for so long he figured she wasn't going to speak. "I've received three e-mails," she finally said. "One from LeaveItAlone, one from BackOffOrElse, and the last this morning, from You'reNotLeavingItAlone. Happy now?"

"Ecstatic," he said grimly, and held firm when she would have shoved free. "Have you had them tracked?"

"Working on it."

He traced a finger over the worry groove between her eyes. "Leave it alone?"

"Yeah." She lifted a shoulder. "Thought maybe at first it was you."

For a moment he couldn't figure out how to speak without losing it. "Jesus," he finally said. "You think so highly of me, I don't know what to say."

"Logic prevailed, all right? I figured leaving it alone is the last thing you want me to do."

"I can't believe you didn't tell me."

"Look, I don't want to do this now." She pushed away. "I have shit to do and . . ." She cast another quick glance over his body, but he wasn't aroused now, he was tense with frustration, anger, and worry.

"Any more secrets you want to reveal?" he asked tightly.

She turned away. "I've got a flight."

So there *were* still more secrets. *Fuck*. He listened to the sound of her boots as she walked away. For distraction, he inhaled the coffee she'd brought him, in desperate need of the caffeine. Then he closed up the hangar, entered the lobby, and accepted the usual fuck-you glare from Dimi. He didn't care. He helped himself to Mel's office and the shower in her bathroom there, which meant that he smelled just like her.

He could smell himself all the damn day as he flew to LA to see a man with a fleet of antique Beechcraft. Not a 1944 in the bunch . . . Bugger it all to hell.

By the time he got back to North Beach, it was late afternoon. He was with Danny in maintenance, looking on the Internet for parts when Char called. "Danny, get your cute buns into the lobby, please."

"What's up?"

"Just hustle."

Danny looked at Bo hopefully. "Maybe it involves food."

On the chance it did, Bo tagged along.

They walked into the café and Char hurried them behind the counter. "Quick, duck!"

Bo ducked down without knowing why until one moment later when Mel walked in off the tarmac, hot and irritated and gorgeous, and everyone leapt up and yelled "Happy B-day!"

There was a huge cake, with decorations hanging over their heads and helium balloons. They pushed Mel onto a chair and sang "Happy Birthday" to her. Ritchie offered to spank her, and then Kellan shoved him and said he'd do it, and then Al hit them both upside the back of the head while everyone gathered in like the tight unit they were and talked and laughed and talked some more.

Al took pictures. Char refilled soda glasses from a frothy pitcher in her hand. Danny kept reaching out to the boom box to change the music from Def Leppard to Green Day, but Char kept laughing and changing it back.

Kellan picked up each present on the table and shook it in turn, stopping at one in particular. "This one sounds like a vibrator," he said hopefully.

"Yeah? Hope it comes with batteries," Mel responded, which had Bo frozen to the spot, his mind caught on the image of Mel using a vibrator on herself. Good God, the image seared his brain, so much so that when Al asked him a question, he could only stare at the man . . . struck deaf, blind, and mute.

Ritchie helped himself to one helium balloon at a time, sucking in the gas, amusing himself and the others by singing along to the radio in a high-pitched squeal.

Mel had a smile on her face, a real one that Bo hadn't seen before, and it stopped him cold. Her eyes were lit, sparkling with life. She wore a pair of jeans and two tank tops layered over each other, black and white. Her hair, all that long, thick, glorious red hair, hung over her shoulders and down her back, and he knew just how it would smell if he buried his face in the silky strands because he'd smelled just like her all the damn day long.

She glanced at him once, her gaze briefly dropping to the buttons on his Levi's.

She was thinking about this morning, about his morning erection, and what a horny little secret keeper he was, and he waited until her gaze lifted before he arched a daring brow.

She blushed. *Blushed.* He'd had her naked and writhing in his arms, he'd watched her come all over him, and she was blushing, after being caught looking at his package. "I don't have a present," he said to her. "I didn't know it was your birthday."

She shook her head. "I don't expect a present from you."

Right. Because he wasn't part of her life. He didn't fit in, she didn't even want him to. All around him was an easy affection, even love, and he felt a pang. A deep, dark pang that he didn't understand. All he'd wanted was to get his father's money and get out of here. He hadn't wanted to belong. Or like these people.

So how had it happened that though he wanted the first he had already done the second?

Char lit the twenty-seven candles on the huge cake, decorated with—what else?—a plane.

"Blow hard," Char suggested.

Mel glanced at Bo and blushed, once again giving away her thoughts. *Blow hard*.

In his dreams.

"Don't forget to wish!" Dimi told her.

"I won't," Mel said, eyes still locked on Bo, thinking . . . what?

He didn't know but he'd have paid a lot to find out.

Mel sliced up the cake, extremely aware of Bo on the outer edge of everyone, looking in but not really a part of the party.

Everyone took a piece of cake but him, and with the gang talking and laughing and occupied, she stepped close and offered up a plate.

He hesitated so briefly she couldn't be sure she hadn't imagined it, then took the plate. He stabbed a bite with his fork, but brought it to her lips.

Over his fork, their gazes met, the air charged. No need to wonder what he was thinking, it was there in his green eyes— a desire so potent it rocked her world. As she opened her mouth and took a bite, licking off a dollop of frosting from her lips, his eyes flamed some more.

God. Her knees shook. What was she doing? Having no idea, she turned away, but he came up behind her.

She knew it was him by the sheer heat that flooded her body. He pressed close, his shoulders brushing against her back, his thighs to hers, a big, warm hand setting low on her spine.

"What did you wish for?" he asked, his voice a low murmur, his lips grazing the sensitive skin just beneath her ear.

A set of delicious shivers chased each other down her spine and she told herself to get a grip. He was hardly touching her. Her body was just overreacting. She turned her head to meet his eyes. A mistake, as they were still on fire. "World peace."

His mouth twitched. "And?"

"And for the answers to my fave TV show, *Lost*."

"And?"

"If I tell, it won't come true."

He looked at her for a long beat, his fingers very slowly gliding beneath her tank top to stroke her bare skin just above the waistband of her jeans.

Then those clever fingers dipped just beneath, toying with the elastic on her panties.

Yeah, that pretty much dissolved the bones in her legs. With him this close, the view of everyone else was blocked out by his broad shoulders, so that all she could focus on was him; his solidness, his scent, the way he was looking at her.

It did something funny to her tummy, and longing twisted and coiled through her. *Longing*. For this man.

Hadn't she already talked to herself about this? *He was a bad idea.*

Luckily, Ernest distracted them all with his latest jar filled with an eight-legged occupant, and then Kellan juggled salt shakers while Danny polished off the rest of the cake, and Ritchie once again sang "Happy Birthday" in his helium-high voice, and then everyone was saying good-bye for the night.

Skin still burning from Bo's touch, Mel gathered all her things and headed out.

The heat had softened with the setting sun, and as she walked toward her car, she was suddenly more exhausted than she could remember being in a long time, and that was saying something. All she wanted was a hot bath and bed—No. Remembering the other day's bath fiasco, she decided to make it a shower.

With no unexpected company. She wanted to be alone.

Liar, liar, pants on fire . . .

In the parking lot, she fumbled through her myriad pockets looking for her keys, and when she lifted her head, her gaze locked with Bo's.

Instant heat wave. Sweaty palms, dry mouth, the whole deal, and now that she was twenty-seven, this whole uncontrollable teenage hormone thing was really getting annoying.

He was leaning back against her car, arms and feet casually crossed, looking like trouble waiting to happen. More than just her hormones kicked in now, something deeper, and inexplicably unnerving.

The longing was a bummer, but she could live with that. He'd put his hands on her many times now and her body knew what they could do, and fact was fact: the man had it going on, and he could make her purr like a kitten.

But beyond that, beyond the physical, something else was happening. She was beginning to know him—that he liked Char's music, always picked the chocolate donuts in the morning, and didn't like tea but coffee, black and hot. More than that, he was an amazing aircraft mechanic, and also a sharp-as-hell business man; more than that, he missed his father, and was loyal to a fault. It was as if she could suddenly see beneath all of it, beneath the Aussie charm and wit, to a man who had as many questions as she did, and just wanted answers. There was hurt there, too, and if she looked even further, vulnerability.

The big, badass Bo Black felt every bit as off his axis as she did. And the knowledge staggered her.

He pushed away from her car. "I figured out your present." He handed her what looked like a legal document, folded in thirds. "Happy birthday."

Mel opened it, scanned the header, and went still. *Oh, my God.*

"It's your lease for Anderson Air here at North Beach. I've renewed it at the same rate you've been paying for years."

They both knew her rate had been highway robbery, and yet . . ."This says it's a twenty-year lease—" She choked out a laugh, then stared at him. "My lease was only good for another six months."

"I know."

Her gaze was caught in his, and everything there. "You've done this so that if you sell I'd be okay," she breathed.

"Maybe I did it so you'd take me home with you and show me how grateful you are."

"Bo. Don't ruin this by being stupidly male. My God." She was blown away by the implications, by how much he cared about her future to have done this. "Bo—"

"If you're suddenly overcome by a need to talk, you owe me your thoughts on that file I gave you."

She also owed him an orgasm, if they were keeping score. That unspoken thought floated in the air between them. Her blush must have given her away because he said, sounding quite irritated, "Just a talk, Mel. *Jesus*. You don't have to look like you're going to the guillotine."

She took in his tight jaw, his flat eyes, and felt herself soften toward him all the more. "My house," she said softly. "Meet me there."

He looked at her for a long moment, then opened her car door for her without a word. He followed her home, and she used the ten-minute drive to give herself a reality check. He'd probably renewed her lease for twenty years at the same price to ease his guilty conscience for having the deed in the first place, or for considering the possibility of selling.

But even if that was true, what he'd done went over and above the call of duty. The stability and security he'd given her would allow her to breathe easy, to take her charter business in any direction she saw fit.

He'd done this, asking nothing in return.

When she pulled into her driveway and got out of her car, Bo followed, waiting until they were inside and she'd flipped on a few lights before he spoke again. "Tell me what you really wished for."

She turned to face him. "How do you know I wished for anything?"

"I saw you concentrating. You squeezed your eyes really tight, like it meant something to you."

He saw a hell of a lot, more than the people in her life, more than she wanted him to.

"I watched you," he said quietly. "And thought, there she goes, mate, wishing you'd never shown up here."

She stared at him, feeling a totally unexpected and unwelcome lump rise in her throat, threatening to choke her. Yeah, she'd wished on the candles, but not for what he'd thought.

She'd wished for security, for stability, for a damn night without stress, without worry.

And with the lease, he'd just given that to her on a platter. What kind of a bad guy did that?

He stood there, unusually solemn, unusually *not* cocky. Watching her.

Not a bad guy.

She moved to the couch and sank down on it, pulling out the file he'd given her the other night. "You going to sit?" she asked.

"I'm thinking no."

"Why not?"

"Because when we get close, our clothes tend to fall off."

"My clothes," she corrected. "You mean my clothes fall off. You have yet to get naked."

His eyes blazed. "Don't tempt me."

Chapter 18

Mel stared up at Bo, who still stood in her doorway looking a little tense and a whole lot sexy.

Not giving an inch.

"Come here, Bo."

"Really bad idea," he said, shaking his head. "Colossally bad idea."

Interesting that when *she* was making the moves he held back. But she didn't want his famed control now, she wanted to give him something back, to show him in spite of the hell around them that she appreciated him, that she cared. That she got him.

He still wasn't moving forward. Fine. She'd go to him.

His mouth went grim as she stood up and headed toward him, his body going more tense. "Mel—"

"Yeah." She set her hands to his chest, came up on tiptoe, and brushed her mouth to his. "I know. Bad idea, right? It's also stupid. I know that, too."

"Don't."

But she did, kissing him again.

Grabbing her arms in his hands, he hauled her up to her

toes, a tic in his jaw. "Don't mess with me, Mel—we're supposed to talk. *Talk*, not—"

Leaning in, she nibbled at the corner of his mouth.

"Fuck." This was uttered roughly as he held himself rigid while her mouth hovered a breath from his.

He was waiting breathlessly for a kiss, she could feel him quivering for it, but instead, she bit his lower lip.

He was up to the challenge. With a hissing breath, he yanked her up against him and covered her mouth with his, taking full advantage when she opened to him, gliding his tongue along hers.

She'd had some half-baked thought that this would be sweet and lovely and just what she needed. Ha! They'd said too much, been through too much for sweet and lovely, and anyway, she didn't really want either. She got hot, and wet, and oh, my God, the real deal. His arms banded hard around her. In fact he basically crushed her to him, kissing her longer, deeper, harder . . .

She loved the way her breasts mashed up to his chest, loved how big and strong he was, how he made her feel so feminine and so excited she could hardly stand it. "Ohmigod, Bo."

"We're supposed to be talking." Turning her, he pushed her against the wall, then spread his legs open on either side of hers, so that his very impressive erection pressed into her belly. He dipped a little, rocking his penis lower, right where she . . . wanted . . . it . . . the most.

"You don't feel like you're up for much *talking*," she quipped.

"Yeah, one guess for what I *am* up for."

Her heart drummed so fast she was shocked she could even hear him, but she didn't need to hear anything because then he cradled her head in his big hands to hold her head still and took her mouth again. In less than one second they were wild, straining against each other. *Lost*. He pushed up her tank tops, flicked open her bra, and groaned as her breasts popped free. "God. Look at you." Bending, he sucked a nipple into his mouth while rasping his thumb over the other, and though she'd never thought of her breasts as particularly sensitive to a man's touch, her vision grayed, and she couldn't see or hear anything over her own blood rushing through her veins.

But she could feel, and oh, my God, what she felt—

And then his mouth was gone. "Bo—"

He dropped to his knees, jerked down the zipper on her pants, and yanked. Head level with her belly, he stared at her tiger-striped panties. "A wildcat," he said, sounding a little hoarse. "I think this says a lot about you, darlin'." He traced a strip from hipbone to between her legs, where the silk clung to her, making him groan.

"My boots—" She couldn't get her pants off until he removed her boots, and she needed, right this very minute, for him to sink into her body.

Instead, he slid the tiger material aside and exposed her to his gaze. "You're wet. Is it for me, Mel?"

"Yes," she choked out, then nearly fell to the ground when he leaned in and kissed her, *there*, would have fallen if his hands hadn't gripped her thighs, holding her upright.

"I want you to come like this, with my mouth on you."

"I can't—"

"Yeah, you said that before, too. What did you mean, you can't?" Still holding her panties to one side, he leaned in again and sucked her into his mouth, using his tongue to slowly stroke her.

Her head thunked back against the wall.

"Mel?"

"Yeah. Um . . ." She'd meant for him not to put too much effort into trying to get her to come because she usually couldn't without a big production and a lot of effort on her part, but explaining it was like throwing a big bucket of ice water on her lust. Even thinking it was a turnoff . . . "I just want you inside me." *Please*.

"You don't come with men?"

She sighed. "Well, certainly not now that we've stopped to chat."

She tried to twist away but he held her still, kissing each thigh. "Chatting is nice, too."

No, she was done, thank you very much. "Forget it. I'm going to bed—"

"Shh."

Oh, no he didn't. He didn't just . . . *shush* her! This was grounds for homicide, but then he leaned in and put his tongue on her again. He knew just the right pressure, the right rhythm, and suddenly, unbelievably, she was back on the very edge, trembling, panting for breath, when normally she'd be working so damn hard for an orgasm it wasn't worth the effort. "Oh, my God."

The bastard let out a soft laugh while she sank her fingers into his hair and held on, thinking if he stopped, she was going to kill him.

But he didn't stop. In less than three minutes, he had her shaking and sobbing for breath. "Please," she gasped, and then he slid a finger inside her.

And another.

She exploded, his name on her lips as she shuddered and completely, utterly lost herself in a collision of a thousand sensations.

When she came back to herself, he'd stood up, was in fact holding her up as well. "You all right?" he murmured, kissing her jaw, her throat.

Okay, maybe he wasn't a complete bastard. And she wanted more, fast, now. "In me," she said. "Now."

"Now works." Scooping her up, he turned and tossed her to the couch, then followed her down. She tried to wrap her legs around him but her pants, still around her ankles, caught her. "Damn it—"

"I've got it—"

"Hurry—"

"Yeah, I got that part." Scooting down her body, he fumbled with her boots. "Christ, how many knots do you need?"

She was pulling off his shirt, her eyes gobbling up his shoulders, his chest, those gorgeous six-pack abs she just wanted to sink her teeth into.

He was still fighting with her first boot, and she slapped his hands aside to undo the laces herself, then his hands moved in again, yanking off the boot, tossing it over his shoulder while she kicked the denim off that leg. Not waiting for the other boot, she tugged at his jeans, her fingers entangling with his as together they shoved the pants to his thighs.

"Oh," she murmured in pleasure, holding him, stroking him.

With a groan, he grabbed her hands and lifted them over her head, pressing his hips to hers. "Let me in, Mel."

Helpless to resist, she arched, wrapping her legs around his waist. Dipping down low, he rubbed his jaw to hers and smiled.

God, his face. Gorgeous, yeah, but the way he looked at her . . . She opened herself up to him, glided her hands down his smooth, sleek back, urging him on. "Now, Bo . . ."

"Wait. I want to—"

Arching up, she tightened her legs around him, pulling him toward her so that he almost pushed into her. The sensation dragged a rough groan from him and a helpless cry for more from her.

"Mel. *God*." He pulled back a little, then slowly pushed back in, fully seating himself within her this time, her wet, sensitized flesh hugging him tight.

She was going to come again, an unbelievable feat—

"Wait," he gasped, sounding strained. "Mel, wait—"

No. No waiting.

Her hands squeezed his squeezable butt as she tried to get him to move. Harder. Faster.

"Hold on," he begged. "We can't—" His voice was hoarse,

serrated as he pressed his pelvis to hers, the pleasure all over his face. He was, in fact quivering with it, but he didn't move again. "I don't have a condom."

That stopped her. She looked up, met his gaze. He held himself rigid above her. There was a line of sweat down one temple, his jaw clenched tight. His muscles stood out in sharp relief, quaking faintly. "Not in your wallet?" she whispered.

He shook his head.

"Not—"

"Nowhere."

"How could you not—"

His expression was close to pain, and frozen with intense concentration. "I didn't expect—"

"I'm going to cry," she whispered. "I swear it."

"Mel—"

The torture in his voice assured her that it was worse for him, far worse, as he hadn't already gotten off like she had, not the other night, and not tonight.

And in that moment, it changed for her. Somehow she went from frantic to warm and fuzzy, soft. He was breathing hard, shaking, and she knew what to do. "It's okay," she whispered, stroking her hands up his chest, feeling his hot, damp muscles jerk beneath her touch. "Let me."

"Let you what—"

She shoved hard and he fell off the couch, but she fell with him, rolling so that he landed on his back, with her straddling him.

"*Jesus.*"

"Are you okay?" she asked breathlessly, running her hands up his arms. She'd dislodged him from inside her body but she could feel him, hot and silky hard pressing against her. "Did I hurt you?"

"You're killing me." He groaned when she slid down his body and wrapped her fingers around his hot and silky length. "*Killing* me."

"Shh." Smiling at how she'd finally shushed *him*, she leaned close, letting her hair fall and graze his belly, his thighs, eliciting another groan from deep in his throat, which turned into a strangled sound of immense pleasure when she took her tongue on a tour over him, from base to tip. "Mmm," she said, and did it again.

The sound that escaped him was half-laugh, half a desperate plea. "*Mel.*"

She could hear his need, and lowered her head to fulfill it. It didn't take long, he was hard and hot and primed to go, and watching him, listening to him surrender to his body's need as he came, gave her far more pleasure than she could have imagined.

Afterward, the only sound as they lay flat on their backs was their ragged breathing.

"I don't know whether to thank you or apologize," he finally managed.

Sitting up, she smiled. She felt him eye her as she began to straighten her clothes. She still had one boot on. Leaning in, he helped her with the knot, then he stood, staggering for balance before he righted his own clothes and zipped up his jeans. "Before you kick me out, we were going to talk."

Body still humming, she blinked. "Kick you out?"

"You tend to do that."

"Oh. Yeah."

He sat heavily on the couch and looked at her. "I've got more information. I'm going to tell you now, if you can handle it."

"And if I can't?"

"I'm going to tell you anyway."

"Ah." She nodded as her lingering pleasure faded away. "So the lease was, what, a peace offering? A way to loosen me up?"

"Maybe a little of both."

"Nice."

"I never pretended to be nice, Mel."

No, but oddly enough, he was. Or at least he wasn't quite as badass as he'd let her believe. "And what do you call what we just did?"

"Fan-fucking-tastic, if you want the truth." He pulled her down beside him. "How about a game of truth or dare without the dare? Truth: I came here to see Sally, but that's never going to happen. Is it, Mel?"

She looked into his eyes and felt the foundation of her world crack.

"See, I've been researching Sally on the net," he said. "Interesting thing. She's vanished. And she vanished a long time ago."

"Well . . ." Mel winced. "Sort of."

He looked at her for a long moment, his eyes dark, reproachful. *Hurt,* damn it. "You let me think she was on a trip, that she'd be coming back."

"I never actually said a trip."

"Why don't you *actually* say then?"

She paused, but knew she had to tell him everything. "I don't know where she is."

"So you've said. Now say more."

"I planned on telling you," she said. "I told Dimi I was going to tell you."

"So tell already."

"She used to call in every month or so. But it's been awhile, and when I called her, she didn't get back to me." She grimaced. "And . . ."

A muscle in his jaw jumped. "And . . . ?"

"And now her cell phone has been disconnected."

"So you've lost touch completely," he said flatly. "That's convenient."

"But true."

He sighed, and she knew he was frustrated as hell. "And you're getting e-mails, vaguely threatening e-mails."

"Yes," she agreed.

Tension radiated off him in waves. "From Sally?"

"I don't know."

Disbelief flashed in those jade eyes. Disbelief that she'd allowed this, that he couldn't do anything about it. "And you didn't feel the need to mention any of this sooner—why?"

Mel chewed on her lip.

"Mel."

"Because I didn't trust you."

He stared at her. "Jesus." He surged to his feet, shoved his fingers through his hair, and turned in a slow circle. "I have no idea why that hurts." He swore softly, then shook his head. Turning, he headed toward the door.

She leapt to her feet. "Bo, wait."

"Can't," he said curtly.

"But you said you'd found something else."

He laughed a little harshly. "That I did. But I don't think I'll be sharing it."

She stared at him in disbelief. "You're not going to tell me?"

"Give the girl an *A.*"

"I want to hear it, Bo."

"I bet you do. But it seems we were playing truth or dare all along, and I've just joined the game. I pick dare."

"I wanted to tell you sooner," she murmured. "But—"

"Too late." When he looked at her, all of his hunger and desire was gone, replaced by the same mocking amusement she'd seen in the beginning. "I keep forgetting, I'm on my own."

He shut the door quietly behind him.

Mel stared at the wood, her throat tight, her pulse points still randomly jumping from the amazing sex.

The most amazing sex in her entire life.

"Happy birthday to me," she whispered, and the words echoed around her mockingly.

Chapter 19

Bo stalked through the airport the next morning, cultivating what some might call a bad attitude. Yeah, he'd gotten off last night, and yeah, that should have mellowed him, but she'd been holding back on him, his Mel. Why that was surprising, he had no idea, but the opposite of mellow had happened. He was looking for trouble now and he knew it, but he'd wasted nearly two weeks doing what he'd said he wouldn't.

Trusting.

His gut—and more computer research—told him Sally wasn't coming back, that the money and plane were long gone, and if that was the case, then there was really nothing to be done except for taking over North Beach, fixing it up so that he could sell, and getting the hell out of Dodge.

He thought of how Mel would react to that, how hurt and destroyed she'd be, and he ruthlessly shoved it aside because he didn't care. She had the lease he'd foolishly given her, she'd be fine. Everyone else, if they were good at their jobs, would be fine, too.

But from the far end of the lobby came Mel's voice, and

just like that, heat flooded through his body, pooling between his thighs, pissing him off because she'd gotten under his skin.

"I can assure the both of you," she was saying, "that two pilots are not needed for this flight."

Bo came around the corner to see her facing a man and a woman, both dressed like a million bucks, looking out at a Lear Jet on the tarmac. "I've flown from here to San Francisco hundreds of times," Mel said to them. "It's a simple, pleasurable trip."

The couple were already shaking their heads. They were in their fifties, and judging from the sheer brilliance of the woman's bling alone, they were big money. New money.

"Our usual jet has *two* pilots," the woman said. "Plus a flight attendant to see to our needs."

Mel stood there in her leather bomber jacket and black pilot pants that showed off her long, lean, tough length, pride warring with tact. "I understand your usual charter service is down, which is what brought you here. But Anderson Air doesn't provide the same sort of service as Diamond Skies, and as a result, we're far more affordable. Now if I could just board you—"

"We don't care about the cost," the man said. "I'm going to have to insist on another pilot on board."

Mel's pleasant expression didn't change but she was insulted. Bo could tell by the little pucker between her eyebrows, and the way her smile went just a little tight. Oh, and the smoke coming out her ears was a sign, too. God, she was so uptight she probably squeaked when she walked, and so unbelievably sexy while she was at it. It was a first for him, wanting a woman that he also wanted to strangle.

"Honestly," she said. "Another pilot would just add unnecessary expense—"

"Expense is not a problem. We're just flying into the city for a business meeting and turning right around. We'd make it worth your while."

This did not cheer Mel up one bit. She was in a bind, and there was only one way out.

Another pilot. She looked over at Bo, her face inscrutable, her body, the one he'd had just the night before, tense enough to shatter.

He knew how to banish that tenseness now, he knew just how to touch her. Knew a helluva lot more about her than she was comfortable with, he was quite certain.

She needed him. Differently than last night, when she'd needed him buried deep inside her so that there was no way to tell where he ended and she'd begun, when she'd needed him so badly she'd left fingerprints on his ass and a bite mark on his shoulder, but need was need.

And suddenly, it felt good to be him. "Need help?" he asked, a little more cheerful.

The look on her face was priceless. He'd just put her in a position of having to ask. She'd hate that, of course, which made him even more cheerful than strictly called for.

"Mr. and Mrs. Hutton," she said, shoulders rigid. "This is Bo Black." She looked at Bo. "Can you fly with us today?" she asked, barely opening the mouth that just last night had brought him to such heights of pleasure he'd nearly blacked out.

"Hmmm . . . Can I fly with you today?" He pulled his PDA out of his pocket and made a show of checking it. "Just so happens I'm free."

Mel's eyes were sheer glaciers by now. Oh, she hated this. She didn't want him here, didn't want his help.

But he *was* here, and available. And, as it happened, he owned the place. That made him the boss. He liked that, too, he decided. He liked that a lot.

"Are you a pilot?" Mr. Hutton asked Bo.

Bo purposely looked away from Mel. "That I am," he said happily. "Been flying since before I could drive."

Mr. Hutton nodded. "You'll do."

"Thanks, mate."

"You're Australian." Mrs. Hutton smiled warmly. "Your accent is lovely."

Bo smiled.

Mel's teeth gnashed together.

Mr. Hutton took Mrs. Hutton's arm. "We'll be onboard, waiting."

Mel waited until they'd walked onto the tarmac. "I didn't need you or your 'lovely accent' to interfere."

"Sure? Because I think the bloke was about to cancel on you."

She crossed her arms. "That would have been fine."

"You need the income."

"Nice of you to concern yourself, but you needn't."

"Actually, I do."

Her eyes were flashing, her body practically vibrating with temper. "And how's that?"

"See, Anderson Air is a client of North Beach. I am now North Beach. Your success is my success. Get it?"

"I thought all you wanted was your money back."

"Right. But that isn't happening, is it?" He clucked her beneath her tilted chin. "I've moved on to plan *B.*"

Her eyes narrowed, her mouth opened—to blast him, he was quite certain—but he set a finger against her lips. "Fight me on this," he said softly, "and trust me, you won't like plan *B* very much."

Then, content with the unexpected change in both the day and his luck, he started to whistle as he walked onto the tarmac.

Mel watched him swagger out and took a deep breath, then glanced over at Dimi, who'd been sitting behind her desk but had come to a shocked stand.

"You're not going to let him do this," Dimi said, clearly shaken.

Mel watched through the window as Bo shook hands

with the Huttons, clearly having a lovely chat. Tall, rugged and rangy even from a distance, he understandably appealed to their clients. It was hard to tear her eyes off him. With his hair just on the wrong side of his last haircut, and that dangerous smile, he pretty much screamed, "let me break your heart."

As she watched, he lowered his sunglasses over his eyes and turned toward the window, his face drawn with exhaustion but still sexy as hell, damn him, somehow seeming as if he purposely wanted to remind her of last night.

As if she could forget what it'd felt like to be with him, his hands stripping her clothes off while his mouth glided over her flesh. God. Even now, even in the light of day, she wanted him to start all over again at the beginning.

What was wrong with her?

And then the bastard smiled.

In spite of everything, her stomach tightened, her heart took a little trip. "Face it, Dimi," she grated out, eyes still locked on Bo. "It's beyond our control." He was beyond her control, and really, when it came right down to it, that's what bothered her the most. "Sally saw to that when she signed the deed over."

"She didn't have a choice," Dimi maintained. "Somehow I know it."

Mel sighed. "There's always a choice."

Dimi slowly shook her head. "Mel, Sally loved—*loves*—us. She wouldn't just do this without a word."

"But she did."

Dimi stared at her, hurt and frustrated, but before either could say a word, Ernest came in and slapped a jar down on the desk.

Yet another spider wriggled its legs at them.

Both Dimi and Mel gasped and shrank back against each other.

"A daddy longlegs, and he's harmless," Ernest said. "Harmless; you big babies. Plus he eats the bad guys." He waggled a finger in Mel's face. "He's one of the good guys, and if I'd cleaned the closets out like you'd wanted, missy, I'd have ended up killing him."

"Um, maybe you could take him outside. Where there are no closets at all."

"I plan to." He snatched up the jar. "Your e-mail problem?"

Mel turned a wary gaze on him. "Yeah?"

"Spam mail. Can't trace it to one person."

It'd taken him long enough. "Okay. Thanks."

"That was the good news."

She blinked. "And the bad?"

"This morning? I was the first in." He slapped an envelope down on the counter. It had MEL typed across the front, and had been opened. "This was taped to the front door."

Mel slid out the piece of paper. It read: *I warned you.*

She eyed Ernest. "Why was the envelope opened?"

"Because I opened it."

She felt a muscle beneath her eye begin to twitch. "I realize that. But it's addressed to me."

"Maybe it was important," he said. "Maybe it was *from* you."

"It says Mel. Implying it's *to* me."

His gaze cut to the damning evidence, then he hitched a bony shoulder. "I've got work."

When he'd walked away Mel stared in disbelief at Dimi.

"Forget him, call the police," Dimi said, and shuddered at the spider. "I wish he'd have taken that thing—"

Ernest came back, and snatched the jar.

Dimi let out a breath. When he left again, Mel stared down at the note. "Yeah. Probably the police is a good idea." She handed the note to Dimi. "See anything unusual about this?"

"It's got our logo on it." Dimi looked down at the paper. "I ordered this paper from Staples. These pads are everywhere inside this place—" She froze. *"Oh my God."*

"Yeah." Mel felt vaguely ill. "It was written from inside the airport."

"Mel. A little freaked out here."

"Join the club." Mel had always been so sure she'd known what had happened with Sally, that Eddie had come along and swindled Sally out of her money, and also the deed to North Beach. That Sally had gone after him, and had destroyed her love for her life here in the process.

But now her disappearance signified something else, at least to Mel, and it hurt to think the things she was thinking. "Okay, I've got to go."

"Let me just cancel your flight," Dimi said. "And then we'll—"

"I'm not going to cancel my flight."

"You're going to fly? With *him?*"

"The note didn't come from him." Mel strode toward the tarmac door. "As for the flight, it's on the schedule. It's mine, and I don't cancel."

"Mel—"

"Not canceling," she called back, her gaze on the tall, gorgeous, enigmatic man on the tarmac waiting for her. "I need the money."

"I think it's more than that."

Mel turned back and faced Dimi's pale, horrified expression. "What more?"

"Face it, Mel. You're falling for him."

Mel's heart tripped, giving her away, at least to herself. "I'll be on the radio."

And she strode out the door.

"I realize we've put a moratorium on trusting each other," Mel said to Bo shortly after takeoff.

Bo took his gaze off the horizon and eyed the woman who until now had pretended he wasn't on the same flight with her.

She looked away, down at the pristine wilderness of the Channel Islands beneath them, a rugged chain about twenty-five miles offshore to her left, shimmering on the horizon. "But there's, um, something you should know," she said.

Her aviator sunglasses blocked her eyes from him, leaving him little clue as to what she was thinking. "What is that?"

"About the two e-mails."

"You found out who they're from?"

"No." She licked her lips. Checked her altitude even though they were perfect. "But it was three e-mails."

"Three."

"And I also got two letters. One in the mail, one taped to the front door of the airport this morning. It said, and I quote, 'I warned you.' "

Bo stared at her, a barrage of emotions hitting him like a one-two punch. Renewed fury that she'd been threatened at all, frustration that she hadn't seen fit to tell him, and a fear for her safety that felt a little too huge for his own comfort. "Did you call the police?"

"Soon as I get back."

He had to breathe for a minute. "When were you going to tell me?"

"Now."

He shook his head, pinched the bridge of his nose, and wondered why, when he'd been a patient man all of his life, that this woman seemed to drive him to the very edge of sanity without even trying.

They fell silent again, Mel distracted by reports in her headset of unfriendly weather over the Bay Area, Bo by the passengers, who were asking him to find them an old biplane for Mr. Hutton's father, who used to fly one. After that they needed him to pour them drinks and check the temperature, then to get the Mrs. a pillow for her stiff neck. Bo resisted the urge to tell them to do all this themselves, it was Mel's business to make sure they were content. It wasn't that he didn't want to deal with them, but more that he wanted to shake the hell out of Mel.

"You make a pretty flight attendant," Mel deadpanned when he finally came back to the cockpit.

He looked over at her and smiled. "Maybe I'm enjoying getting your butt, your very nice butt, I might add—out of a sling."

"You did not save my butt."

"Really." He hitched a shoulder toward the back, where the upscale, elegant couple was engrossed—finally—in their respective laptops, complete with headphones. He imagined they were listening to something classical, while checking their stock portfolios. "Because I'm pretty sure I did."

Her jaw tightened, but that might have been the storm on the horizon, which they'd been carefully eyeing for the past half hour. It was going to be a hell of an issue for the return flight.

Not that he'd mind an overnight stay in San Francisco. He could find fun and entertainment wherever he went. But truthfully, Mel was providing most of his entertainment at the moment. God, the way her eyes flashed at her every single thought. She eyed the horizon, and the churning gray and black clouds there, then swore beneath her breath.

"Did you know you wear your thoughts out on your sleeve for everyone to see?" he asked conversationally.

She glanced at him, her eyes pissy. "Really? What am I thinking now?"

He laughed softly at the fuck-you glare. "Ah, that's too easy."

Her mouth actually quirked in an almost smile before she turned away to once again eye the storm, then her instruments.

"We're going to be okay."

She nodded. "I know. But getting back—"

"Yeah, we're not going to get back. Not tonight."

"We are not staying overnight."

"What's the matter, you afraid of a little sleepover?"

At that, she tossed back her head and laughed. He already

knew he enjoyed her temper. He enjoyed her thought processes, too, and he most definitely enjoyed her body. But her laugh. The woman had a laugh that reached out and grabbed him by the throat. And south of that as well—his heart.

And also south of *that* . . . Yeah, he thought, she slayed him through and through.

"Funny that you accuse me of being afraid of a sleepover," she said. "When you're the one who stood with a couch between us, because you were afraid I was going to rip your clothes off."

And yet still his clothes had come off. "You think I was afraid?"

"I know it," she said smugly.

He opened his mouth without quite knowing what he was going to say to that. Because, seriously? She was dead-spot right on.

He *was* afraid of her.

He'd come here to the States half-cocked, ready for bloodshed or whatever came his way, including destroying everything Sally had worked for, but something had happened.

Or someone.

Melanie Anderson, temperamental, stubborn hard-ass. But now he knew she was also strong, loyal, dedicated, passionate . . .

God, he had it bad.

"Damn," Mel breathed, and then the plane jerked. Dipped. Her jaw went tight as she touched base via radio to air traffic control.

Bo didn't need to hear the short, clipped conversation to know. The storm had worsened ahead of schedule.

Turbulence ahead; both outside the plane, and in.

Mel glanced at her instruments, at the horizon. They were fifteen minutes out of San Francisco, that was all, but it was going to be a rocky ride. Proving it, the plane hit an air pocket and shuddered and dipped again.

Behind them, their passengers took off their headsets, glancing up worriedly. Bo motioned for them to stay seated. "Just turbulence from the storm," he said calmly. "Hang tight, we'll have you on the ground in fifteen minutes."

"I could have said that," Mel said to him from beneath her breath.

"You're flying."

"Yeah." Her muscles were tense as granite as she scanned the horizon, which by now was completely socked in by cloud coverage. The plane dipped again and she fought the controls, feeling a drop of sweat glide down between her shoulder blades.

Their passengers gasped again. And as before, Bo turned to them and smiled . . . "Don't worry about a thing, you're in great hands."

Mel didn't take her eyes off the vanishing skyline. Vanishing, because the cloud coverage was taking over. Deep breath.

And then another. "Handy having a flight attendant."

"I guess it is," he finally said, sounding amused at himself. "At your service, darlin'."

She risked a quick glance at him. "As if you'd ever be at my service."

"Try me."

Something deep inside her leaped but the plane took another stomach-dropping dip. She bit her lip and gripped the controls.

"Easy," he murmured. "Just stay on it."

"I know how to fly." She scanned the horizon, but all she could see was a solid, sickening gray.

"I'll tell you what," he said quietly. "You just concentrate on what you do best, and we can get back to the servicing later."

"Been there, done that," she said, referring to the other night.

"Yeah, but it's worth a repeat."

"I don't know," she quipped, eyes scanning the horizon, teeth clenched as she tried to make light. "I mean, sure, the first time was pretty great, but I doubt you could repeat the performance."

He let out a low laugh of disbelief. "A dare, Mel? You know better than that."

They dipped again. "Goddamnit," she muttered, leaning forward as if that could help her see through the clouds that were thicker than cream soup.

"Stop wasting your time searching for a visual you're not going to get. You've got the instruments, use 'em."

Right. Damn it, he was so right, and that pissed her off enough to jolt her into the rock-solid concentration that had eluded her until now. She focused in on the controls and breathing, and once she did, her instincts kicked in.

The plane shuddered and dipped and shuddered again, but she was in firm control.

Behind them, Mrs. Hutton gasped. Her husband put an arm around her. Outside the plane, the wind and rain battered the plane while Mel began their descent. Another trickle of sweat ran down her back but she didn't think about that now, thought about nothing but the work right in front of her. Flying was like breathing, and breathing was second nature.

Bo didn't say another word, and for that, she felt grateful. She knew what to do, she didn't need direction, and that he didn't butt in was testament to how much he trusted her.

She'd think about that, and the implications of that trust, later, but not now. Not when her heart still raced, adrenaline flowing through her like a raging river.

When the wheels touched down, the Huttons let out a collective sigh. Shocking her, Bo became the consummate flight attendant, getting the passengers off with their luggage, through the driving wind and rain, and off the tarmac as quickly as possible.

Then he was back for Mel. "I swore I wasn't going to do this," he said, then yanked her into his arms, his voice low and rich in her ear when he spoke. "That was some class-A flying, Mel."

She resisted for all of half a second, then hugged him back, her insides still quaking. "Thanks."

He looked at her, his smile fading, desire and heat filling the spot. "Ah, hell. Hold on darlin', here comes another storm." And he kissed her, his mouth warm and knowing, his tongue sweeping in her mouth as if it belonged there.

She certainly enjoyed the invasion, and as amazing as it seemed, with his hands in her hair, on her back, pressing her as close as she could get, the rest of the world faded away. She was reduced to nothing but the sensation of being held against his body and how he made her feel—which was alive, vibrantly, wonderfully alive. When he finally pulled back, he smiled. "It's time."

She was still breathless. "Time?"

"I believe there was a question of servicing."

Oh, God. Now that they'd actually been together, she knew exactly what he meant, and how good he was at it. Her thighs trembled. Between them she went damp, at just his voice, his words. She was worse than Pavlov's dog! "I don't think so. I have to prepare for the flight back."

He laughed softly. "We're not going back tonight. You know that. No one is flying in this." As if to solidify this statement, lightning cracked. Thunder boomed. Rain and wind slashed at the plane.

"Hotel room," he said. "Shower. Dinner. And then . . ."

Her voice was not steady, not even close and yet she couldn't help but ask. "Then?"

His smile looked like sin personified, wicked and naughty to the nth degree. "Then . . . Let the servicing begin."

Chapter 20

After Mel's charter left Dimi found herself craving chocolate. It was all Bo's fault, she decided, as she inhaled a Hershey's bar from Mel's hidden stash. Bo's and . . . damn it, Mel's.

Yeah, that's right. She really wanted to blame Mel for not fixing this the way she'd fixed everything else over the years, even as Dimi hated herself for the thought. It drove her to go for yet another chocolate bar, after which she felt like crap and was filled with self-loathing, a sense of worthlessness, and a fear for the future she couldn't eat away.

"Damn it." She reached for the phone and called Brian, the tall, dark, and hunky guy she'd drooled over at the gym the other night while watching him go through his weight-lifting routine.

He'd worked out shirtless, wearing only shorts, looking amazing at every single station. When he was done, his body taut and quivering and damp with sweat, he'd swiped his face with a towel and locked gazes with her.

She'd felt that familiar thrill, that age-old "gotta have him" lurch deep inside, and she'd smiled.

His eyes had bloomed with heat and a good amount of trouble as he'd smiled back, and her engine had revved.

When she'd gotten to her car after her own workout, he'd left his card on her windshield. Brian Desota, attorney at law.

Yum.

Even better, he answered his phone, he was available, and thirty minutes later, he picked her up at North Beach, looking hot in all black as he drove her to a new restaurant in town.

It started out good, with lots of potential, so it shocked Dimi when he insulted the waiter. He'd also, she remembered, been rude to the valet. And no matter how many drinks Dimi ordered, he still got uglier and uglier.

She sure could pick 'em.

Finally the meal was over and they stood outside his car. She didn't want to get into the passenger seat and let him take her home, despite the fact that it was fifteen miles from North Beach, it was raining cats and dogs, and she was more than a little tipsy. But in truth, she'd rather risk life and limb, and walk every single one of those miles barefoot than spend another moment with him.

"Get in," he said, adding a little nudge to the small of her back.

Another problem: having met her drink for drink, he wasn't feeling any pain, either. Always, that had seemed like a turn-on for Dimi, a man who could drink right alongside her.

But suddenly, it felt old. She wanted to get to know someone and *remember* what they had to say. She wanted to wake up without a headache, wanted to get through the afternoon without yearning for a glass of wine.

She wanted to look in the mirror and not see a woman who looked harder and colder every single day.

"Get in," he said again, raising his voice over a boom of thunder.

No. The word was no, but as everyone in the entire universe knew, she had a little problem saying it. "Actually," she began, and sent him a smile she hoped looked halfway genuine, "I—"

"You're not changing your mind about coming to my house," he said. "Not after that expensive dinner."

Her brows knitted. "I never said I'd go to your house."

"Sweetheart, it was implied." His hand, low on her spine, became firm as he tried to get her inside his car.

"No." She lifted her chin, and with rain coming down into her face, looked into his now cooling eyes. *"No."* She backed out of his grip and stood beneath the restaurant awning next to the valet. "Thank you for dinner, but good night."

His jaw went tight, and suddenly not a single bit of that earlier hunkiness she'd seen in him showed.

What was it with her? Did she have a "looking for an asshole" sign on her forehead?

"I won't call you again," he warned.

She nearly laughed, but it would have come out half-hysterical so she bit it back. "I know. I don't want you to."

Now temper filled his eyes along with the annoyance, and she just sighed as he sped off, screeching out of the parking lot. Yeah, she sure could pick them. She opened her cell again and dialed Mel. It took her two tries, which told her she was either a bit more tipsy than she'd thought, or thoroughly shaken. Maybe some combination of both.

"Anderson Air," came Mel's voice, sounding extremely out of breath, and extremely distracted.

Dimi frowned. "You're on your way back from the Bay?"

"No."

"Okay, good." Dimi reached out and gripped the back of the bench beneath the awning for balance, a little unnerved to find herself weaving. "I need a ride from—"

"I'm still in San Francisco. Grounded by the storm."

"Oh." Dimi looked out into the dark night and felt . . . alone. Extremely, frighteningly alone. "Are you stuck in the airport?"

"Uh, no." Mel hesitated. "I'm getting a room, we're nearly at the hotel now."

"We?" Dimi staggered back a step. "You, and . . . Bo?" She realized she'd only been mildly upset by her date, at least compared to this. "Mel. You can't—"

"Look, tell it to Mother Nature, okay? I'm sorry I can't pick you up. I thought you were on a date."

"*Were* being the operative word."

"Oh, God." Mel's voice softened. "What happened? Are you okay? Was he a jerk? Goddamn this weather—"

"I have a feeling I'm better off than you are." Dimi's throat went thick at all the worry and love in Mel's voice. "Hey, listen, I'm okay. But you . . . you be careful."

"Right back atcha," Mel said.

Dimi nodded even though she knew Mel couldn't see her, and closed her phone. The chilly rain brought goose bumps out on her arms, and she hugged herself.

"Ma'am?" The valet stood in front of her with an umbrella. "Do you need me to call you a cab?"

Cabs were few and far between in the city, where most everyone drove themselves. The thought of waiting around seemed to bring her down even further. "No, thanks." She opened her cell again, accessed her saved numbers and tried Kellan. No answer. She hit the next number, which would be Ritchie, and waited.

"'Lo," came the sleepy voice.

Dimi blinked. "Ritchie?"

"Danny."

She stared at her phone. She'd hit the wrong number. Oh, God. Anyone but him, the one guy she'd rather not have see her this way. Not again. "I'm sorry I woke you."

"Dimi." He sounded wide awake now. "What's the matter?"

Just the sound of his voice tightened her throat. Pathetic. She was pathetic being on the verge of a breakdown tonight. So she'd had a bad date. Again. She should be used to it. She wasn't the type of woman who men treated nicely. "Nothing's the matter. Sorry I woke you." She shut the phone and shoved it in her purse. "Idiot," she told herself, huddled beneath the awning as the storm kicked it up a notch. "You're an idiot—"

Her cell began vibrating. She reached into her purse and looked at it. Danny. Slowly she flipped the cell open.

"Just tell me if you need help," he said without a greeting. "Because I sure as hell can't go back to sleep until I know."

She winced, touched the phone to her forehead and scrunched her eyes tight as regret, pride, and stupidity all played tag with each other in her brain.

"Dimi."

She sighed. Oh, what the hell, he'd asked. "I could use a ride," she admitted.

"Your date went bad."

"Just a little bit, yeah."

To give him credit, he didn't say a word about that. "Where are you?"

She told him. "I could just catch a cab—"

"Don't move." Disconnect.

With a sigh, she sat on the fancy bench in front of the fancy restaurant to wait, and tried not to think. In twelve minutes flat, Danny pulled up with a screech, getting out of his big, beat-up truck and into the rain.

Tonight he wore a pair of jeans loose on his lean hips, flip-flops, and a T-shirt worn thin at all the seams that said BITE ME across the chest and was now getting wetter by the second.

She stared at the words on his shirt, feeling something tighten deep inside her.

He was a fellow rebel.

How had she missed that about him? He looked rumpled, sleepy, and unsmiling as he strode right to her, pulled her up from the bench and peered into her face. "Are you all right?"

"I'm sorry—"

"Are you all right?"

"Yes."

He looked her over as if needing to make sure for himself, then let out a breath. "Okay, then."

How was it that she'd never noticed how cute he was? His blond hair, wet now, fell nearly to his shoulders, with a stubborn strand stabbing him in the eyes. His mouth was grim at the moment but when he smiled, which she knew he did with ease, it was never cruel. Nothing mean ever crossed those lips.

Those lips. She couldn't tear her gaze off them, which she had to attribute to the sheer volume of alcohol she'd consumed, because she didn't care about lips. Why should she when she never kissed? Never wanted to?

But from deep within her she craved *his* lips, his kiss. It made no sense, but clearly, tonight, she wasn't about making sense. Compounding error on error, she leaned in and touched his mouth with hers.

His shock vibrated through her, but she did it again, staring into his eyes as she balanced herself on tiptoe by holding onto his arms and kissed him.

He held himself rigid, unmoving, but beneath her fingers she felt the strength of him, and then she felt him tremble.

Tremble.

More. She had to have more, so she touched her tongue to the corner of his mouth, tasting him. "Mmm," she murmured, and finally, *finally,* shattered his rigid control. With a rough sound, he hauled her up against him and kissed her, ohmigod kissed her, head bent, mouth fused to hers, tongue sweeping inside her mouth to claim hers . . .

This was what she'd needed so badly tonight, and all those other nights. If she'd only known what she was missing . . . But no, that wasn't right. It was because it was Danny that she felt such a delicious oblivion. Clearly he knew what he was doing. She could lose herself, she could feel it, and he'd keep her safe. She wouldn't have to think.

Just feel.

Thank God, she thought, and wrapped herself around him, nearly crying in relief, but then she was blinking in surprise because he'd pulled away, supporting her until she nodded, and then dropping his hands from her as if burned, stepping back, averting his face so that she couldn't see into his eyes.

"Danny?"

He was breathing hard, looking extremely unlike his usual laid-back, easygoing self. "I'm not doing this," he ground out. "Not like this. Not in front of a damn restaurant, with you so drunk you can't stand up straight."

"I'm not drunk."

"Plenty wasted, though."

She staggered back a step and tried to figure out how she'd gone from feeling as if she might explode into orgasm from just a kiss, to wanting to crawl into a hole and die.

Without another word he led her to his truck, waited for her to get in and buckle up, and then came around and got in behind the wheel. The both of them dripping everywhere, he shoved the truck into gear and pulled out into the street.

The night was dark, the highway had no lights. The cab of his truck had a slight glow from the instruments on the dash, but she didn't need to see him to feel the tension. Hers, certainly. And also his. He was mad, furious even, and yet for that one glorious moment when he'd held her close, she knew he'd been aroused. Even the thought sent a shiver of thrill through her. *She'd made him hard.* "Why did you come for me?" she whispered.

An oncoming car slashed light over his tense features as he turned to her. "Because you called."

"But you're mad at me."

"One thing has nothing to do with the other."

Her head was beginning to spin, and with a sound of distress, she put her hand to it.

He swore, then jerked the truck to the side of the road and braked hard.

"I'm not going to get sick in your truck," she said. "I'm not that drunk. A pity, really, because believe me, the night sucked."

"I'm not worried about you getting sick. You know how to hold your alcohol. Which isn't a compliment, by the way." A raindrop slid down his jaw, plopped onto his chest. His shirt was plastered to his torso. "I can be pissed as hell at you, Deem, and still be there when you need me. I wish you'd get that through your thick skull."

She couldn't breathe. She could only draw air into her lungs. "That's a foolish thing to tell me. It gives me the upper hand."

His eyes were dark, and extremely solemn as he shook his head. "Actually, what I was hoping it would give you is a sense of . . . I don't know. Security."

Security. Her greatest fantasy, and because it had continually eluded her, also her greatest fear. That he'd so cavalierly throw it around confused her.

And hurt. "You know what? I gotta go." She fumbled for the door handle, but Danny beat her to it, locking it, waiting until she turned to glare at him.

"Go ahead and be pissed," he said. "That'll make us a fine pair."

"Danny—"

"I'm taking you home," he grated out. "All the way home."

"No." She grappled with the lock, but became both horrified and humiliated to find her hands shaking. *Shaking.* "Oh, God." She set her forehead to the glass. "I'm sorry. So sorry. I shouldn't have let you come for me. Not you."

Gripping her shoulders, he pulled her around to look at him, his usually soft, melting eyes furious. "Why, because I hate knowing you're out there every night, all night? Because I hate knowing that one day a phone call in the middle of the night won't be necessary because *you won't be able to make a phone call?*"

Backing away as far as she could, until the door handle

dug into her back, she crossed her arms over her chest and hugged herself. "I'm sorry. I'm so sorry you had to come out here tonight. I'm sorry I've made you mad." She swallowed, blinked back tears. "I'm sorry I kissed you. I don't know why I did that, I never do that."

He frowned. "What does that mean?"

"I don't like to kiss."

He looked floored. "What?"

"Nothing. I don't want to talk about it." She turned away. "And anyway, this is all your own fault."

"How the hell do you figure that?"

She looked out the window, staring blindly into the night and uttered the truth for once. "Because you've never made a move on me," she whispered.

He pulled back as if she'd slapped him. She felt his gaze boring into her but she had exhausted herself with that last outburst and didn't look at him, instead pressed her hot forehead to the cool glass.

The beat of silence stretched out, and in it she wanted to die. Thankfully, without another word, Danny shoved the truck into gear and steered back onto the highway and drove her home.

Which was good, really, because she didn't want to hear him apologize for not wanting her. She'd had enough humiliation for one night.

When he finally pulled into her driveway, she fumbled with the door, unable to get out quickly enough.

"Dimi—"

"Thank you," she muttered, and ran out of his truck and into her place before he could do anything stupid. Before *she* could do anything stupid.

Like beg him to come in.

The San Francisco Regatta Hotel was big and far fancier than Mel would have picked on her own, but the Huttons had insisted that she and Bo join them—so they all climbed into the Huttons' limo waiting at the airport, and drove to the hotel.

Mel was quite certain the Huttons's credit card hadn't groaned and nearly keeled over on the spot at the front desk from the night's rate. Still muttering about it, she entered her posh, elegant hotel room and stood there feeling a bit like a bull in a china shop. Tossing her duffle bag onto the fancy, silky, perfectly made bed, she took a deep, calming breath.

Which backed up into her throat when she realized two things at once. One, her hotel door hadn't shut behind her. And two, that was because Bo stood in the opened doorway, watching her.

Damn it, she was still a little shaky from the adrenaline rush of the rough flight. She couldn't deal with him now, standing there looking disheveled and sexy.

"That was some flying," he said.

She turned away and told herself that her stomach jangled because she was still shaken. "Yeah, well, that's what you get for getting on a flight you hadn't planned on."

"Can't plan out your whole life, you know."

Maybe not, but she'd tried. Planning meant a lot to her. It gave her a sense of routine, and routine was what had gotten her through some incredibly tough times.

He stepped closer. "Sometimes you've just got to wing it."

Such as having sex with him, she supposed. Wild, erotic, earthy, glorious sex during which she knew she'd come with such ease it still blew her mind.

Not fair that he made her yearn and burn, and not just for another orgasm. He made her yearn and burn to be what she'd always secretly wished that she could be: spontaneous, easygoing, and . . . dare she even think it? . . . sexy.

With a soft laugh, he tugged lightly at her hair. "Earth to Mel."

"I'm here."

He looked at her for a moment. "That was a tough flight, and I meant what I said. You pulled it off with grace."

"Imagine that. Me with grace."

He didn't laugh with her. In fact, his face remained utterly solemn as he lifted his other hand and cupped her face.

Oh, God. "Don't," she said shakily.

"Don't what? Touch you?"

"Right. And don't look at me like that, either. Like you're proud of me, like you care about me."

"Too bad, since both apply."

"No, they don't. Not really." She took a step back. "Look, I'm a difficult woman—"

"Wow, there's a news flash."

"I'm serious."

"Me, too. Now, about that servicing."

Her entire body leapt to attention at that, and she took another step back. Her thighs hit the mattress.

He came forward some more, and her hands came up to his chest. Beneath her fingers she could feel the steady beat of his heart. Hers wasn't nearly as steady, but she told herself that that was lingering adrenaline from the flight. She opened her mouth to say something, she had no idea what, but her cell vibrated in her pocket. The ID was foreign, possibly Mexican, and now her poor overworked heart skipped a beat entirely.

Bo cut his eyes to the cell. "Sally."

She hurriedly flipped it open. "Hello?" Nothing. "Hello? Sally?"

More nothing.

She and Bo stared at each other. "Bad connection," she said slowly, closing the phone with great reluctance. They looked at it for a long moment, both more strained than they'd been on the crazy flight here, but it didn't ring again.

"Call back," Bo said tightly.

She punched in all the numbers, then locked gazes with him while it rang somewhere far away, her heart pounding, pounding . . .

No one answered.

"It could have been a wrong number," she murmured. "Not Sally—"

Bo put a finger over her lips, his eyes hot, dark, and fascinating. "I can take a lot, Mel, and have, but no more lies, not from you."

She'd hurt him. She hadn't meant to, but she had. When he'd first shown up here, she'd been prepared to hate him on principle, had wanted to hate him. But then he'd brought in customers when she couldn't. He'd kept the employees when maybe he shouldn't. He'd given her a lease that set her up for a good long time.

He hadn't sold . . .

At least not yet.

All of which was more than she could say for Sally, who'd vanished on them, no warning, no help, nothing.

In sharp contrast, Bo had been here for her, for all of them, and no anger could hold up to that. "I'm not lying to you," she said, and waited until he met her gaze. "I really don't know where she is, I swear it. I never have."

"What about the money you sent her?"

"Always electronically to her account."

"So who's trying to warn you off digging for more info, Mel?"

She closed her eyes. "I don't know."

"Yes, you do. It's her." He put his hand against her throat, then slid his fingers into her hair, lightly tugging on her ponytail so he could stare deep into her eyes. She did her best to convey her honesty, but knew he had no reason to trust her.

"What else aren't you telling me?" he asked.

"Nothing."

"Bullshit."

She licked her lips, and his gaze dropped to them, his eyes glittering. "Seriously," she said. "You know it all now."

He waited, every muscle tense.

"No more lies, Bo," she whispered. "I promise."

"That's quite a promise."

"I mean it."

He laughed a little harshly, but then he lowered his head so that he was a mere breath away. Their gazes locked, held . . .

And then he kissed her, and all wondering and worrying went out the window along with her good intentions and common sense. He changed the angle of the kiss to suit him, opening his mouth, sliding his tongue to hers in a dance as old as time. "Mel," he breathed, just that, and clamped her head between his big hands, nibbling, licking, sucking, and all around driving her right off the edge of sanity and straight into lustville. She was clinging to him, whimpering, panting, desperate, when he pulled back.

"Say it again," he demanded.

She tried to take a step back, and fell onto the mattress.

Bo stepped between her thighs, leaning over her, staring into her eyes with a single-mindedness that brought her out of her fog, barely. "Say it. Say 'no more lies, Bo.'"

She blinked. Focused past the sensual haze in her brain. "Is that why you kissed me?"

"When I kiss you, you become the real Mel, no holding back, no lies, no façades. Just you. It's like a truth serum."

She stared up at him, hurt sneaking in past her defenses. She'd nearly torn off her clothes and begged him to take her. "That's a horrible thing to do. Get out of my room."

"Gee, you must be done talking."

"I'm done with *you*."

Still leaning over her, a hand on either side of her hips, he shook his head. "Look at that, another lie already."

"What does *that* mean?"

"Come on, you feel the sparks, too."

"Yeah, sparks of temper!"

"Yet another lie," he said very softly.

She let out a frustrated growl.

"Fact is fact, darlin'. Our bodies are happy together."

She shook her head.

"Look at me."

She couldn't help it, her gaze ran over him. His well-worn jeans softly cupped his sex, which was obviously aroused. Her mouth went dry.

Worse, she began to perspire again.

"Now you," he said.

She transferred her attention to her body, specifically her own breasts and her traitorous nipples, which poked through her shirt like two gumballs.

He arched a brow.

She crossed her arms.

"Doesn't help," he said. "Now I'm wondering what other parts of you are reacting."

Her thighs actually quivered, and between them . . . more quivering.

As if he could tell, he smiled.

She was shaking as she pointed to the door, because damn, she really hated when he was right. "Get out."

Instead, he laughed. "You don't really mean that."

She opened her mouth to say she did, but the message didn't make it all the way to her brain, and as he came down over her, arms closing possessively around her, she didn't say a word. Instead she moaned his name and met his mouth with hers.

Chapter 21

There was kissing, and then there was *kissing*, and with Bo it was an art form.

Mel had had lovers, a few who even knew what they were doing, but none had ever made her knees quiver with just a touch of their mouth. None had ever made her feel as if his kiss was more important in that moment than breathing.

None had ever made her feel soft and beautiful and feminine.

With Bo, she could hold on and feel her world slide away, feel despair and stress and churning grief over Sally and her deception vanish behind the maelstrom of need and desire and hunger for more of this man's touch. She felt—crazy as it seemed—calmer. So when his tongue teased hers, she teased back. When he reached for her shirt, she did the same with his, coaxing a rough sound of pleasure from his throat, one she helplessly mirrored back to him.

"Love that sound," he murmured, pulling her closer, kissing her as if he meant to inhale her, pressing himself against her as if he needed to be inside her now, now, now . . . making an unbearably sexy noise when his thumb rubbed over a pebbled nipple and it tightened even further.

She'd had no idea how badly she'd wanted this, but she needed to remember one pesky little fact: he'd kissed her simply to get information. That made this a very bad idea. "Wait," she gasped.

"Wait?" His gaze was sleepy-lidded and incredibly sexy. His hair was messed up from her fingers, his mouth wet from hers, his eyes hot.

"We're not taking this any further," she said.

He looked at her for a long moment, as if the words were having trouble sinking in. "You want me to go."

No. "Yes."

He nodded agreeably. "Then I will. Soon as you look into my eyes and tell me you don't want me."

She opened her mouth, ready to tell him anything so she could be alone but nothing came out. "I don't . . ." The words were *I don't want you.*

"Yes?" he asked patiently.

The words sat on the tip of her tongue, a big fat lie, stuck, unwilling to come out. "Damn it!"

With a triumphant laugh, he pressed his face into the tumble of her hair. His voice sounded thick with satisfaction. "All you have to do is say it. Say you don't want me and I'm out of here."

She had to close her eyes against that strong, masculine voice.

"Let's try something easier," he suggested with far too much amusement in his voice. "Say you *do* want me."

"Never."

"Ah, darlin'. Have I taught you nothing? Never say never."

"I don't—" She sucked in a breath when he nipped at her jaw, then her throat as he skimmed his hands down her back. *"Bo—"*

He flicked open her bra and moaned when her breasts spilled into his hand. "Mmm . . . nice."

"We're *not*—" She broke off again when he bent and sucked a breast into his mouth, encircling her nipple with his tongue. "Not. Doing. This—"

Surging up, he popped open the button on his pants.

Oh, God. If he shoved those off, she was a goner. It was bad enough when he had his shirt off because he had the best belly known to man, the kind of belly she wanted to kiss. *Bite*. Frantic, she rolled to her stomach to crawl away.

A big hand clasped her ankle. "You haven't said it." He slowly but inexorably tugged her back, then flipped her over. Holding her down, he smiled with pure wickedness.

"I'm not saying anything!"

"Suit yourself." He pinned her to the mattress, overpowering her, which she allowed, especially when he set his forearms alongside her face so that his fingers could stroke back her hair. The tender gesture startled her. He was heavy but not uncomfortable. The opposite, actually, and even as she wanted to deny it, her body was doing a slow burn for him, and of their own accord, her legs bent, pulling back to let him cradle between. With a rough groan, he rocked his hips to hers. "Mel."

She whispered his name, too, or at least she meant to but it came out a sort of strangled plea for *more, please more* as she strained to fit snugger against him. She told herself this was ridiculous, that they were adults and could stop this at any time, and should. Instead, she wound her arms around his neck and clung.

"Mmm," he murmured, and gently closed his teeth over her bottom lip, tugging just a little, creating a slight sting he stroked away with his tongue. "Still not saying it . . ."

Her skin had heated as if she had a fever, but she didn't feel sick, she felt exhilarated. It was him, he gave that feeling to her with every taste, every touch, banishing away her worries, the mountains of stress on her shoulders. Banishing it and giving her something else instead, something she absolutely did not want to face. "I'm too stubborn to give in," she admitted softly.

"Just one of the things I'm learning to appreciate about you, darlin'. Though I might have said bull-headed instead of stubborn."

Arching up, enjoying his sharp hiss of arousal, she said, "Shut up and do me."

"Oh, absolutely." His low laugh warmed her further, and so did how he kissed his way along her jaw to her ear. "But let the record show you asked."

"Told."

"Begged."

Before she could sputter and shove him away, he captured her mouth with his in a deep, wet, carnal kiss that left no doubt as to his plans, plans he furthered along by stripping away her pants while still holding her pinned to the mattress.

"Not fair," she gasped. *"Your* pants—"

"If I take my hands off you, are you going to play nice?"

"Of course."

He narrowed his eyes, but an aroused man didn't have much in the way of working brain cells, and Bo was little exception. He pulled his weight off her and sat back on his heels as he unzipped his pants, the muscles in his rock-solid chest rippling, leaving her with a shocking need to put her mouth on him. Anywhere. Everywhere.

He eyed her as he slowly pulled a string of condoms from his pocket, dropping them to the mattress by her head as he kicked off his shoes, then came up to his knees to shove his pants to his thighs.

That actually sidetracked her for a beat, as her gaze traveled south and locked on her target. She didn't realize that she licked her lips in anticipation until a choked out "oh, man" escaped him.

When he sat to kick the pants off his legs, she made her move, pouncing, tackling him midchest and taking him down to the bed, making sure to grab the condoms before they hit the floor.

Now he lay beneath her, his pants still at his thighs as she

straddled his hips, gliding her hands along his arms, holding
him down at the biceps, which flexed once, then went still.

"Is this your way of playing nice?" he murmured, lying
still like a panther; poised, patient, just waiting to make his
move.

"Believe me," she said, "what comes next is going to be
nice. Very nice."

"Please be gentle," he quipped, but lay there, surprisingly
pliant.

Ha! As if he'd ever been pliant a day in his life. "Did you
worry about gentle the last time?" she asked. "When you
shoved me against my own front door and had your merry
way with me?"

"Hey, I'm the one with rug burns on my ass."

The memory of him sprawled out on her floor while she
ran her mouth over that edible body tightened hers. "Complaining?"

"Not likely."

Never underestimating him, she remained crouched over
the top of him, the both of them well aware that he could
have easily reversed their positions if he wanted.

"What are you going to do with me?" he asked.

In answer, she tore off a condom.

"Good start," he said sounding a little pressed for air.

With a smile, she went to work protecting them both,
stroking the condom down his silky hard length, probably
taking far longer than necessary but she found she got a vic-
arious thrill out of the sounds he made when she stroked him.
By the time she finished, Bo was sweating and she was shaking. "They should make those things bigger," she said, and he
let out a laughing moan. She bent over him again, pressing
her lips to his jaw, then his throat, overcome by a sudden
need to be gentle.

He gripped her hips, his laughter also gone. "Mel?"

"Yeah?"

"You're killing me."

"Oh! Sorry!" She tried to lift her weight off him but he
held her still.

"No, not too heavy. I meant because I'm going to explode
and you haven't done anything to me yet."

She eyed his penis, which twitched. "Ah. Well . . ."

"What?"

"I hate to ask . . ."

"Ask," he said, looking a little desperate.

She stroked a finger over him, loving how that made his
back arch up a bit, his hips push almost helplessly toward
her. "I was thinking . . ."

"Seriously," he grated out. *"Anything,* Mel."

Power surged through her at that. "Maybe you could beg
me for a change."

His eyes locked onto hers. His fingers tightened on her
hips, and the air charged, crackled, and popped around them.
She'd bet her Hawker that he'd never begged for a single
thing in his entire life. Never had to.

He slid one hand from her hip to low on her back, nudging her forward just a tad. Now the very tip of his erection
teased her right where she wanted him the most. It tore a
sound from deep in her throat, a sound that came awful close
to begging so she clamped her lips shut, her hands flat on his
pecs, her head bowed, air panting in and out of her mouth as
if she'd just raced a marathon in the snow, uphill both ways.
"Beg me, damn it."

His lips quirked, though she could feel him tremble as he
cupped a breast. "I'm getting to it."

"Clearly," she managed, biting her lips to keep a gasp in
when he used his long fingers to tease her nipple, "you are
not desperate enough, a state you put me in quite effortlessly."

He shot her a cocky grin. "Is that right?"

Damn it. "Oh, that's *so* it. *Prepare for desperation.*" Reaching down, she wrapped her fingers around his hot, velvety
length and stroked him against her, for her own pleasure.

His fingers tightened on her hips. A rough groan tumbled from him.

Hmmm. Now they were getting somewhere. She stroked him over her again until he glistened with her own excitement, and then again right . . . where . . . she . . . needed . . . him . . . the . . . most—

"Christ," he said thickly. "Look how beautiful you are."

She skimmed her free hand up over her own belly, her ribs, then her breast.

"Oh, God." His eyes darkened. Went opaque. "Definitely feeling desperate here, Mel."

"If you were desperate," she panted, desperate herself, thank you very much, "you wouldn't be able to talk." Again she stroked him over her, but that turned out to be a two-edged sword because her own body was reacting, heating, tightening. Begging. Because she had to, she allowed the very tip of him to slip inside her, stretching her sensitized flesh, stretching and filling—

"More." Breathing hard, he arched up. *"More."*

She was dying for more, but she shook her head. "Not yet."

With a groan, he pushed his hips up, his hands trying to urge her closer, to let all of him in. His abs were tight, his nipples tight, his skin hot and damp, his eyes all but flaming as they held hers, letting her see everything he felt, which was possibly the sexiest, most arousing thing she'd ever experienced.

And just like that, with his fingers on her breast and only the tip of him inside her, she began to lose it.

"Oh, yeah," he murmured, and grazed his thumb over her clit.

That was it, all she needed, and she was gone, completely gone, in a spectacular orgasm that left her deaf, blind, and mute. *"God,"* she finally breathed as she sank down over his chest like warm putty. "What *is* that?"

"I don't know, but stick around, there's more."

Stick around . . . The thought might have made her sad

because he *wasn't* going to stick around, but then he thrust up into her, filling her to bursting.

His hands gripped her hips, set her rhythm as she rode him, and when she heard him call out her name in a hungry, heated voice, it—unbelievably—sent her skittering over the edge again.

He joined her that time, and as she fell, she thought . . . It's so easy with him. So damned easy, it terrified her.

"Hungry?" The word came out rather smothered, as she lay sprawled face down and sideways on the bed.

Bo trailed a long, work-roughened finger down her spine, continuing farther, dipping with wicked intent where other treasures lay, making her gasp.

"Oh, yeah," he answered. "I'm hungry." Flipping her over, he put his hands on her inner thighs and gently pushed them open, then groaned at the sights before him.

"Bo—"

"Shh, darlin'. Don't interrupt a man when he's eating." And he bent his head to the task.

Far later, the water sloshed out of the lush hotel tub, hitting the fancy tiles with a splash, dousing the candles they'd lit, prompting Mel to say, *"Bo,"* in that voice he loved, all low and throaty, and sexy as hell.

"Careful." She laughed breathlessly from her perch astride his legs. "We'll cause a flood."

He skimmed his hands up her gloriously wet, taut curves to cup her breasts, loving how her breath caught at his touch. "A little water never hurt anything. Christ, you have a body."

"Right back atcha." She looked him over and made him hard. Or harder, since he'd been in this state for two weeks now.

She lifted the soap. "Remember. No funny business. We're just getting soaped—" Her eyes glazed over when his thumbs rasped over her nipples. *"Bo."*

"Right. Have at me then. Soap me up." Because he couldn't help it, he made one more pass of his thumb . . .

She dropped the soap.

Between his legs.

"Whoops." He grinned. "Someone's going to have to get that."

She laughed, a sound he was beginning to love, and he laughed, too, which backed up in his throat when her hand dove into the water after the soap . . .

Mel woke up alone; naked and sore in spots she'd forgotten she owned. She staggered into the bathroom and eyeballed the empty condom packet on the floor.

And the second on the counter.

A third had actually made it to the trash.

Her body let out a traitorous little shiver of remembered delight. She loved the way he touched her, looked at her. The way he drew her hands to his chest, moaning his encouragement when they lowered. The way he reared back, driving her higher and higher still, face and body tight. Loved that it had been her name on his lips when he'd come.

God. What was she doing, thinking of him this way, romantically, softly, with a dreamy smile on her face? She knew that was a one-way street to Hurtville.

He'd left her a note.

Mel,
  Wanted you to catch a few extra winks if you could. I'm going to the airport to fuel you up and run the preflight check.

                                   —Bo

Hmmm. So he hadn't gone running from morning-after fear. She took a shower and catalogued her wounds. Whisker burns on a breast and between her thighs. Hickey on her throat. Swollen lips. Bite mark on her ass, which she'd had to twist around to even see.

She hoped like hell Bo had some marks on him, too, then took that back. No! No marks! No proof of the digression! This little interlude was over. Back to the real world for them, she thought, looking around at the empty hotel room. Apparently starting right now.

Chapter 22

In the lobby of the hotel, the Huttons were waiting for Mel. Bo had already caught his own cab to the airport.

Good. That meant she didn't have to see him quite yet.

But that ended all too soon on the tarmac. He boarded the passengers while she went through the preflight check. When she was finished, he stood there, those deep, unwavering jade eyes fixed on her.

"What?" she asked, a little defensively, unconsciously straightening her shoulders as she prepared for battle.

He only shook his head, moved toe to toe with her, cupped her face, fingers gliding into her hair, and then kissed her.

Not a hello peck, either, but a long, melting one that had her staggering back. "Man." She couldn't recover. *"Man."*

He simply smiled and boarded, and for the entire flight— blissfully uneventful—she felt incredibly aware of him sitting next to her. Everything he did seemed to spark a reaction within her, whether it was sliding on the headphones over his come-as-it-is hair, or covering his eyes with those mirrored sunglasses, stretching out his long legs, talking to air control with that low, effortlessly sexy voice, dealing with her passengers with far more patience than she ever could have managed . . .

They were nearly back to Santa Barbara when the conversation turned to the hotel. The Huttons went on and on about the incredible service, then asked about Mel's room.

Bo glanced at her. "Yes, did you sleep well?" he asked.

In fact, she'd hardly slept at all, as he very well knew. "Yes."

"Did you enjoy the service?" he pressed.

It was all she could do to maintain her composure. "The service was . . ."

Bo raised a brow, lips quirking. He thought he was so funny. Well, she was funnier.

"It was okay," she finally said with a shrug.

The Huttons expressed their surprise, then after a few minutes of small talk, busied themselves with their laptops, leaving Mel and Bo to their own.

"Only okay?" Bo murmured.

Mel stuck her tongue out at him. Immature, but there it was.

He only laughed softly. "I have a better job for that tongue," he said.

"I bet."

"Watch your altitude."

"Altitude? Or attitude?"

He laughed. "Both."

She glanced down at the instruments and sighed. "Are you always right?"

He met her gaze again, and suddenly he wasn't playing. "Usually."

Her smile faded. Yeah. He'd been right about a lot of things. Sally, for instance. After meeting his gaze for a long beat, she looked out at the horizon. No visible storm, but that didn't mean the one brewing inside her heart wasn't going to be a Category 5. "If the money in those accounts you found was your father's, then where is it now?" she asked quietly.

"Maybe she bought an island and is drinking her lazy days away."

Mel shook her head. "Then why ask Dimi and me to send her cash over the years, leaving us so strapped all the time?"

He didn't answer. The implication being, of course, because Sally could.

Mel absorbed that for a time, flying in silence.

He let her, and if she hadn't been in such a bad place inside her head, she might have admitted that she liked that about him. No rushing, no forcing of his opinions. "I'm going to get a private investigator."

"How about *we*? *We* get a PI. We start with Mexico, and that last call you received."

She paused. "I think I should do this alone," she said carefully. "And talk to her first."

His eyes went dark, inscrutable. "You want to warn her away from me."

"I want to make sure she's okay, and that she wasn't a victim."

"And . . ."

"And nothing," she said. "That's all."

Jaw tight, he shook his head but didn't say another word. The truce, if there'd ever really been one, was over. Tentative trust shaken if not gone completely.

The next day, in between charter flights, a broken tow, fuel deliveries, and filing a police report for the e-mails and notes, Mel pulled out the local phone book and picked a private investigator.

Matt Thomas promised to investigate Sally's whereabouts, which should have made her feel good but instead left her feeling like she'd betrayed her own mother.

The next two days moved like a blur. Bo took a flight to

test-fly an old Douglas he was looking at in Los Angeles. Mel stopped what she was doing to watch him take off, wondering when things would ever get back to normal.

Or if he'd ever want her again . . .

One afternoon, Char fed her, standing in her small kitchen fanning air with her shirt as she grumbled about the heat.

"It's not that hot," Mel said.

"Well, you're not facing early menopause, are you?" Char lifted her top. "Look at me."

"Um . . ." Mel couldn't help but take in Char's slightly curved belly and full breasts straining to escape a black cotton bra. Her skin was flushed beet red and dewy. "Maybe you could open the window—"

"It doesn't matter. I could take the roof off, I'd still be too hot."

"Charlene, Jesus." Al came around the corner and blocked the view of his wife's breasts and belly. "What are you doing?"

"Didn't you hear me? I'm hot! Hot, hot, hot—"

"You're flashing the customers!" He craned his neck to the tables, found them empty, and lost some of his bristle. "Okay, fine, there are no customers."

"Hey," Mel said. "I'm right here."

"You don't count." Char smiled up at Al. "You don't want to share my breasts."

"Nope. All mine," Al murmured, and pulled her against him.

Mel rolled her eyes and hightailed it out of the den of love. The *hot* den of love.

She stayed late that night, working on the Hawker. When she was done, she hopped into the shower in her office bathroom, closing her eyes in bliss, letting out a long breath as the tension finally began to drain from her body.

"That sounded like a loaded sigh."

With a startled squeak, she blinked one Bo Black into focus.

One soon-to-be-*dead* Bo Black.

The walls of the shower were glass, clear glass. He could see everything of her. *"What are you doing?"*

"Same as you." Eyes on hers, he kicked off his shoes.

"Oh, no." Even though she still had shampoo in her hair, she slammed off the water. "Go away!"

He pulled off his shirt, and her gaze dropped to his shoulders and chest, gilded from the sun, the sleek flesh delineated with long, sinewy lines of muscle.

An undeniable surge of anticipation coursed through her.

He reached for the waistband of his jeans.

"Don't you dare!" she said.

"Now what have I told you about daring me?"

"We just had sex a few days ago." She eyed his unmistakable hard-on. "You're still mad at me. You can't want it again."

"I've got a part of me that says otherwise."

"Well, you're not supposed to think with that part."

"It's how us men are made, darlin'. Ridiculously easy." Pop, pop, pop went the buttons on his Levi's.

Boom, boom, boom went Mel's heart. *"Stop."*

To his credit, he did. Thumbs hooked in his opened jeans, he lifted his head, a specimen so magnificent he took her breath. Her body quivered for more. *Just looking,* she told herself. *That's all, just looking.* "Fine," she relented, already breathless at the thought of his nude body. "Go ahead and get naked, then. That'll make us even."

"Even is good."

"But we're not doing anything." She tore her gaze off his body and looked into his eyes, which were lit with humor and heat. *Gulp.* Lots of heat. "I mean it, Bo."

"Remember the other night?" he asked.

Remember? She could do little else!

"Yeah, you remember," he said. "You know it was off-the-charts amazing. *You're* off-the-charts amazing."

"Are you trying to butter me up?"

At that, his eyes positively smoldered. "Do you have butter?"

"Oh, my God, you are so male!"

"I'd think you'd be grateful for that." His smile was slow and wicked and did things to her belly, not to mention her nipples and between her thighs.

"Oh, this is ridiculous."

He merely turned away to make sure the door was shut.

Um, yikes. "Bo . . . We don't even trust each other, so—"

"I want to trust you. Can you say the same?"

She absorbed those words as he slid the bolt home, the click echoing in the bathroom. "I'm naked here," she said. "Which surely displays a certain level of trust."

"I'm looking for more than that."

More? What more?

"Finish your shower," he said, leaning against the door. "You need the relaxing."

"I'd loosen up if you'd get the hell out of my bathroom."

"You asked so nicely, but no. Sorry. Careful, you're going to get that shampoo in your eyes. And don't use all that hot water."

"You're ever so romantic, you know that?"

He grinned. "I'm not trying to romance you, Mel. Trust me, if I was, you'd already be panting my name."

"Ha ha." The shampoo was beginning to burn her eyes. "Stay right there."

He lifted his hands innocently. "Staying."

Incredibly aware of his gaze on her, she ducked her head back beneath the spray to rinse off the shampoo. Everywhere the suds slid down her body felt like a caress; over her shoulders, her breasts, her belly, her thighs . . .

Then the shower door opened, and she squeaked, opening her eyes. "You cheated!"

That devastatingly slow, sure smile stretched across his mouth as the water sprayed him. "I'm an Aussie. We don't cheat. We just take advantage of any given situation." Gaze still holding hers, he shoved down his jeans.

Oh, my. Oh, my my. He was aroused. Extremely aroused. *Hugely,* extremely aroused. She tried not to look, honestly, she tried, but her eyeballs appeared to have a mind of their own, and took themselves on a happy tour.

As she already knew, Bo Black really had it going on.

He stepped into the shower with her, not cockily, but completely unselfconsciously, easily showing her everything he had as if it was the most natural thing in the world to do so.

He'd always done that, from the very beginning, shown her everything.

For a moment that truth hit her so hard she couldn't even breathe.

His smile faded. "Mel?"

"I'm okay."

"Yeah, you are. Let me in," he urged softly, stepping close. "I'm getting cold. Certain things aren't pretty when they get cold, Mel."

"Bo—"

"Look, there might be trust issues between us. Truth issues, too. But one thing we don't have is a chemistry issue."

She stared at him, then scooted back, giving him room beneath the water with her.

He took it, and more, pulling her wet, naked body to his.

The next morning Mel was on hold with Matt when Bo stuck his head in her office.

"That number in Mexico," Bo said. "It's to a place called *El Pelicano Blanco.* The White Pelican."

"The number is to *El Pelicano Blanco,*" Matt said, back on the line.

Mel stared at Bo.

"And," Matt continued in her ear, "one interesting thing. That return address stamp on that letter you got via USPS!"

"Mexican?" she asked weakly. "From the same zone as the White Pelican?"

"Yep."

Mel hung up and looked at Bo. It didn't escape her that he was still sharing all his info, when she wasn't quite sure if she'd have shared hers.

"Get your passport," he said.

"I don't suppose there's any point in telling you I'm doing this by myself."

"No point," he agreed. "We'll take the Gulfstream."

They left immediately, going through Los Angeles for customs, and then landing in Hermosillo. Mel had grabbed a picture of Sally along with a small overnight duffle bag, which she really hoped she wouldn't need because that would mean another night with Bo.

Probably a naked night. Sweaty, too, with what would undoubtedly be myriad orgasms, all in a delicious, delirious blur.

Her body tightened in anticipation at his knowledge of her body and all he could do to it, and how easily he could do it, but she knew another morning after would kill her.

She wasn't so good at this casual-sex thing. It lingered in her mind, messed with her heart and soul, affecting her job, her everything.

How was it going to feel when he finally left?

Plus, they had a mission here. Find Sally once and for all. Figure out what the hell was going on so that Bo could get on with his life and Mel with hers.

The thought brought a pang to her heart but in the long run, it was for the best. She wasn't a happily-ever-after sort of woman. She'd never dreamed of a white wedding dress and kids all around her. All she had dreamed of was flying, and she had that.

There was no need for more, she reminded herself as they deboarded and headed through the small airport and toward an old, beat-up rental car. The sun was bright and bloody hot above, but Bo stopped Mel next to the car. They had a map, they knew where they were headed, so she looked at him impatiently.

"You okay?" he asked.

She stared up into his face, his lean jaw, his unsmiling mouth, at those green eyes that had seen so much. There was genuine concern there, and for a moment she let herself think . . . Maybe they could make something of this . . . "If we find her here, what's going to happen to her?"

"I want her to stop threatening you."

"And . . . ?"

"And I want answers on what happened all those years ago."

"And . . . ?"

"And . . ." He shrugged. "And then I'll accept it and move on."

To Australia. He didn't say it, he didn't have to. His home country was an innate part of the man.

"Australia isn't that far away, you know," he said quietly.

She laughed. "Are you kidding? It's on the other side of the world."

"We could—"

"No," she said flatly.

"You don't even know what I was going to say."

"That you'll e-mail? Call? Fly to come see me a couple times a year? Not going to work for me."

He looked as if maybe he was going to press her about it, but she brushed past him and headed for the driver's seat.

He grabbed her by the back of the shirt. "I'm driving."

"Why?" she asked. "Because you have the dick?"

"And the balls, mate. Let's not forget the balls."

"You got to fly all the way here."

She had him there, and she got behind the wheel. He was both a good sport and a good navigator so he got them to the *El Pelicano Blanco* in no time.

At night the building might have passed for a bar but by day it was nothing more than a dive. A few dead trees spotted the lot. The windows had no glass, just boards. The front door was open wide, and from within came the strong smell of alcohol and cigarettes.

To the left of the front door was a public telephone booth, no bench or phone book, just a beat-up-looking telephone.

Mel and Bo looked at each other. Had Sally called from right there?

A woman swept the dusty floors inside, a chicken at her heels following her like a dog. She looked up when Bo and Mel stepped inside and shook her head. *"No servicio."*

"Do you speak English?" Bo asked.

"No."

Mel began to flip through the English-to-Spanish book she'd bought at the airport, muttering, "How do you ask if she knows Sally?"

Bo rattled off something in Spanish, and Mel stared at him. "You speak Spanish?"

"Enough to get by."

"Enough to get by," she repeated to herself. "You might have mentioned."

Bo said something else to the woman, sounding quite fluent.

"Ah, sí," she said, and followed with more quick-paced dialogue.

"You catching any of this?" Mel asked Bo out of the corner of her mouth.

"Shh."

Damn it, she hated when he shushed her, but he was listening intently, clearly having to concentrate, so she decided not to kill him. At least not right then.

Bo said something with Sally's name in it, then turned to Mel. "Show her the picture."

Mel pulled out a photo she'd brought of Sally standing in front of the sign of North Beach, smiling.

The woman's eyes locked on Sally, and hardened. "Rosario," she said. "Rosario Lopez."

Bo's gaze met Mel's for one beat before turning back to the woman. "You know her?"

The woman's eyes were flashing good now. "Rosario, *sí.*" She turned her head and spit on the ground.

"I take it they're not old friends," Mel murmured.

The woman pointed to both of them, then to her eye, then back at them, saying without words that she was watching them, then left the room.

"That's probably not good," Mel said. "I think she just put a curse on us."

"Or something." Bo took her arm and pulled her toward the front door, but before they got there, the woman was back with a man, a big man who was growling, fierce-looking, and . . .

Gulp.

Carrying a gun.

"Fuck," Bo said softly, then tried to shove Mel out the front door ahead of him, stopping short at the very audible click of a gun cocking.

Together they slowly turned back.

The man jerked the gun toward them and spit out something in rapid-fire Spanish.

Bo raised his hands. "Raise 'em slowly," he said softly to Mel while the man raved on and on in Spanish, eyes bulging, practically foaming at the mouth. "Let's not piss him off any more than we already have."

Mel's heart was in her throat, pounding so hard she was

shocked she could still hear anyone speak at all as the man railed on and on in loud, staccato Spanish.

The woman barely came up to his shoulder. She was trying to get his attention by tugging on his sleeve, but he was still yelling, gesturing with the gun pointed right at Bo and Mel, having gone berserk.

The woman stomped her foot but that didn't get the man's attention, either. Finally she poked him in the highest place she could reach well.

His belly.

With a roar, he turned to her.

"Let them speak," she said in perfect but heavily accented English.

"Hey," Mel said. "You said you couldn't speak English."

"Ixnay on the arguingkay," Bo murmured as the woman and the man had turned on each other now, furious, yelling at each other in Spanish.

"She doesn't want him to kill us," Bo said quietly, translating. "I think she's my new best friend."

The woman actually reached in and snagged the gun, turning it around, pointing it at the man, jabbing him with the loaded thing still cocked, trying to get him to go back to the kitchen.

The man balked and she jabbed him again, right in the ass.

He started moving, but not before glaring at Bo and Mel. If looks could kill, they'd be six feet under, but finally, he vanished into the kitchen.

Or the rock under which he'd come from.

Mel let out a sigh of relief, until the woman once again leveled the gun at them. "What do you want?" she demanded in her accented English. "Why do you come here looking for that woman?"

"She gave you trouble?" Bo asked.

"Trouble? *Trouble?* She destroyed my brother!" She lifted her chin and the gun. "And if you are her people, I will destroy you back."

"How did she hurt your brother?" Mel asked, but Bo lowered the arm closest to Mel, setting it across her middle, trying to push her behind him.

"We're not Rosario's people," he assured the woman.

"Bo—"

"You," the woman said to Mel with a fierce scowl and a jab of the pistol. "Be quiet. Keep talking," she said to Bo.

"She stole from my father. Then vanished. Now some threats are being made, and we want to find her."

"She's not here, I ran her out."

"How long ago?"

"A few days."

"Do you know where she went?" Mel asked from behind Bo, frustrated when he wouldn't let her out from there.

"If I knew," the woman said chillingly, "she would no longer be breathing."

Mel swallowed hard.

"Can you tell us what happened?" Bo asked.

"She came here crying *poor American woman, lost in Mexico*. She told us she'd been taken by a man who'd fooled her into giving him her property, everything. She was so devastated, so sad. And willing to work hard. So we let her stay, we even gave her work at our airstrip running the radio."

Mel gaped, then stared at Bo, who looked at her, eyes and mouth grim.

"My brother fell for her," the woman continued. "She claimed to fall for him, too. Lies, all lies. But we did not know that then. She got him to marry her, then broke his heart."

"How?" Mel whispered.

"By stealing his money, and the deeds to his properties."

"How long ago was this?"

"Last year. After she left, she sold the properties, and now we're little more than laborers in our own place."

Mel had been sweating but now she went cold. "A year ago?"

"*Sí.* We hadn't seen her in all that time but she came back just last week, where she tried to buy my silence. With my brother's own money!"

From the kitchen came the sound of breaking glass, as if someone had just tossed down a dish in anger.

The woman's eyes hardened. "I should have killed her. Instead, I hit her with my broom, batted her right out of here. I won't be so kind next time."

"Are you sure she stole—"

The woman aimed the gun between Mel's eyes, then squeezed the trigger, at the last minute lifting her hand so that the bullet bounced off the ceiling and toward the floor, lodging into one of the tables.

Mel began to sweat.

"I am sure," she said.

Bo shoved Mel behind him again, keeping his eyes right on the woman. "I'm sorry," he said evenly. "Terribly sorry that you got hurt, too. But we want to find her. We want to stop her from doing this again to anyone else."

The woman nodded. Mel simply reeled. Sally had been here. She'd done these terrible things, eerily close to what Bo said she'd done to Eddie. It was all true, and suddenly so overwhelming she could hardly stand it. She didn't realize she'd staggered a step backward until Bo's hand came up to grip her arm, giving her his strength.

Sally had stolen from this woman, from her brother.

From Eddie.

Deep down Mel had already begun to know this, to understand, but it didn't make it any easier to take.

"She is evil," the woman hissed.

"I'm very sorry for your loss," Bo said quietly. "But we want to help."

Mel stared into Bo's eyes, and knew he meant it. There would be no mercy for Sally if they caught her. And if she was guilty, she deserved none.

God, Sally, what have you done?

Bo pulled out a business card from his pocket, handed it to the woman. "If you see her again, call me. Collect."

The woman looked down at the card. "I want my brother's money back."

"If I find her, and there's still money, you'll get it back," he promised.

The woman studied him for a long moment, then, much to Mel's relief, lowered the gun and nodded. "Go, then."

They didn't have to be told twice. Outside, the harsh sun had Mel blinking but Bo grabbed her hand and pulled her quickly to the car. He shoved her into the passenger side and she decided not to argue that he got to drive because truthfully, she didn't think she could keep them on the road while shaking like a little poodle.

"Delayed shock," he murmured, and pulled her seatbelt across her shoulder for her. "You'll be okay."

"I know." The sun streamed in the windows, baking them. Mel swiped the sweat on her forehead with her arm, not breathing until they were out of sight of the bar.

"Mel."

Feeling a bit numb, she stared out the window, realizing several minutes had gone by, and that Bo had pulled off the road a bit, and they sat on some deserted stretch of highway.

A million miles from absolutely nowhere.

"She's probably using a different alias now," she said in a voice that seemed to come from far away. "If we can get that name, maybe we can catch up with her."

"Mel—"

"I'm sure the police would be interested—" Shit. Her voice broke just a little, and she forced herself to draw a deep breath, which caught on the emotion balled in her throat.

"Mel, goddamnit, look at me."

When she didn't, he reached across the gearshift and console to grab her shoulders and physically turn her toward him. "Do you think I can't see what this is doing to you?" he asked grimly.

"And do you think I don't know that it doesn't matter to you what it's doing to me?"

"Fuck!" He gave her a little shake. "I'm that unfeeling, am I? Really? I'm that much of a bastard?"

"That's rat fink bastard," she whispered, and felt her eyes fill.

"Mel." He sat back, looking horrified. "Don't you even think about crying."

"I'm not." She waved a hand in front of her face, trying to cool it. "I'm really not." But she was. She sniffed. "I'm really not."

"God. *Christ*. I don't want you to cry."

"Then you're not going to like what's coming next." And she burst into tears.

"Shit." But he pulled her into his lap, no small feat in the car that hadn't just seen better years but better decades. *"Shit."*

"I know!" she sobbed.

"Ah, Mel." He held her close, stroked his hand up and down her back. "I'm so sorry, darlin'. So damned sorry. I know you wanted to find her."

All she could do was cry harder at that, and he simply held her. "You feel like you lost her, I get that." He pressed his face against her hair. "If it helps, I know what it's like to lose someone, someone you think you can't live without. Someone you think you need more than air."

She clung to him. "Your dad?"

"Yeah. It's going to hurt like hell for a long time, Mel, and that's okay. It means you're alive. It means you're okay. It means you can learn to live with it, and go on."

She kept her face to his throat, thinking he was truly a miracle in her life. And God, he smelled good. He smelled like soap, like warm man, like . . . like every secret hope and dream she'd ever had. To make herself feel better about *those* scary thoughts, she wiped her nose on his shirt.

He narrowed his eyes. "Did you just wipe your nose on me?"

She let out one last sniffle. "No."

"Yes, you did."

"Okay, a little. I'm okay now."

"Mel."

"I am." She started to climb out of his lap but he held her, his gaze meeting hers.

"Truth," he said.

"Maybe not so okay. We were nearly shot. Nearly *killed!*"

"Nearly doesn't count except in horseshoes and hand grenades," he said, and stroked a big hand up her back.

"It's a new experience for me."

"I just feel . . ." *So much.* "Jarringly, exceedingly . . . disconnected to my body, like I have a surplus of . . . adrenaline, or something," she tried to explain.

"I know."

She felt like she was going to jump out of her skin if she didn't do something. "I have to get rid of some of this energy, Bo."

His gaze dropped to her mouth. Heated. "Keep talking."

"Really? Because I'd really rather do this." And she kissed him.

One rough sound escaped him, then he was in. In her mouth, in her clothes, and with some swearing and desperate rustling, inside her body.

"Good Christ," he breathed, the both of them going still after that first hard, quick plunge.

The feel of him, hard and throbbing inside her, simply couldn't be put into words. Her shirt was opened, bra shoved down, one boot in the backseat, jeans around one ankle. She had her head back, eyes closed, absorbing the barrage of sensations. His flesh was stretching her, his fingers gripping her hips, his mouth pressed to the side of one breast.

And she thought, *I could stay like this forever.* "Bo."

Opening his mouth on her nipple, he breathed her name,

loosening his grip on her hips so that she could move, so that she could take them both where she needed to go, where the only thing she could do was feel this, him, and nothing else.

Chapter 23

The ride back to the airport was silent. Well, not completely silent. Bo and Mel were sweating like crazy in the insane heat, and with no air conditioner, their breathing sounded ragged and rough.

He could still hear the slightest catch in Mel's, the kind of catch that came from great sex and an explosive orgasm. The way they devoured each other every single time, without a lessening of the painful want, confused and baffled him. And made him afraid.

Maybe he was going to always want her like this.

Jesus.

Or maybe he was an idiot, and she was simply breathing like that from her crying jag.

She'd cried. If there was anything more soul destroying than watching a woman as strong and tough as Mel completely lose it, he didn't know what.

And had he ever, in his entire life, felt so helpless? Like he could punch his fist through a wall of concrete, or curl into a ball of misery himself?

Maybe, he could admit. Maybe in that dark time right after his father's death. The senselessness of it all, the loss. Yeah, he'd felt helpless then.

And he hated that Mel felt it now.

He wasn't sure when he'd even started taking her feelings into account. Maybe that was a side effect of another realization: she was on his side. She didn't like it but she was.

The truth was, he was falling for her. Talk about terrifying. He parked the car in the brutal sun at the airport and watched her get out, hair tumbling around her shoulders, mouth unsmiling, eyes tired.

Not falling, he corrected. But *fallen*. He'd fallen for her, done deal.

She did a double take in his direction. "You just went pale as a ghost. What's the matter?"

Pale? Yeah, that sounded about right.

"Bo?"

He opened his mouth and said the first stupid thing to hit his tongue. "I came inside you without a condom."

She whipped her head back toward him, stared for one blink, then looked away. "Oh."

"Oh. Is that all you have to say—*oh?*"

"Okay. Oops. Is that better?"

He scrubbed a hand over his face. "I've never done that before."

"Don't worry."

She sounded so quiet, so weary, he dropped his hands from his face. "Are you on the pill?"

"No, I meant I would never hold you back from doing what you've got to do about the airport, and then going home."

"Home."

"Back to Australia."

"You wouldn't hold me back from leaving here, even if you're pregnant," he said quietly, then watched temper spark in those gorgeous whiskey eyes of hers, the ones that had been so soft and heated only a few minutes ago.

"Of course not!" she snapped. Crossing her arms over her chest, she turned her head away.

Putting his hands on her arms, he tried to pull her back around, not an easy task because she was strong and pissed and didn't want to look at him. "Mel. Look at me. Please?"

She did so with clear reluctance.

"If I got you pregnant, I'm sure as hell not going to walk away."

"There were two of us forgetting a condom, and I take responsibility for my own mistakes, thank you very much."

"I am just saying that I'm not going to desert you."

"If I'm pregnant."

They stared at each other for a long . . . well, pregnant beat. Then Mel walked into the airport. Bo followed, kicking his own ass all the way to his plane. They flew for a full hour in silence, during which time he thought far too much.

Could he really walk away? Go back to Australia as if nothing had happened? As if he hadn't begun to think of North Beach as his home, too? As if the place hadn't captured a good part of his heart, and Mel the rest of it?

"Here." Mel reached over and flipped open the ice chest they'd stocked way back in North Beach before they'd come. She pulled out a soda. "You look like you need a hit of sugar."

"I'm okay." But he took the can, noticing that she even opened it for him. He must look like death warmed over for her to be babying him like this.

Customary cool long gone, he downed the soda, the icy drink wetting his parched throat but not making him feel any better.

He didn't know if he *could* feel better. Could he go back to Australia?

And if he couldn't, how would Mel take that, when she couldn't wait for him to get the hell out of her life, he wondered.

"You sure you're okay?" she asked.

"You're hovering, Mel."

She pulled back as if slapped. "Excuse me."

He swore to himself. "I'm sorry. I just need some quiet."

"Fine."

"Fine." Yeah, he was an ass. An ass with the words *you've fallen and you can't get up* running through his mind over and over.

He went back to sweating.

"Why did you tell that woman at the bar you'd try to get her money back? What about *your* money? Wouldn't you take whatever you found for yourself?" Mel asked him.

"I have the airport."

She stared at him until he squirmed. "What?" he finally demanded.

She shook her head. "That's the first time you've ever said such a thing, admitted that maybe North Beach has equal value to what you've lost."

He cut his eyes to hers, then looked straight ahead to the horizon, the two of them silent again.

"Why did she go back there to try to buy their silence?"

This from Mel some time later. Clearly she'd thought of little else.

Bo shrugged. "She knows you're looking for her."

"But she doesn't know why."

"You don't know that."

She shook her head. "I just keep thinking that there has to be a good reason for what she did, both to Eddie and those people we just met. She wasn't a bad person, Bo."

He grimaced, and she read his thoughts. "Look, I know people can be bad, damn it. I'm not naive. But Sally . . . God." She blew out a breath. "She was everything to us. I just can't . . ." She shook her head. "I just can't put it all together and make sense of it."

"I'm sorry," he said. "If I could have done this any other way—"

That actually tore a laugh out of her. "Oh, no. You prided yourself on being honest, so don't start lying now just to save my feelings."

"I mean it. Look, I know I was hell-bent on coming here and wrapping my fingers around Sally's neck—"

"And then mine."

"Well, yes," he agreed with a small smile. "But for different reasons entirely."

She played with the condensation on her can of soda. "I keep wondering . . ."

"What?"

She looked at him, her whiskey eyes guarded. "What is it that you want from me?"

"Honesty."

"You've got that now."

"Affection," he said before his self-editor could stop the revealing words from escaping.

She paused. Looked out the window. "You have that, too," she said to the glass.

Then your heart, he wanted to add, but she'd probably put on a parachute and jump. So he let out an easy smile. "Then I have it all, don't I?"

She stared down at the landscape below, pensive, silent for a long time. "Those things?" she murmured softly just before they landed. "Honesty and affection?" She was speaking to the glass. "I want them, too."

He waited until she looked at him, and smiled with what he hoped was his heart and soul. "They're there for the taking, Mel."

And, apparently, much more than that as well. Certainly more than he'd ever bargained for. And given the look on her face, she felt the same.

*   *   *

They got back just before closing time. Outside a new storm brewed and flights for the morning were already questionable, while inside North Beach something else brewed . . .

Ernest left after Mel and Bo's arrival, without so much as a grumpy word, dirty look, or spider in a jar. Char and Al were in a "discussion," which meant Al had done something stupid and Char had told him so in no uncertain terms, and they weren't speaking to each other. Danny was also unusually quiet. Well, if one could call the air compressor and gadgets he used for plane maintenance *quiet,* not to mention the head-banging music he played so loud the entire hangar shook with each thumping beat.

Dimi had incense going everywhere, but if it was supposed to have a calming effect, it'd failed. Bracelets jangling on her wrists, stress in her gaze, she followed Mel into her office. "Tell me how it went. Oh, God, I can see by your face. It's bad, right?"

"Define bad," Mel said, sinking to her chair.

"Aw, hell."

"We found an ex of Sally's. And Sally had been with him under a different name, Rosario Lopez."

"What?"

"Yeah, hold on to yourself, it gets worse. While she was married to him, she had her name put on the deeds of his properties, then divorced him and sold those properties out from beneath him. Then vanished."

Dimi covered her mouth, shook her head, and also sank to a chair.

"And what's bothering me is, I'm getting this sinking feeling that there are more men out there who've been equally screwed. I'm going to call Matt and ask him to find out what other aliases she's used."

"Ohmigod."

Mel leaned forward and squeezed her fingers. "You know what comes next, right?"

"We bury our heads in the sand and pretend none of this ever happened?"

Mel shook her head.

"We put on red glittery shoes and click the heels three times and chant, 'There's no place like home, there's no place like home'?"

"I'm sorry," Mel whispered. "Please don't freak out."

"I don't freak out." Dimi opened Mel's bottom drawer and pulled out three candles that Mel had never used.

"Dimi."

She was going through another drawer, probably looking for yet more incense. Mel put her hand over hers. "Hey, let's get out of here, okay? Get some dinner—"

"You mean let's babysit Dimi so she doesn't go somewhere and get drunk, right?"

Well, hell. Yes. But Mel couldn't say that, not when Dimi's hand beneath hers was shaking, not when her bestest, oldest friend on the planet, her only family, was biting back tears and looked an inch from a meltdown.

"I haven't had a drink in six days," Dimi said in a low voice, then looked Mel in the eyes. "Did you know that?"

Mel shook her head, ashamed of herself for not noticing. "No," she said quietly. "I didn't."

"I wanted you to notice. I mean, I realize for normal people six days is no big deal but—"

"I should have noticed. I'm so sorry."

"No." Dimi closed her eyes and sighed. "None of this is your doing."

"Nor yours."

"Yeah, but it's all in a person's reactions, I've noticed." She opened her eyes. "I've come to some realizations lately, one of which is that I'm my own person, with my own life. I can't take the path of others, you know?"

Mel nodded. "I know."

"Yeah, you've always been good at taking your own road. I'm not going to fall apart, Mel."

"I know you're not." Mel reached in and hugged her tight. "We're going to be okay."

Dimi held on and let out a shuddery breath. "It's funny, but I never really believed that before, that we were going to be okay. I think that was the problem. Even when everything was status quo, before we knew about the deed, before Bo even showed up, I never really believed we were okay. I worried, I stressed. I never slept at night."

"You never said," Mel marveled. "You just lit your candles and found your calm."

"Yeah, shocking how much alcohol can help with pretenses. At least on the outside." Dimi sighed. "The weird thing is, now everything's as messed up as it can possibly be, and yet I feel okay for the first time in forever. How is that even possible?"

"Because you're amazing. We're both amazing."

Dimi laughed and hugged her again, hard, no longer shaking. "I always thought it was because of Sally."

Mel pulled back. "Maybe it started out that way, but we deserve credit, too. It's about time, don't you think?"

"Yeah." Dimi looked down at her perfectly manicured fingers. "I wanted to talk to you about your lease."

"Yeah, me, too. I want Bo to add you—"

Dimi was shaking her head. "I don't want to be added."

"I'll put you on Anderson Air's payroll instead of North Beach's, and that way—"

"Mel."

"—Because then he wouldn't be responsible for—"

"Mel."

She stopped talking and now *Mel* felt a little shaky because she knew. Damn it, she knew.

"I'm thinking of doing something new," Dimi said softly.

Oh, God. *"Dimi."*

"I'm applying to UCSB."

The university at Santa Barbara. "College?"

Dimi smiled. "Maybe eventually I'll become that nurse I always dreamed of, working in-flight care."

Mel gaped. "But . . . you hate flying."

"No, I don't hate it. It scares me. But if you can overcome your fears, then so can I."

"I haven't overcome any fears—"

"You're letting a man in."

"Bite your tongue! And since when was that a fear of mine?"

"Since your mother left you. Since your father left you. Since Sally left us. Now you have a leaving thing, which means you walk before anyone else gets the idea to do the same. Just ask any guy you've ever dated and then dumped."

It made Mel's chest ache to think about it. It actually hurt so much she had to lift a hand to rub at the spot, but it couldn't be assuaged. "I'm not afraid of letting people in. I let everyone here in; Char, Al, the guys . . . I let you in, didn't I?" She forced a smile that faded at Dimi's next words.

"You let us in because we need you, each of us in our own way. Mother-hen-to-chick type of relationships. Face it, honey, you don't know how to be the little chick. You don't know how to lean on someone, or need them."

"This conversation is about Sally," Mel said, shaken. "About her illegal tendencies. About how she didn't just screw *us*, she apparently screwed a whole line of people. How the hell did we end up talking about me and all my faults?"

"Because your faults are so cute."

Mel snorted.

Dimi opened her mouth to say more but she was staring at something over Mel's shoulder, lost in thought, eyes a little dreamy, mouth soft.

Mel craned her neck to see what—or who. Danny had come into the lobby, looking lean and lanky and tough.

Dimi stared at him, gone, just completely gone, including mouth sagging open and drool pooling.

Mel craned her neck to get a better view of Danny to see what she was missing. He had his blond hair pulled back from his face with a plastic tie wrap, his baseball cap on backward, knees ripped out of his coveralls, looking like . . . well, Danny.

And Dimi was now drooling, practically soaking him up as he headed toward the café. He smiled at Char, who handed him a soda, then leaned his head back and drank.

And from thirty-five feet away, Dimi sighed, audible only to Mel.

When Danny put the drink down, he glanced over. From across the long expanse of the lobby he caught Dimi's gaze, then held it for a long beat before walking back outside, his long, rangy body moving with his usual laid-back ease.

Dimi let out a breath. "Yeah. Still mad at me."

"What? Why's he mad at you?"

"Forget it. He's just a man. A jerky man."

"A jerk?"

"He's got a penis, doesn't he?"

"Dimi. The two of you are close friends."

"Were," she said toughly, then sagged. "Oh, who the hell am I kidding? It's me. I screwed up, bad. And now I feel funny around him, like I can't breathe normally. I even *sweat*. It's awful."

Mel sat back, let out a low laugh. She recognized those symptoms! "You're falling for him."

"No. I'm just getting a bug or something." She picked up her purse. "I'm out of here."

"Dimi—"

"I'm going to be fine, Mel. We both are."

"What about Sally?" Mel asked quietly.

"Oh, no doubt, that one hurts like a son-of-a-bitch, we both know it."

"She was everything to you. And I've just dropped a bomb in your lap." Mel wanted to hold on to her and keep her safe. And busy. Very busy. "I think we should go—"

"I told you, I'm fine." Dimi kissed her cheek, then walked out as well, leaving Mel staring at the door, wanting to believe it.

Needing to believe it.

Chapter 24

Dimi got all the way out to her car before she let out a shaky breath. Okay, not quite as steady as she'd thought, but at least it wasn't alcohol related. Nope, this was purely emotional stress. *God, Sally*.

Annoyed at herself for thinking about it, she fumbled through her purse, looking for her car keys, finding instead a pen, her favorite lip gloss, a tampon . . .

No keys.

"Damn it." Finally, she dumped the entire contents out on the hood of her car. There was her library card, and that receipt she'd been looking for, but still no keys, though look at that, there was her missing book, with the gorgeous firefighter on the cover, and the wild sex between the pages.

She stared at the mess on her hood, the mess that didn't include keys, and felt the tears building that she hadn't allowed before. Why couldn't she get herself organized? Why couldn't she get it together?

Why had Sally done this to them?

Dimi had built her life on what Sally had done with hers. She'd emulated a woman she admired more than life itself because she'd never had anyone to admire before.

Sally hadn't asked for the hero worship, she'd just lived her life fast and hard and without looking back, as if it could all end at any moment. It had taken Dimi to glom on to that and live that way as well. Her own doing . . . but to find out that Sally hadn't been worthy of Dimi's admiration at all, that maybe Sally wasn't even her real name . . .

God.

She felt as if her very foundation had been kicked out from beneath her. Did she still know who she was? Or who she wanted to be? Did she really?

Just a week ago she might have settled the matter by going to a bar and getting shit-faced, then going home with someone gorgeous who could take her mind off everything for a few hours.

But that thought exhausted her now. And left her sad. She wanted . . . something. Needed . . . something.

And yet she couldn't put her finger on it. But it sure would be nice if she could put her finger on her keys!

Behind her, someone opened their door. She turned and froze.

Danny.

Perfect. He had his surfboard in the back of his truck, and he'd changed to go surfing, wearing a pair of faded yellow board shorts and battered old flip-flops. His T-shirt was the same color as his baby blue eyes, nearly hidden beneath the baseball cap he had on.

"Hi," she said, a little breathlessly, painfully aware they hadn't talked since that night he'd driven her home. She missed him, with an ache that nearly brought her to her knees, just from looking at him. But the loss of the friendship had been her own doing. She'd pushed to keep him at a certain distance for years, then breached that distance by asking for help as she'd needed it.

Was it any wonder he'd never made a move on her?

God, the memory of that night at the restaurant made her cheeks burn.

He looked over at her. "You okay?"

It took her a moment to figure out how to answer that but before she could, he let out a low laugh and shook his head. "Never mind. You're fantastic, right? Just like always."

"Actually," she said. "I'm not. Fantastic, that is."

He went still, his gaze not so hidden now.

"And truthfully?" she whispered. "Haven't been for a long time."

He moved around his truck to come toe to toe with her. "Someone bugging you?"

"No, I don't need rescuing or anything." She stared down at his feet. They were clean and tanned, and big enough that an inane thought went racing through her mind.

You know what they say about the size of a man's feet . . .

"I never minded helping you out when you needed it," he said.

But he *had* minded. It had upset him when she'd gone bar hopping. And bed hopping . . .

As her friend, he'd worried. And she owed him for that.

He lifted her chin, his fingers on her jaw. His eyes were deep, and filled with things, things that made her swallow hard because she'd never really let herself see them before.

She was seeing them now.

"It's okay not to be fine once in awhile," he said. "Long as you face it."

Face it. Something she'd never really tried. "I had some bad news today," she said. "And it made me sad. That's all. I'm not off to do something stupid or anything."

"Of course you're not."

"So you don't have to worry that I'll call you needing—"

"Dimi—"

"Just go surfing, damn it." She turned away and began to

scoop her things back into her purse. She really hoped he'd leave before she had to admit she couldn't find her stupid keys, that she once again needed rescuing. In fact, she'd eat her own purse before admitting she needed help. Again. "Better hurry," she said. "Before the wind kicks up—"

He pulled her around to face him. "You're finished drinking. Why don't you be finished running, too?"

"What?" Her heart started to pound thickly, heavily. "What are you talking about?"

"You haven't had a drink since that night I picked you up."

She hadn't kissed anyone, either. She couldn't imagine ever kissing another man now that she'd kissed him. But that he'd noticed she hadn't had a drink . . . He could have no idea how much that meant to her. "Maybe I go home and get raging drunk every single night."

"No." He shook his head. "Your eyes are sharp. You're sharp. You're on your game again. Welcome back, Deem. Now go all the way and face your crap."

She let out a harsh laugh. "Yeah. Look, not facing my crap is what I do."

"That's a nice excuse."

"It works for me," she quipped, but he didn't smile.

"You didn't drink for pleasure," he said. "You didn't serial date for pleasure. You did it because you were looking for something."

"Yeah, looking to lose myself."

He just looked at her.

"Okay, I was looking for the mind-numbing oblivion."

He shook his head. "Deem."

"Well, you got me," she said with a shrug as if it didn't matter, as if her heart wasn't clogging her throat. "I have no idea."

"You asked me a question last time we talked," he said.

Yeah, she'd asked him why he'd never made a move on

her. She couldn't go there now. She was too fragile to go there. "Listen, I've got to—"

"We've been friends a long time."

She closed her eyes. *Friends*. "Yes, I know." She managed to look at him even though doing so made her chest feel too tight. "Danny—"

"We've talked about everything—work, life, stuff, but . . ."

The but. She hated the but. She stood there feeling bare-ass naked.

"But you always held a part of yourself back," he said.

Her secret defense. Laid out.

He put his hands on her arms and gave her a little shake. "It's me, Deem. Me. You can trust me with anything. Especially yourself."

At that, she opened her eyes, shocked and embarrassed to find them wet.

"I should start with this," Danny said, looking mad at himself. "You asked me why I never made a move on you— I never did because you've never been open to the kind of move I'd make—"

"Honestly, Danny, we don't need to do this—"

"The permanent kind of move."

She went still, eyes closed.

"Open your eyes, goddamn it. Maybe the thing you've been looking for is right in front of you."

She stared at him.

"And maybe," he went on, his voice low and frustrated, "maybe I'm tired of waiting for you to see it."

Oh, God. He had no idea. No idea at all. She'd learned so much about herself, just in a week of clear thinking. The partying, the men, none of it appealed anymore, but he appealed. So very much. Still, it hadn't been long enough, and she wasn't ready to trust her heart.

"It's just that I don't want to wake up in the morning after a night of great sex and find you running for the door," he said roughly. "I don't want to call you and listen to your voice mail because you recognize my number and won't pick up."

She swallowed the shame and managed to keep looking at him.

"You see yet? I never made a move on you because I knew if I did, it wouldn't last."

Staggered, she could only stare at him.

"And I don't intend for anything with us to be our last."

Oh, God. Could he see her heart getting ready to leap right out of her chest? "I . . . I didn't know that."

"I realize that. You still don't know all of it. Which is that I'm in love with you."

Her mouth fell open but nothing came out except maybe a squeak.

A laugh escaped him. "Yeah, and I can see that thrills the hell out of you." His mouth twisted into a grimace, and he turned back to his truck. Opened the door.

He loved her. He *loved* her. He loved *her*.

By the time she found her voice, he'd already gotten in. "Danny!"

He had his hands on the steering wheel, gripping tight. "Yeah?"

She leaned into the truck to get a good look at his face. His comfortable, kind, and yes, damn sexy face. It was her own shame that it'd taken her so long to see it. "It did."

"What?"

"It thrilled the hell out of me." She gulped in a breath. "You know. To hear it. No one's ever . . ." Here she faltered, but only because it was so important that she get it right. "No one's ever loved me before. Well . . . Mel does, but I'm thinking that's a different kind of love."

His smile was slow and real and loosened the vise she'd had on her heart for too long. "Yeah, different."

"Danny, I have to tell you, I need time to—"

"I know. I'm not going to rush you, don't worry."

"I have no idea how long I need."

"So we'll just let it all play out. Get in." Leaning over to the passenger side, he opened the door.

"But . . ."

He smiled, and her entire inside melted. "Trust me?" he asked softly.

She smiled helplessly in return. He was the most passionate, wonderful man she'd ever met.

And hot. He was damn hot. "I think I do, actually. But . . ." He'd said he loved her. She hadn't said it back. She didn't know if she could ever say it back—

"You're thinking too much," he said.

"I don't want to hurt you."

"Deem, I'm not taking you to elope. Just a ride."

"Oh." She laughed at her foolishness and got in.

His smile warmed her as she'd never been warmed. "Been surfing lately?"

Pulling on her seatbelt, she shook her head. "I don't have my bathing suit."

"Been skinny-dipping lately?"

She tossed her head back and laughed. *Laughed.* "No," she said, the first thing she'd been certain of all day. "I haven't."

"Well, then." His grin was adorable, with a pinch of wicked tossed in.

She loved wicked, and as they peeled out of the parking lot, she laughed again.

Mel couldn't sleep. It wasn't the heat, which felt unusually sultry and steamy as thunder clouds moved in. It wasn't worry about her future, she'd signed the lease, which lay folded on her table.

But still, the restlessness rolled through her.

Giving up on bed, she moved to the dark living room, sitting in the picture window as the storm hit, arms curled around her legs, chin on her knees, lost in thought about what she'd learned today about Sally.

It was nearly impossible to reconcile her memories: Sally teaching her to use a wrench, letting her take the controls in the air at age thirteen, showing her how to carefully run a preflight check, and never, ever scrimp on the details ... Sally letting her land for the first time, ruffling Mel's hair and saying, "Good job, kid, you're a natural, just like me."

Sally hugging her hard after getting her pilot's license, her eyes filled with tears, saying, "Stay just as you are, kid, just as you are."

And Mel saying, "But I want to be just like you," and Sally slowly, sadly, shaking her head.

"God." Mel drew a deep breath, and another, but her throat still felt tight, her eyes burned. "Goddamn." Because how was she supposed to have these good memories while knowing Sally was a criminal who'd hurt innocent people?

She was not going to cry again; earlier today had been enough to last her years. She should have been mortified at that, but Bo had made it okay. What was it about him that always made it okay?

She'd always thought of herself as work. All work. But she was coming to understand there was more to life, and also, more to her.

And that no matter what happened, she was going to be okay.

But a little part of her couldn't help but wonder, what would it be like if Bo wanted to stay at North Beach? With him in her life, she'd do much more than fly, that was certain now.

She'd love.

The thought knocked her back a few breaths, and then the soft knock on her door startled her further. Padding to the door, she frowned. "Dimi?"

"Try again."

Bo.

Everything within her reacted to that unbearably familiar voice. Everything within her wanted to throw open the door and jump him, but she set her forehead to the door and told herself that she had to give him up at some point, the sooner the better. She'd probably have managed to resist him if he hadn't knocked again.

Chapter 25

Mel closed her eyes. *Resist.* She could do it. She *had* to do it, because this was much more than a physical want. This was the kind of ache that couldn't be assuaged with just another quickie, amazing as that quickie would be, and Bo couldn't, *wouldn't,* offer more.

He was leaving.

Damn it, hadn't she given herself enough disappointments?

He didn't knock on the front door again, and she breathed a sigh that she told herself was relief, which backed up in her throat when another knock came.

The back door, this time.

She saw him through the glass. Lightning flashed, revealing his face, his eyes, which glittered with a whole host of things she couldn't begin to guess at.

"Mel."

She stared at him. Shook her head. She felt too weak, too vulnerable.

"Open up." He spread his hand on the glass. *"Please?"*

Ah, hell. It was the please, uttered in that Australian drawl, in that low, husky voice that followed her into her dreams.

She pulled open the door, let him slip in, then walked away from him, back through the living room to her large picture window.

Putting her hands on the sill, she stared out into the dark night, extremely aware of the man behind her in the dark, silent. Waiting.

The wood floor creaked beneath his feet as he came close in the charged silence. Around her the awareness heightened, and she drew a shaky breath.

Still, neither of them spoke.

The rain hit, slashing at the windows. Bo came closer still, moving without a sound but she didn't need to hear him, *she felt him,* with every fiber of her being.

Go away. Please, go away.

Don't go.

With her mind and body playing tug-o-war, she felt a little off center. "I can't do this, Bo."

"I haven't asked anything of you."

His voice came out of the dark. Disembodied.

But not distant. Never distant. She had a feeling she could be in a coma and just hearing that low, whiskey, Aussie voice would bring her out and awake.

And aroused.

Without looking at him, she pressed her forehead to the window. Looking at him would be bad, like looking at an open box of donuts.

Irresistible bad.

Gotta have one bad.

Can't stop at just one bad.

In fact, if she looked at him and he spoke, the combination would probably cause her to spontaneously combust.

From behind her, he touched her hair.

So close. He was so close she could feel the strength of him, his breath at her temple. "Mel."

"It's late," she whispered, still pressing her forehead to the glass.

"I know. I was in bed, staring at the ceiling."

"Ah." She felt the reluctant smile tug at her mouth. "A noble bedtime activity."

"I can think of a better one."

Her entire body tingled, reacting in the predictable way as she squeezed her eyes shut. "Is that why you came?"

He touched her again, trailed a finger over her neck, nudging her oversized T-shirt off one shoulder. Simple touch. Complicated feelings. "Bo."

"I was lying there."

"Studying the ceiling."

A huff of breath escaped him. "Yeah. Picturing you here. Devastated from today."

She craned her neck to look at him now, the low light casting his face in bold relief. "So you drove over here to what, make me undevastated?"

A grimace crossed his face. "It sounded good from flat on my back."

Flat on his back. She wanted him flat on his back, with her straddling him. She turned back to the window, set her hands on the wood-lined pane and desperately took in the sights.

Ocean pounding the shore.

Sky unleashed.

"Mel." He set his hands on her shoulders, which he began to knead with such a knowing touch, the first moan escaped before she could stop it. "You've got a rock quarry going on here."

"Yeah. Listen, Bo . . . I called Matt and asked him to run Sally for more aliases."

"I'm searching, too."

Right. Of course.

"Stop thinking, Mel," he said softly. "At least for tonight." He had magic hands, talented fingers . . . both of which she already knew. Beneath them she nearly slid into a pool of boneless putty as he drew out each and every tense muscle in her neck and shoulders and arms, concentrating in silence, until finally she sagged back against him.

His chest brushed her back, his thighs hard and tough to her softer ones. She hadn't taken a good look at him on purpose, but she could feel his T-shirt against her shoulders, absorbed his soft denim jeans against her bare legs. Because she was weak, very weak, she rocked her bottom, wriggling just a little.

The sound that escaped him managed to perfectly convey his desire, as did the hard bulge she felt pressing into her bottom. She'd told herself they weren't going to do this, but then his hands slid up her sides and down, gripping her hips when she helplessly arched into him again. Still holding on to the wood for dear life, she murmured his name.

His hand skimmed up her belly, taking the hem of her T-shirt with him, higher, slowly higher, exposing her breasts to the night air, and then to his fingers.

"I dream of this," he said a little hoarsely. "Just about every night. I wake up hard and aching for you." He slipped a hand inside her panties, let out a rough sound of pleasure when he found her wet, and slid a finger inside her.

God. She pressed his hand against her, needing more, which he gave by adding another finger. He kissed her shoulder, her neck, the sweet spot right beneath her ear; hot, wet, open-mouthed kisses that went in tune with his clever fingers.

She opened her eyes and caught her own reflection in the glass. Hair, wild. Face, hungry. T-shirt shoved up, one breast bared, nipple hard and pouty, the other covered by Bo's big hand. Her belly rose and fell as if she'd been running. His other hand, between her legs, was still moving, the sight so erotic she almost had to close her eyes but she blinked rapidly, trying to watch, wanting to watch, because she'd never seen herself like this before.

Then she looked up and caught Bo's reflection. He wasn't

looking in the glass, but at the real thing, his head bent as he took in her body and what he was doing to her. His expression curled her toes. "Bo."

His thumb flicked over her and she couldn't help it, she bowed back, body tight and quivery. As she shifted, a breast brushed the cold glass, making her gasp.

He stroked her again.

Her mind shut down, reduced to nothing but sensation. Hot fingers inside her. Cold glass against her breast. Bo's mouth on her throat, his erect penis pressing into her bottom. *"Please,"* she managed.

That was all he seemed to need to hear, and in the next moment, he dragged down her panties and opened his jeans.

Something hit the ledge and she looked down. A condom packet.

So they weren't going to compound their errors.

And then she couldn't think at all because he'd dipped down a little, his thighs on the outside of hers, and slid inside her with one powerful thrust.

She cried out, and so did he as she pushed back against him for more. Please more. *"Bo."* She couldn't stay still, couldn't, but when she wriggled, desperate, his hands gripped her hips, his voice low and rough in the dark. "Don't move. Christ. Don't move—"

But she couldn't help it. He was huge inside her, filling her to bursting, and when his thumb pressed over her again, she began to come. At her first shudder, he groaned, his fingers digging into her hips, gripping hard as he began to move, too, thrusting into her again and again, so that she burst once more, or maybe that was *still*. She didn't know, didn't care, as long as it went on and on . . . And then he came, pulsing powerfully inside her, sinking to the floor with her as if his legs could no longer support them.

"So," she finally managed, flat on her back. "We ended up ceiling-watching here, too."

He let out a strangled laugh, and still breathing hard, rolled to his side, hauling her into the curve of his body. "It's better with you."

"I went off like a bottle rocket." She was a little embarrassed, actually, at how fast she'd come.

"Twice." He grinned down into her face.

"You counted?"

"I didn't have to, you screamed it to the moon."

"Did not."

"Did, too."

She felt herself blush, and he laughed again. "What, you're shy now?"

"Did I really scream?"

"My name," he said, looking quite pleased with himself.

Yeah, well, all he had to do was touch her and she went up in flames. Hell, he *looked* at her and her body temperature soared off the damn chart.

Truth was, she could get overheated just thinking about him.

And yeah, he'd made her scream. She shook her head and struggled to her feet. "Okay, time for you to get out of here."

He was shaking his head before she straightened. "I'm not leaving town yet, not with you still getting threats. Not with this whole thing unresolved."

She stared down at him. She'd meant for the night, but that his leaving the country had been forward enough in his mind to assume she'd been talking about *that* . . .

She crossed her arms, suddenly extremely aware that she was naked. "I, um, meant it was time for you to leave my house."

His lazy, satisfied, cat-in-cream smile vanished. "Mel."

No. No, she didn't want to hear it, and she whirled away.

"Shit, you're a genius," she heard him mutter to himself as he got to his feet, but she sped up as she headed toward her bedroom.

"Mel—"

She shut the door, and in the dark went straight for her dresser, planning on putting on clothes. All of them. She needed armor, she needed—

A lock on her bedroom door, apparently, because Bo walked right in, still butt-ass naked. "Mel—"

"It's late," she said in the coldest voice she could muster, which wasn't very cold with him standing there looking like some kind of pagan god.

"I know. Mel, about me leaving the States—"

"I don't want to talk about it."

"Mel—"

"Seriously. Don't want to talk about it."

"I was careful not to lead you on," he said quietly. "I never led you to believe I was staying—"

"No. You were careful," she agreed. "Now please go."

He looked at her for a long moment, during which she tried to remain cool and, more important, not lose it.

"I'm guessing this is nonnegotiable," he said.

"Give the man an *A*."

Chapter 26

For the first time in memory, Mel's inner alarm clock didn't go off and she overslept. By the time she entered North Beach, she was fifteen minutes late and found herself the target of a handful of gazes, all staring at her in shock.

"What?" she asked a bit defensively to everyone sitting around the café bar still eating their donuts. "I'm a little late, so what?"

"Two times in as many weeks," Char said, concern all over her face.

"Yeah, did hell freeze over?" Kellan asked.

Ritchie snickered, then sucked it in at the glare from Mel, who grabbed a donut and lifted her chin. "So I slept in, no biggie." On second thought, this was a two-donut morning, and she snatched another, double-fisting, before stalking off to her office.

Neither the lemon pastry nor the jelly-filled donut appeased the hole in her gut. She sat at her desk organizing her flight schedule, trying not to think about last night in Bo's arms, and how for one glorious moment she'd completely lost herself in him. She also tried not to think about the day before, flying to Mexico to find Sally, finding instead more information that had only made her feel worse, and then nearly getting shot in the process . . .

Tried not to think about any of it . . .

It didn't help that as the day passed, she realized something else. Morale seemed to be up at North Beach, and bad attitudes down. People were happy. Content. Char was singing at the top of her lungs to Bon Jovi. Nothing new, but she'd hugged everyone three or four times today already. Al, out of the doghouse, had sold some photos, and also had a gallery interested in his work.

Oh, and Dimi was smiling. *Smiling,* answering phones, charming customers . . .

Mel would have suspected alcohol but she knew Dimi had given it up.

Even Kellan and Ritchie seemed different. They'd been on time and awake. A miracle in itself.

And then there was Ernest. He hadn't moaned, groaned, complained, or so much as set a spider jar on her desk, not once the entire day. And he'd even offered to bring her lunch.

She'd nearly fallen off her own chair at that one. Ernest, offering his own money up for lunch.

How was it possible that everyone around her was getting cheery again, feeling excited and hopeful, and she'd lost all taste for it?

Oh, yeah. Because Bo Black was going to walk out of her life.

Shortly after noon, Char popped into Mel's office.

Mel's nose twitched at the delicious-smelling something in Char's hands, and perked up slightly. "I hope it's carbo-loaded."

Char set down a tuna melt, with the cheese and tuna squeezing out the sides of the thick French bread. "For you? Always."

Mel took a bite and moaned. "You are a goddess."

"Yeah. A pregnant one."

Mel stared at her as the food stuck in her throat. "What?"

Char sank into a chair and put her hands on her belly. "Got myself knocked up. Think Al's going to kill me?"

"If it's the delivery boy's."

Char laughed, but grew serious quickly. "He's going to think I did this on purpose, but I didn't. Remember last month, when we went camping?"

"You mean when you guys went for the overnighter specifically to 'do it in the woods'? Yes, I distinctly remember the feeling of my brain matter coming out my ears as you told me how great it was."

"We got carried away before using a condom." Char sighed. "But these things happen."

Mel thought of yesterday, and how after facing down that gun in their faces, she and Bo had pulled over on some deserted Mexican road, and right there in the heat and the dust had ravished each other in order to remember they were alive.

They'd gotten carried away as well. "Yeah. These things happen," Mel said weakly. Oh, God. What if it happened to her, too? "I thought you were getting hot flashes. Doesn't that mean you're done with all this stuff?"

"Apparently not." Char smiled. "Look, we're married. We have a decent home and we love each other. Now we'll have something to show for that love, that's all." She paused. "Did that sound good, or did I rush it?"

"Depends on Al's mood."

"Yeah, well, let's hope it's a good one."

"So, you happy?" Mel asked.

"Oh, yeah."

Mel hugged her tight. "Then I'm happy for you."

Char patted her still-flat belly. "Thanks, honey. Hey, you notice Dimi skipping around this morning? She didn't even light her candles or incense. And she was smiling. She looks so pretty when she smiles. Anyway, I'd say she must have gotten lucky, but you know what? I think in her case, it's the

opposite. I think she's finally learning to make herself happy."
Char leaned in and hugged Mel. "One down, now only one
to go."

Mel frowned. "What does that mean?"

"You, honey. I mean you. You have to learn to make yourself happy." And then she left Mel alone to wonder how exactly to do that.

At the end of the day, Dimi buzzed Mel in her office.
"Line one," she said. "It's *him*."

Mel stared at her phone as if it was a coiled rattlesnake.
She didn't have to ask who. It was Matt, with possible news
on Sally.

"Tell me exactly what he says," Dimi instructed. "Every
word."

"I will."

"Unless it's bad news. Oh, God, do you think it's bad
news?"

"Bad in comparison to what, Dimi?"

"Right." Dimi drew a ragged breath. "Right. Maybe . . . I
know this sounds crazy, but maybe he's calling to tell us he
found out it's all some sort of mistake."

Mel had no hopes left, false or otherwise. "What kind of
mistake involves taking money and property that doesn't belong to you?"

"Yeah," Dimi sighed. "Wishful thinking and all that."

"I'm going to take the call now," Mel said gently. "I'll just
buzz you when I'm off—"

Before she'd even finished her sentence, Dimi opened
Mel's office door and slid inside, breathing heavily. "Well?"

"Uh, I haven't taken the call yet," Mel said dryly, then
clicked over. "Mel Anderson. Can I help you?"

"How many aliases for Sally are you expecting?" Matt
asked.

"Well?" Dimi whispered. "Is she alive?"

Mel held up her finger. "As many as you can find, Matt."

"I've unearthed four without any effort," he said. "I'm not a betting man, but you can be sure if it was this easy, there are more."

Four aliases, minimum. If there'd been only the one, someone could argue that Sally had had a good reason for vanishing under a different name. Fear, danger . . .

But four.

Four.

"There's more," Matt said. "The last alias on record, Tara Louise? She was married for two years to a man who just recently died in New Orleans. Suspiciously. She's wanted for questioning but has vanished."

Mel gripped her phone tight. "Oh, my God."

A man dead.

Until Bo had arrived, Mel had faced only a moral dilemma. Yes, Sally had vanished, but she hadn't done anything to Mel, at least nothing criminal. So what right did she have to dig?

But now . . . Now there were many reasons; for the rights of the victims, for one.

For Bo's father.

For Bo himself.

The thought came out of nowhere. Mel wanted answers for Bo, for that eighteen-year-old who'd lost so much, for the man who'd never lost his belief in his father.

And then there was the fact that Sally had instructed Mel and Dimi to act criminally without their knowledge.

"Melanie?" Matt asked. "You there?"

"Yes, thank you. I'll get back to you." She hung up and stared at the phone.

"Four aliases?" Dimi sounded as dazed as she felt, and staggered to a chair. *"Four,"* she said again, stunned.

"Maybe more," Mel told her. "Probably more. And let's not forget the coup de grâce: an ex, dead under suspicious circumstances."

"Two," Dimi whispered. "Two ex's dead, if you coun[ ]
Eddie. Do you think . . . my God . . . Do you think she some[ ]
how killed Eddie?"

It was too terrible to even think about. "We have to fac[e]
facts right now, Deem," Mel said, her voice trembling. "*To[ ]
gether*. Sentiment doesn't have a place here. Sally's in bi[g]
trouble and we both know we can no longer help her. But w[e]
can help the people she's hurt."

Dimi reached for Mel's hand. "Don't worry. I'm not fallin[g]
apart. And I'm all yours, at least for the duration of this dis[ ]
aster."

"For the duration? That sounds a little . . . temporary."

"Yeah." Dimi stared at their joined hands. Hers were smaller[ ]
more delicate, with a perfect manicure and silver bracelet[s]
lined up her left wrist, jangling prettily. "You remember[ ]
told you about wanting to be a nurse."

"Yes."

"I've decided to go to a nursing school and the one I wan[ ]
to go to is in San Diego. I've registered, just today. Classe[s]
start in the fall."

Just two months away. "I see."

"Do you?" She scooted closer. "Do you really, Mel[?]
You're not mad, upset, freaking out? Because I freaked out a[t]
first, the thought of leaving here, of being separated from[ ]
you, but it's just . . ." She paused, her eyes misting. "Damn[ ]
it, I don't want to cry."

"It's okay, I get it. It's what you have to do."

"Yeah." One tear escaped and with a sound of frustration[ ]
she swiped at it. "But I'll be back. I want to work out of the[ ]
hospital in town, only ten minutes away. That won't be s[o]
bad."

"It'll be good," Mel assured her, and they hugged hard[ ]
Mel feeling her own eyes go damp. "Shit."

They laughed a little over the waterworks, then Dim[i]
spoke. "See, so I'm not leaving you for long. Or Danny."

"Danny?"

"We're going to try things out." She smiled with her entire heart in her eyes. "It'll be from a distance at first, but that's okay. I need the time."

"You and Danny?" Mel repeated, surprised.

Dimi's face closed a bit, her shoulders straightened. "I'm not going to hurt him, I wouldn't do that. Why do you think I resisted facing the truth about my feelings so long? The last thing I'd ever do is hurt—"

"Oh, honey, I'm not worried about *him*. He's a big boy, and he knows what he wants. I meant you. I'm worried about you."

"You shouldn't be. I'm a little fragile, I know, but like I said, I need some time." Dimi shook her head. "What Sally did sucks, and it hurts . . ." She pressed a hand to her gut. "Hurts like I didn't know I could be hurt. But with Danny, I just feel . . . *alive*. Like I haven't felt in a long time." Her eyes were clear. Happy. "Whatever happens," she said with intense pride, "I know I'm going to be okay."

Mel nodded, understanding perfectly. She felt alive, too, vibrantly alive, and she had a feeling it had something to do with Bo. Everything to do with Bo. "I'll miss you," she whispered, and they held each other for a long time. Mel didn't want to let go. For as long as she could remember, they'd been a team. A duo.

But it was the end of an era, and that was okay. Things changed. She'd live. When Dimi was gone, Mel stared sightlessly out at the tarmac, wondering what their future held. She'd always assumed that for her, it would be this place. North Beach.

Now . . . who knew?

"Looking pretty serious, mate."

Mel's heart clutched. Her everything clutched as she turned and faced Bo. "What would you know about serious?"

With a cocked eyebrow, he shut her office door behind him and leaned back against it, arms and feet casually crossed as he smiled at her. "You're uptight again."

"Let me guess. You have just the cure?"

"You know it."

"Doesn't thinking with your dick ever get tiring?"

"Oh, I do more than think with it."

Yep. And no one knew that better than she. "I'm busy. You need to get out." She rubbed her temples and remembered the reason. Matt had called. She had to tell Bo. She owed him. "Damn it, I have to tell you something."

The amusement was gone in a blink. "What's wrong?"

She laughed a bit harshly, and he frowned just as her computer beeped. Incoming mail. She glanced at it, then went still.

Bo took one look at her face and moved close. "Another one, then?"

Standing behind her as he was, he surrounded her, a hand on either side, gripping her desk. His chest brushed her back. His jaw was so close to her head that a strand of her hair stuck to the day-old growth of stubble there. She craned her neck so that her gaze met his. "A new one." She could have hidden it, but no more secrets—well, except one. But she doubted he wanted to hear how much she'd gotten used to having him around. How much she'd begun to feel for him.

Want him.

"Is this the first e-mail since the last one you showed me?" he demanded.

"Yes."

His gaze scanned her face. Looking for honesty, no doubt, but then he let out a breath. "Either you're getting better at lying, or I'm going soft on you, but I actually believe you."

"You're . . . going soft on me?"

"Jesus, Mel, you can't tell?"

"I like words," she said carefully. "There's less misunderstanding with words."

He opened his mouth, but before her eyes, his own shuttered, and his smile was strained and humorless. "You're trying to distract me from your incoming mail."

"I'm not."

"Prove it. Show it to me."

"I will. But you should know, Matt just called me. He unearthed four more aliases for Sally. The last one, the most recent . . . She was married, but her husband died. Suspiciously."

They looked at each other. "Now Sally's wanted for questioning," she added softly, and clicked on the new e-mail, gasping at who it was from: Tara Louise.

"Let me guess," Bo said grimly. "One of those aliases is Tara Louise. Probably the one with the dead husband."

"Bingo, you win the prize," Mel murmured, still in shock.

"If it's you on a platter, count me in."

"This is serious, Bo."

"Yes, I'm serious as a heart attack. Mel, look at me."

She lifted her head. He was close enough to kiss. Close enough to look into his eyes and see the utter honesty there for her to take. He wanted her. But she already knew that much, he'd made it abundantly clear. Her body mesmerized him.

Well, they were even there.

The problem? More than just his body mesmerized her. *Yeah, don't go there.* She leaned in to read the e-mail, but cupped her face and held her gaze.

"We're scaring her. You know that."

"She can join the club, then."

He slid his fingers into the hair at her temple, his eyes unusually solemn. "She's on the run, she's scared and she's pissed. She's going to blame us. Me, I'm more than ready for the face-off. You—"

"She won't hurt me."

"Mel, she's threatening you. She's threatening you because of me, because I came back and dug all this up. I'm the catalyst, not you."

"No—"

"I'm not going to let anything happen to you," he said fiercely.

"Nothing's going to happen to me, she's long gone now."
With that, Mel clicked open the e-mail.

Dear Mel,
   I'm sorry. God, I'm so sorry for every-fucking-
thing. But please, if you ever cared about me at all,
even a fraction of what I feel for you, please stop trying to trace me. Please, Mel. Save my life. *Stop trying
to find me*.

                                        Love,
                                        Me

Bo leaned in farther, his jaw actually brushing her as his
fingers pushed hers aside and started clicking on the keyboard.

"What are you doing?" she asked, watching as he opened
her browser, and pasted something from the e-mail on to the
page. Then his fingers were clicking over the keys, far faster
than she could type, and she couldn't follow what he was doing.

"Fuck," he said softly, and straightened away from her.

"What?" she asked, but he was already running. Leaping
up, she grabbed ahold of his shirt at the door. "Bo."

"That e-mail," he grated out. "It came from within the
airport. It came from one of your computers right here on
the premises."

Chapter 27

With Mel on his heels, Bo went running through the lobby, skidding to a stop at the front desk's computer so fast that she plowed into the back of him, hard.

He could smell her shampoo as her hair slapped him. And if he closed his eyes, he could still feel the way it'd stroked his throat and chest when she'd straddled him, when she slid down his body, her silky hair and mouth driving him to the edge of sanity.

Focus, mate.

Dimi sat behind the front desk, a pair of reading glasses perched on her nose, legs crossed, holding a ledger, which she dropped at the sight of them.

Leaving in her hands a paperback novel that she shoved behind her back. Bo didn't care what she was reading, it was her computer he wanted to see, and he moved around the desk, turning her screen to face him.

"Hey," she protested. "Paws off."

Ignoring her, Bo clicked on a few keys, then looked up at Mel and shook his head.

"Of course not," Mel said in quick defense of Dimi.

"Do we have any customers onsite?" Bo asked.

Dimi shook her head. "No. But what—"

"I'll be back to tell you," Mel promised. "Hurry," she said unnecessarily to Bo, then pushed ahead of him to run out of the lobby, along the tarmac toward the maintenance hangar.

And the computer there.

Danny was at that desk, leaning back, feet up, flipping through a manual while sipping a Big Gulp soda. "Hey guys, I found a new distributor, with cheaper— What are you doing?"

Bo had leaned right over him to hit a few keys.

The computer stayed dark.

"It's not on." Danny eyed them both with a growing frown. "It froze up a few hours ago and I shut it off. I didn't need it right now so I never turned it back on. What's happening?"

"Someone just e-mailed me," Mel said. "From inside North Beach."

"Must have been one hell of an e-mail," Danny said quietly, taking in their tension.

Mel looked at Bo. "Yeah, a hell of an e-mail. That's it, Bo, except for Ernest's old laptop that we use as a backup, but—"

"Wait." Bo stared at her, it was all sinking in. The only common denominator and they hadn't seen it. Christ, they'd been stupid. *"Ernest."*

Again they went running, this time with Danny on their heels.

Ernest wasn't in his office.

And neither was the laptop.

"What does it mean?" Mel gasped, trying to catch her breath. "What does it all mean?"

Bo looked at her, and he saw the instant she got it. *"Sally was here,"* she breathed. "But why now, why after all this time?"

"Because she needs us to shut the hell up. She's facing

some unpleasant jail time with me showing up and stirring the old news. She can't risk us finding out exactly what we did—that she's a career con."

"Where's Ernest?" Danny asked. "What's his part in this?"

"That's a bit complicated, actually."

They all whirled to face Ernest in the doorway. He looked grim. That is, grimmer than usual. In his hands he held the big ring of keys that would open any door within North Beach.

Shit, Bo thought.

"Ernest," Mel said softly. "What's going on?"

"You already know." He looked pale. Very pale. "You know everything, you just didn't put it all together in time."

"Sally sent me an e-mail from your computer," Mel said.

Ernest shook his head. "I sent the e-mails."

They all stared at him as if he'd grown another head, and he sighed. "Sally came to me weeks ago and asked me for help."

Weeks, Bo thought. Right around the time he'd first shown up.

"I tried to scare you off," Ernest said to Mel. "You began digging, and Sally got nervous. She asked me to make sure you didn't find . . ."

"Find what?" Bo glanced at the keys in Ernest's hand. "Something that would implicate her," he guessed. "Something she needed to stay hidden."

Ernest nodded.

"You two go way back, don't you, Ernest?" Bo asked. "She knew you were someone she could trust."

Ernest looked at Mel. "Yes. We go way back. All the way back."

"You've been in contact with her all along?" Mel asked, shocked. "All this time? *Years?* When I needed her, you were talking with her and didn't tell me?"

Another nod, jerky now.

Mel looked as if she could be knocked over with a feather. "And do you know what she did?" she demanded. "Do you know how she ruined people's lives?"

Ernest stared down at the keys, his usually placid face a mask of pain. "I thought she was the most beautiful, wonderful, compassionate woman on earth. I thought she was amazing. I thought . . ."

"You were in love with her," Mel breathed.

Ernest fumbled with the keys and said nothing.

"You were as fooled as we were, weren't you?"

"She changed," he said tightly. "It's my own shame that I didn't see that before. Soon as I did . . ." He met Mel's gaze helplessly. "I stopped helping her. I was still trying to scare you off, though, but by then it was so that you wouldn't get hurt."

"Where is she now?" Bo asked.

Ernest shook his head.

"You don't know, or you won't tell?"

"I've been covering for her all these years without knowing it," Ernest said quietly, looking at Bo. "I've been fooled, the same way your father was, the same way the others were. But no more. Here." He thrust out the key ring, with one key in the forefront. "This is yours. It should have been yours this whole time, and saying sorry doesn't seem good enough, but I am. It's been waiting here for you."

Bo took the key, eyed the number on it. Number thirteen. "Ironic," he murmured and turned and left the hangar. He knew the others were following him, with Mel immediately on his heels. He could feel her dismay, her anger, and when she set her hand on his back, her *support*. Damn if that didn't mean far too much. They moved along the tarmac to the rental hangars, stopping at the second-to-last one.

Ernest's.

Bo unlocked the side door and came face-to-face with the same stacks and stacks of old boxes he'd seen before. But

Ernest reached out and pushed at them, and they fell over. "Empty," he said.

"Nice cover." But Bo didn't feel amused as they flipped on the lights to find . . . more boxes. He shoved those out of the way as Ernest had. Like the others, they fell easily aside, revealing—

"Holy shit," Bo breathed at the sight of the Beechcraft.

His father's first plane.

Mel gasped at the sight of the antique aircraft. It'd clearly been neglected, but was probably still worth close to three quarters of a million dollars as is.

"Right under our noses," Danny said, and let out a low whisper. "Christ, she's a beauty."

Bo didn't say a word, *couldn't* say a word as he walked up to the plane and stroked the steel.

Mel covered her mouth at the stunned, almost overwhelmed look on Bo's face as he reverently touched the Beechcraft. She still couldn't quite believe it. All these years, it'd been right here. How was that even possible . . . ?

But it made sense. Perfect sense. Sally had been keeping tabs on them. She knew Bo had never shown up.

God, it was all so amazing, how it'd worked out. Mel thought back to how Bo had been when he'd first arrived: ready to take on all of them to get back his father's good name, not to mention what had been rightfully his. She knew Bo now, knew him better than she'd ever meant to. Yes, he was cocky and sarcastic and far too good looking for his own good. But he was also fiercely loyal, passionate, and utterly honest, bluntly so at times.

And he'd never lied to her.

He never would.

There was comfort in that, unbelievable comfort. It was a shame that she hadn't given that comfort back to him. She hated regrets, but now she moved to Bo's side and stared her biggest woe right in the eye. "I didn't know it was here," she said softly.

"He loved this damn thing—" His voice was rough with emotion, his hand still on the plane as if he couldn't bear to stop touching it.

"Bo." She turned him to face her. "I swear it. I didn't know."

His gaze went suspiciously bright when he nodded. "I know."

Not thinking, simply reacting, she pulled him into her arms.

He resisted for a half a second, then with a roughly muttered "fuck," fisted his hands on her shirt at her spine and held on tight, burying his face in the crook of her neck. "I miss him, Mel. I still miss him."

Words failed, so she just nodded and held on tighter.

After a minute, he lifted his head and looked at her from those gorgeous green eyes that always stopped her heart. "A piece of him is here." He glanced at the plane. "Which means me coming here was the best thing that could have happened out of all this."

"Because you can sell it?" Ernest asked. "And be rich?"

"Megarich," Danny added.

Mel knew what the money would do for Bo. It'd give him the nest egg he needed to get the restoration business off the ground. It'd give him a down payment on land in Australia, where he could run an airport like North Beach if he wanted. It'd give him freedom to go anywhere, do anything. And she found herself holding her breath as he eyed them each in turn, finally his gaze landing on her for the longest beat of her life. She managed to smile at him, through a throat so thick she could scarcely breathe.

"Whatever you do," Danny said, pulling out his cell phone, "we need to call the police."

Ernest went green. "We do?"

Bo looked at the older man. "Yeah, we do. The paperwork is in Sally's name, right?"

Ernest nodded.

"I want to get this all straightened out. It's going to be a mess."

"I didn't really do anything illegal, you know," Ernest said.

Mel narrowed her eyes, but before she could open her mouth, Bo said, "It's not you I'm after."

Ernest nodded but still didn't look happy, knowing he could end up in jail.

It didn't take the police long to arrive, and they all had a long chat, spilling everything they knew, from the beginning. By the time that was over and Mel got into her car to drive home, she was exhausted.

But not sleep exhausted.

Heart exhausted.

She parked outside her place and sat there for a long time. She looked down at her passenger seat, at the signed lease lying there. She'd never given it to Bo, but now seemed as good a time as any.

So she started her car again, heading to the condo Bo rented. It was dark outside. As she got out of the car, she could hear the waves crashing onshore in rhythm, a soothing sound. Still, her chest felt too tight, her heart squeezed into too small a space as she knocked on Bo's door.

He answered wearing a pair of shorts and nothing else. She could tell by his tousled hair and sleepy eyes he'd been lying in bed.

"Um . . . hi," she said. "Is it too late?"

"Depends. Too late for what?"

Bo waited for Mel's answer. His brain was still befuddled from lying on his bed, sleepless, tossing and turning, thinking of the woman now right in front of him, the woman with the biggest heart of any he'd known, with a smile that could melt him at one hundred knots.

It was as if he'd conjured her up from his fantasies, except in his fantasies she didn't have on a pair of jeans and a tank top, she had nothing on but a sexy smile as she dropped to her knees in front of him and—

Instead, she slapped the signed lease against his bare chest. She was trying not to look at him, but her gaze kept dropping to his chest in a way that made him extremely grateful to be a man.

He loved that she lusted after his body. He'd love for it to be more than lust as well, and was banking on talking her into that with some more time.

"I took your deal," she said. "I know you're probably halfway out the door, and I just wanted to say good-bye. Alone. Just you and me."

"Mel—"

"No." She stepped over the threshold and slid her arms around his neck. "I don't want to talk. I don't even want to think. Okay?"

Not thinking worked for him. He'd done so much thinking his brain hurt; about his father, about the past, about what the fuck to do with himself now that he'd come here with destruction on his mind but instead had ended up actually enjoying himself.

He missed Australia, but if he left here, he'd miss this, too. He loved the ocean, he'd discovered. He loved the lush landscape.

He loved the woman wrapped around him like saran wrap.

She sank her fingers into his hair and pulled his head down to kiss him, dancing her tongue to his, and just like that, he was a goner. Send in a rescue plane, he was going down. "Oh, yeah," he breathed, and tossed the lease over his shoulder, hauling her up against him, kicking the door closed.

"A bed," he murmured against her mouth. "I want you in my bed, beneath me, panting my name, coming . . ."

"Yes."

But halfway there he had to press her back against the wall in his hallway, kissing her mouth, her neck, anything he could reach. She rocked against him with a sexy little whimper, and he could barely stand it, this need to inhale her whole.

"God, Bo—"

"I know." He stripped off her tank top, then ripped open her jeans, unable to get to skin fast enough to suit him. Her jeans got caught on one leg, her tank on his arm, but she just laughed breathlessly and held on.

Held on as if she never intended to let go.

God, the amazing rush that gave him. For a moment he pressed his forehead to hers, just breathing her in, wanting to stop time right at this moment so he could soak her up. Lap her up. *"Mel."*

She wrapped her arms around his neck and arched up, her legs around his waist, pressing the wet heat of her where he wanted it the most.

I love you. The words wanted to burst from his throat, and it stunned him, the power of them, so that he could only stare down at her.

Her eyes were half-closed, with that sexy little smile curving her lips as she rocked against him again, that hot bod feeling so damn right against his. "I thought you wanted me in your bed," she murmured.

Yeah, in his bed. And in his heart and soul, for the rest of his life, but he kept his mouth closed as he gazed down at her because he didn't want the words to escape, not when she might attribute them to just lust.

Because this was so, so much more.

"Please, Bo," she whispered.

Yeah. He'd please. He'd please if it took all damn night.

Somehow he got them to his bed, then crawled up her body and slid inside her.

"Oh, my God." Arching up, she closed her eyes.

"No, leave them open, Mel. Look at me."

Her eyes fluttered open as if at great effort, then locked on his. "You are so beautiful," he breathed.

She started to shake her head but he just nodded. "You are. So damned beautiful I can't stop looking at you."

She stared up at him, her arms locked around his neck. She sent him a shaky smile that he managed to return, but it backed up in his throat as he began to move, as she gasped and pulled him even closer, struggling to keep her eyes open on his. She moved with him, and with their eyes locked, something extremely deep and real passed between them. *I love you*, he thought again, his last coherent thought for a good long time . . .

Mel woke up in Bo's bed, burrowed beneath the covers, a pillow over her head. Seemed she'd gotten pretty comfortable, sleeping easily next to his muscular, warm body . . .

The thought of him brought a smile to her lips and she pushed the pillow away and blankets off. The early-morning sun slanted across her face. Squinting, she turned her head and reached across the bed.

Still warm, but no Bo.

The shower was running, and she lay back and grinned up at the ceiling, wondering how long he'd been in there . . . if he still had enough hot water left so that they could make it a twosome.

Odd, this wanting-to-stay thing. A first.

And here was another: she loved him.

Goofy with it, she sat up in the bed just as a scream sounded from the bathroom.

A *female* scream, followed by a gunshot.

Chapter 28

The gunshot was accompanied by a crash and a thud, a second gunshot, and yet another scream.

Mel's heart stopped as she leapt out of bed and went running for the bathroom in nothing but Bo's T-shirt. She hauled the door open, then gasped in shock.

Bo stood in the shower, the door open, water raining out on the floor, holding a gun. There was glass everywhere, and above them, the light had been shot out.

On the floor, wet and looking extremely pissed, sat . . . Sally.

The years hadn't been particularly kind to her. Oh, she was still carefully gorgeous, with her long hair and wild blue eyes, with tanned, toned skin and a body most men would drool over, but she looked as if she'd been ridden hard and put away wet. She looked cold. Rough.

Mean. "Ah, *shit!*" she said at the sight of Mel. "What are *you* doing here?"

Dealing with stressful situations was like breathing for Mel, but this was beyond anything she'd ever experienced. She was looking at the woman she'd loved, deeply loved, after years of absence. This person was holding her arm and bleeding profusely all over the floor.

Mel's gaze whipped toward Bo, who still stood there, naked, water streaming down over his back and shoulders, holding a gun on Sally. "She tried to kill you," Mel guessed, horrified.

"Luckily, she's a bad shot." His eyes were still trained on Sally, gun steady.

"Bullshit, I'm a bad shot," Sally spit out. "You grabbed my shooting arm."

"And shot her?" Mel gasped.

Bo's mouth tightened, but Sally laughed harshly. "I damn well shot myself, thank you for asking. The bastard was going to wrestle me to the floor, the gun went off twice."

"Oh, my God." Mel put her hand to her mouth. He could have been killed. Just like that. Before she'd told him—

"Don't move," Bo told Sally, who was creeping toward the door. "Don't fucking move."

Sirens went off in the distance. "Well, that's just perfect." Sally thunked her head back against the tile, pale and exhausted looking. "It's over. You should have left it all alone, Mel. Why couldn't you just have left it alone?"

"You gave Eddie the deed. You never even told us," Mel said slowly, so many things going through her mind she could barely speak. "How did that happen? *Why* did that happen?"

"It was mine to give."

"You should have told us."

Sally laughed again, a cold sound. "It was just a means to an end."

"The end being?"

"Cash." Sally opened her eyes, and they were shockingly filled with honesty. Pain.

But no regret. Not even a little bit. "Men are scum of the earth, Mel. You know that by now. You've always known it. Look at your father. They all deserve what they get."

"If that's true, why did you marry two of them?"

"Eight."

"Eight?"

"And each of them left me a fortune, stupid bastards. It was a great gig, too. Until you started digging your nose in. That's when things began to unravel."

"Yeah, you were in control right up until that point," Bo said dryly, reaching behind him to turn off the water, gun still on Sally.

"I'm not going anywhere, stud," Sally told him. "You win. You can lower that bad boy now."

Bo kept the gun on her.

"Aw, jeez, at least wrap yourself in a towel." Sally scooted a little closer to the door. "Not that you aren't impressive or anything . . ."

He was. Standing there naked, dripping wet, all his muscles seemed to glow. Unfortunately for Bo, he couldn't move without getting cut on the glass splintered at his feet, but he reached out and grabbed a towel, holding it in front of him.

The sirens grew louder.

"So let me get this straight," Sally said to Bo, still bleeding profusely, and beginning to shiver in shock. "You sleeping with her to get back at me?"

Bo didn't answer, just kept the gun on her. Mel's heart took a little dive.

"Because I can see why you'd want to fuck her," Sally said conversationally. "It'd be like fucking me over, right?"

A muscle jumped in Bo's jaw. "Stop trying to get to the door, damn it. You're not going anywhere except to a nice cold cell block."

But Sally laughed harshly, then lunged for the door anyway, knocking Mel over as she went.

Surprised, Mel fell to the glass-covered floor.

Bo flew out of the shower and tackled Sally. They went rolling into the bedroom, out of Mel's sight.

The gun went off again.

Mel heard a scream, realized it was her own, and crawled out of the bathroom to see Bo and Sally locked together, rolling . . . blood everywhere. Again her heart stopped because she couldn't see who'd been hit. "Oh, God, oh, God!" she cried, terrified Bo was going to die, or maybe he was already dying. There was a planted pot on the nightstand, which she grabbed and ran over to the locked pair. Bo was on top and she raised the pot, thinking *move, move, goddamn it, move,* until finally, they rolled again.

Now Sally was on top, lifting her head, laughing coldly down at Bo. "You bastard—"

Mel cracked her in the back of the head with the pot.

Sally slumped and went still, and Bo crawled out from beneath her. Mel dove for him. "Where are you hit, Jesus, where?" Her hands ran all over him, everywhere she could touch.

"I'm okay, Mel, I'm okay."

But she couldn't stop touching him, skimming her fingers over his body, which was, in fact, utterly free of bullet holes.

"Mel, stop." He gathered her hands in his. "I'm okay. It's you." He dragged her into his lap. "You're the one who's hurt," he said hoarsely.

Yeah, she knew that, and the cuts were beginning to make themselves known, little bits of fire along her knees and feet, but she couldn't stop touching him. "I thought you were shot. I thought—"

"I'm okay, I promise."

But she still flung her arms around his neck and let herself cling, just for a minute. "You feel okay."

"I am. Mel, look at me." Cupping her face up, he looked into her eyes. "I'm fine."

"Good." She gulped in air. "Because I'm not."

"I know. You're cut from the glass." His voice was hoarse with fear, for her, she realized, as he carefully lifted her and set her on his bed.

"No, it's not the cuts. Bo—"

"I didn't sleep with you to get back at her," he said.

She looked into his eyes. "I know."

"Do you? Do you really?"

"Yeah. I do. But Bo? I, um, did something a little out of the norm for me. Like on Mars out of the norm, something . . ." She swallowed hard, managed a shaky smile. "Well, I sort of fell in love with you."

Sally rolled to her back and groaned. "Are you kidding me? I'm lying here dying and you two are going to have a moment? Seriously?"

Bo lifted the gun on Sally again, all without taking his eyes off Mel. "Qualify 'sort of.'"

"Sort of," Mel said. "As in did."

"Hey, my life is flashing before my eyes, people!" Sally yelled.

"You fell in love with me," Bo repeated to Mel, looking dazed.

"Yes."

"Unbelievable," Sally muttered.

"Shut up!" both Mel and Bo said to her at the same time.

"I know we're still working on the trust thing," Mel said to Bo. "And I also know you're leaving, but it was just too much for me to keep inside, I'm sorry. It just popped out, without permission."

He had a funny look on his face so she rushed to finish. "I don't mean to burden you, or make you feel—"

"You don't want to burden me with your feelings," he repeated slowly.

"Right." Why was he sounding like a parrot? "Or make you feel like you have to see me when you come back into town, I just—"

"Make me feel like I have to see you." He shook his head. "Mel, have you ever known me to do anything I don't want to?"

"Well, no."

"Or let someone *make* me do something?"

"No. But—"

"Yeah. Look, you're a little crooked on all this. Especially since I love you back."

"You . . ." Her breath caught. "You do?"

"Oh, yeah."

"Oh, my God. I didn't imagine you'd—"

"Why not?"

"It's just that you have it so together, and I never seem to, and—"

"It's you."

"What?"

"If I have it together," he said. "It's because of you."

Mel's eyes filled. *Damn it.*

"For years something's been missing," Bo said to her. "I always thought it was my dad, or that I couldn't get the restoration business going, or maybe location . . . I always had a reason for not feeling . . . whole."

Undone, she put her head to his chest. "Bo."

"It's you, Mel. You make me feel whole."

Her heart was so full she could hardly stand it. "Really?"

"Oh, yeah." He sounded as if maybe his throat was as tight as hers, and his eyes were as shiny as they'd been when he'd first seen the Beechcraft again. "And I do love you, Mel. So much." He took a deep breath. "But you're bleeding. You probably have glass embedded in your flesh, and I'm feeling a little drafty here, so—"

Two cops burst into the room, guns drawn. "Hands up!"

"Right on cue," Bo said, and lifted his hands.

Mel, still on his lap, lifted her hands, too.

Sally just groaned.

"No one moves," one of the cops said. "Until we straighten this out."

Bo looked at Mel. "Actually, I'm good right here."

Mel laughed through her tears and kissed him. "Me, too."

Epilogue

Three months later . . .

AC/DC blared from the boom box on the counter, next to a tray fat with fresh donuts. Standing around the counter chowing down on said donuts was the usual morning crowd.

With some obvious differences.

Dimi was on a school break from her nursing program. And though the hour was obscenely early, she was smiling—*grinning,* actually—up into Danny's face. She had a sunburn across her nose and cheeks from yesterday afternoon's surfing lesson.

"You almost stood up that last time," Danny told her proudly.

Dimi was learning to surf.

And to love.

"Shhh!" Char cranked up the music from ear splitting to glass cracking. "I love this song!" she shouted, and began to boogie her pregnant belly around the kitchen floor.

Al caught her up in his arms, laughing as he nuzzled his wife's neck. "Hey, don't drop my kid."

Ernest rolled his eyes, grabbed his broom, and stalked off, muttering about displays of public affection.

Some things never changed.

Bo turned down the music. "Sorry, Char. I just want to say something." He looked at Mel, whose entire heart gushed at just the sight of him, as it had every single day since he'd walked off that Gulfstream so many months ago now. "Mel and I would like to announce a new adventure."

Char gasped hopefully.

So did Dimi.

Mel kept her face even, knowing what they thought. "We're merging Anderson Air and Black Aviation," she said.

"Oh." Twin faces fell.

"What's the matter?" Bo asked. "Aren't you happy for us?"

Danny shook Bo's hand. So did Al.

The women, both of them, tried to even out their clear disappointment. "Yes, of course," Dimi said. "But I already knew that."

"But what you don't know," Mel said, "is the new title for the company."

"Black," Bo said, letting his grin escape as he stole a peek at Mel, making her heart tip right on its side . . . "and Black Aviation."

Dimi blinked.

Char blinked.

Black and Black Aviation.

As it sank in, they both squealed together and began jumping up and down as they crossed to Mel and gathered her in close.

"Does this mean—" Dimi started.

"That you're getting married?" Char finished.

"Does it?" Dimi demanded.

"Tell us!" Char demanded.

Mel laughed and hugged them both, pulling back to show them her finger.

And the brand-new diamond on it.

This caused more screaming and more squeals, and Mel endured it all, finally pulling gently away to look at Bo. "Maybe we should have called the new merger Just Plane Trouble."

Bo laughed, and snagged Mel's heart all over again. He knew, as she did, that it didn't matter what they called themselves, as long as they were together.

Try something different from Jill Shalvis, OUT OF
THIS WORLD, coming in October!

I SHOULD HAVE STAYED IN BED

Three weeks ago I, Rachel Bond, inherited a bed-and-breakfast.
In *Alaska*. Just this morning I was in my warm bed in LA but
now here I am, up north—and this is, like, nosebleed north—
sorting it all out. So:

PROS:

1. Bears and wolves and moose can't be any worse than
   LA guys.
2. You've heard of "starving artists?" I'm about to faint.
   So it's probably time for a change.
3. My good friend Kellan—you'll like him, unlike me,
   he's cool under pressure—suddenly has this animal
   sexiness I've never even seen before.

CONS:

1. ALASKA.
2. The house chef can't cook, and the guide can't read a
   map.
3. Kellan's sudden hotness is getting very hard to ignore.
4. I just got hit by lightning.

And I'm not sure if this is a pro or a con just yet, but since
that lightning bolt, I can see through everything. As in completely transparent. That was before things started to get
really weird . . .

#4093 THE GREEK'S FORGOTTEN MARRIAGE
by Maya Blake

Imogen has finally tracked down her missing husband, Zeph. But he has no recollection of their business-deal union! Yet as Zeph slowly pieces his memories together, one thing is for certain: this time, an on-paper marriage won't be enough!

#4094 RETURNING FOR HIS RUTHLESS REVENGE
by Louise Fuller

When self-made Gabriel hires attorney Dove, it's purely business—unfinished business, that is. Years ago, she broke his heart...now he'll force her to face him! Yet their chemistry is undeniable. Will they finally finish what they started?

#4095 RECLAIMED BY HIS BILLION-DOLLAR RING
by Julia James

It's been eight years since Nikos left Calanthe without a goodbye. Now, becoming the Greek's bride is the only way to help her ailing father. Even if it feels like she's walking back into the lion's den...

#4096 ENGAGED TO LONDON'S WILDEST BILLIONAIRE
Behind the Palace Doors...
by Kali Anthony

Lance's debauched reputation is the stuff of tabloid legend. But entertaining thoughts of his attraction to sheltered Sara would be far too reckless. Then she makes him an impassioned plea to help her escape an arranged wedding. His solution? Their own headline-making engagement!

HARLEQUIN
PLUS

Try the best multimedia subscription service for romance readers like you!

Read, Watch and Play.

Experience the easiest way to get the romance content you crave.

Start your **FREE TRIAL** at
<u>www.harlequinplus.com/freetrial</u>.